A TALE FROM THE BADLANDS

THE BOOK OF MYSTERIES

J. R. WALLIS

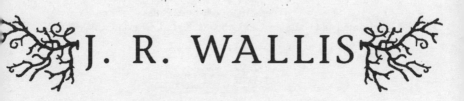

SIMON & SCHUSTER

First published in Great Britain in 2020 by Simon & Schuster UK Ltd

1 3 5 7 9 10 8 6 4 2

Simon & Schuster UK Ltd
1st Floor
222 Gray's Inn Road
London WC1X 8HB

www.simonandschuster.co.uk
www.simonandschuster.com.au
www.simonandschuster.co.in

Simon & Schuster Australia, Sydney
Simon & Schuster India, New Delhi

A CIP catalogue record for this book
is available from the British Library.

PB ISBN 978-1-4711-8333-1
eBook ISBN 978-1-4711-8334-8

Typeset in Goudy by M Rules
Printed and bound by CPI Group (UK) Ltd, Croydon, CR0 4YY

MIX
Paper from
responsible sources
FSC® C020471

*For anyone hoping to make the world
a kinder, more inclusive place*

'The *Ordnung* has stood the test of time, enabling the Badlander Order to thrive for centuries. I expect this rule of law to stand for all future time too.'

*The Apprentice's Guide to
the History of the Badlander Order*

by Edgar Holt

'As their name suggests, Lucky Drops can indeed change your fortunes. But beware, their ultimate purpose is to teach Badlanders that greed and ambition are not virtues but vices.'

*A Guide to the Rare and
Wonderful in the Badlands*

by Crispin Boulter

'The ælwiht (pronounced a-l-why-t) is a dangerous creature, particularly the pregnant female, for reasons that will become clear as you read on.'

*The Badlander Bestiary
Pocket Book Version*

ONE

When the breeze blew a little harder, click-clacking the bare branches of the trees, Jones caught the scent of the *ælwiht* again. It was eye-watering, like too much vinegar poured over hot chips.

As the breeze dropped and the trees fell silent, the scent faded and Jones reminded himself to stay focused. The *ælwiht* had already proved it was extremely dangerous, springing like a trap in the dark to grab him, talons tearing through his overcoat like it was made of wrapping paper and he was the gift inside. He'd only escaped by slipping out of the coat and leaving it behind on the grassy path.

Shivering in his T-shirt, Jones cursed not only because he was cold but because everything in the pockets of the overcoat was gone too. The one consolation was that he was still alive, for now, at least. The cut on his forearm was starting to sting, making Jones wonder if the *ælwiht* could smell something of him too.

It was impossible to know where the creature was or how close it might be. The ramshackle farm buildings had lots of hiding places. In the moonlight, Jones had counted two old barns on either side of the yard as he'd peeked round the wall. He'd seen the deserted farmhouse too, with its black windows.

'Are you okay?' whispered Ruby, giving his shoulder a squeeze.

'Fine,' he hissed. Jones had already decided he'd give her a piece of his mind later on, if they survived tonight.

He'd lectured her before, of course, about how jumping feet-first into any situation without thinking could be fatal when they were hunting monsters in the Badlands. But his words hardly ever seemed to stick. Especially if Ruby thought she knew better. And that had been happening a lot more recently because of the historic vote the Order were preparing to take. So Jones hadn't been entirely surprised when she'd gone striding off again after the *ælwiht* this time, despite his protestations about them needing to be very careful about how to proceed.

A rustle in the undergrowth cut Jones's thinking dead and Ruby squeezed his arm harder. The night had spun round in the opposite direction now that the *ælwiht* was hunting *them*.

Jones peered back down the farm track towards the small copse where the creature had surprised them. He couldn't see anything moving. Despite being a regular boy who went to school, he was a Badlander too. It was his job to hunt monsters and keep ordinary people like his mother and father safe as they slept soundly in their beds. And hunting monsters was something he was very good at indeed.

2

As the moon crept out from behind the clouds again, he slunk along to the end of the wall with Ruby behind him, shivering as he wondered what to do now he didn't have his overcoat and all the usual items he kept in its pockets. Some of them would have been pretty useful around about now.

The farmyard was bumpy with potholes, the largest ones full of black water and stars. On the other side was a line of stables, with most of the doors open or missing. In the weak moonlight, Jones could see enough to know many of them were empty. But it was difficult to be sure about the ones furthest away.

Ruby tapped his shoulder and pointed to the farmhouse.

'We could set a trap for it in there.'

'One of those stables would be better.'

'It's more likely to be tricked into the house, isn't it? It's not stupid.'

'Yes, I think we already know that, Ruby.' Jones felt something red hot rising in his belly and he wanted to shout at her but he managed to hold back. 'All cos of this blooming vote,' he muttered. 'You weren't thinking straight. We shouldn't have come after it once we found out it was pregnant.'

'What's that supposed to mean?'

'Because now it en't gonna give up till we've killed it or it gets us first.'

'So? That's what Badlanders do, isn't it? Hunt monsters?'

Jones cursed and shook his head. This was not the best

time for an argument. But the red-hot feeling kept rising inside him. 'I knew it. You never read up on the creature like I told you to, did you?'

'Jones, why are you so worried? I *can* use magic now, remember?' Ruby pursed her lips. 'In fact, let's stop hiding and find out where this thing is so we can go home. I'm freezing.'

'No, Ruby.'

Jones grabbed her wrist as she pointed a hand at the sky and muttered a couple of words. A silver spark burst out of her finger like a firework, and instead of shooting into the sky, kept low to the ground as it flew across the yard, its shimmering light sweeping back the dark. Crashing into a stable door it pinged back into a puddle, hitting the water with a hiss and sending up plumes of steam.

Ruby glared. Before she could say anything, Jones glimpsed a tall figure dart out of a dark corner of one of the stables and sprint through the steam towards them.

'Run!' he shouted, pointing at the farmhouse. For a split second, Ruby thought about using her magic, but the boy had taken off so quickly, she felt a sudden sense of panic and instinctively raced after him.

It was supposed to have been a reconnaissance night, exploring a town called Wighton after Jones had found a local news article on the Internet about strange events there. Surfing the web, they'd realized, was a more efficient way of discovering something that required investigation than randomly exploring places the way Badlanders were traditionally used to doing. Neither Jones nor Ruby felt duty-bound to stick rigidly to the Badlander code of conduct called the *Ordnung*, which followed particular rules such as not using modern technology, because they were a unique team that made their own rules. At least, that's how they thought of themselves: an ordinary boy, who missed working in the Badlands where he'd trained as an apprentice, and an extraordinary girl who hunted monsters with him, something only men and their boy apprentices had done before.

The article had described how two horses had been killed a day earlier, the bodies so mutilated their elderly owner had suffered a stroke. The journalist had suggested the savage attack could only have been the actions of a deeply disturbed individual. But Jones and Ruby had their suspicions that what had killed the horses was, in fact, not human at all. The details, or lack of them, were odd. It had not been a full moon. There had been no strange markings in the earth. The date, September the 25th, had not been significant according to the Badlander Calendar in the Pocket Book Bestiary. But there had been reports of an odd smell lingering in the autumnal air, according to the locals who'd been interviewed.

Jones's mother had brought them milk and cookies and gently reminded her son about his homework when she noticed the article on the computer screen. Both Jones's parents knew about the Badlands and the terrors there, having been freed from a Witch's curse by Ruby over a year before. Ruby had presumed that becoming a Badlander was going to be all about saving people, especially after receiving the gift of magic and being officially allowed into the Order, the first girl ever to be given such an honour. But the High Council had been keen for her to catch up on the education any boy apprentice would have been expected to learn. In fact, Randall Givens, the head of the Council, had made it *very* clear just how much learning she needed to undertake. So, over the past few months, there had been a lot of studying and gardening – growing herbs in particular – in between the supervised hunting trips she was allowed to take with Jones who was supposed to make sure she put all her studying into practice.

She'd snuck out a good few times on her own, of course, because Ruby was not the sort of girl who liked to be told what to do. These solo hunting trips had increased after Givens had told her about the vote he was proposing, that the Order should decide on whether to allow girl apprentices as well as boys. It was to be his great legacy, changing the Order for the better, despite all its centuries of tradition. So, Ruby was eager to build up a casebook describing all the creatures she'd despatched, and leave as many *mearcunga* as she could, the special marks that Badlanders left to prove what monsters they'd killed.

Therefore, as she'd munched on her cookies, listening to Jones talking through possible explanations for the horses' deaths and recommending she read up on a creature called an *ælwiht* as part of her studies, she had really been thinking about what an opportunity Wighton might be.

They had started their reconnaissance that Monday night, walking around in the evening gloom to see what snippets of information they could pick up. The pubs and bars were busy, so there were punters on the streets drinking and smoking and chatting away. No one paid attention to two kids. Ruby made sure the gun in her waistband was covered up so it couldn't be seen or indeed heard, since it was charmed to speak and liked to give an opinion on most things.

Ruby and Jones had paused after hearing two men discussing the murdered horses in hushed tones. Apparently, the mutilations had been very extensive, the hind legs pulled off and never found. Ruby and Jones had exchanged glances and decided to go straight to the field. It had yielded no clues except for a tuft of coarse animal hair snagged on a hedgerow ripening with big blobs of blackberries. Any ordinary person might have presumed it to have belonged to one of the horses. But an ordinary person would not have held it up to the moonlight to check for a blue sheen like Jones had done.

'Definitely an *ælwiht*,' nodded Jones as he put the hair in the pocket of his trousers. 'A pregnant one.'

'How about over there?' said Ruby, pointing across the field to a small copse.

'We'll come back tomorrow night,' said Jones. 'An *ælwiht* like this needs careful—'

'Preparation, I know!' groaned Ruby. But she turned and started to walk across the field towards the copse.

'Oooh,' said the gun, as she pulled it out of her waistband, 'that dark and rather scary-looking set of trees looks interesting.'

'Let's hope so,' said Ruby, tramping over the grass as Jones muttered something behind them.

'What's got into him?' asked the gun.

'No idea.' Ruby walked on towards the trees, focused on the tingle of magic in her veins and flexing the fingers of her free hand to keep them warm and sharp.

Jones banged open the door to the farmhouse and smelt something foul. He wondered what must have died here, before a nasty growl rose outside in the yard.

'We wouldn't be in this situation if you'd done your reading on the *ælwiht* for your studies like I'd told you to.'

Ruby folded her arms. 'I did some.' She stared defiantly back at Jones and tried not to wilt under his glare. 'Enough to get the general idea, anyway,' she continued. 'It's a very dangerous creature. Vicious. Smelly. But one I can take out *if* you give me the chance,' she said, flexing magical sparks around her fingers. 'I could have sorted out everything back there if you hadn't run off.'

Jones grunted and produced the tuft of hair from his trouser pocket and held it up to the window so the moonlight caught it. The blue sheen reminded Ruby of a kingfisher she'd seen once flashing upstream as she'd walked down a towpath. She'd been with her parents, who had been arguing, of course. Or at least the drink in them had been. That had been a long time ago in a different life. She whirled the sparks faster around her fingers to prove it. 'Let's find out what spell works best on this particular creature.'

'Be my guest.' Jones dropped the tuft of hair to the floor.

Ruby muttered some Anglo-Saxon words she'd been practising and fired magic at the hair. It bounced away. She muttered some different words but the same thing happened again. And then again.

Ruby frowned. 'The Pocket Book Bestiary said a fireball, death-shot or blood-boiler are the most common ones to use.'

'I guess this pregnant ælwiht is an unusual one, then?' said Jones as he glanced out of the window into the yard, watching closely for any movement, listening for any sound.

When he looked back at Ruby she snuffed out the sparks at the ends of her fingers and sighed.

'Okay, so I didn't do *all* of the reading. I skimmed some of it.' Jones seemed to bristle in the murky dark as he gave a snort. 'Fine, I skimmed all of it. What's your bigger point here? Because there obviously is one.' She pointed a finger at the tuft of hair on the floor.

'When an ælwiht is pregnant, its hair gives off a blue sheen in the moonlight, its stench increases and, if you'd read up like I told you to, you'd also know . . .' He paused and rubbed his forehead as though there was something painful lurking there. 'The creature becomes immune to magic too.'

Ruby opened her mouth and then closed it.

'So now we're trapped, Ruby. No magic, no weapons . . .' Ruby raised the gun and it coughed loudly. 'No *decent* weapons. And no Slap Dust because the bottle we used to

9

get here was in my overcoat pocket along with everything else that would have been useful in a situation like this. And all because you thought you could handle a creature like this on your own, without reading up on it, just like you always do. There's nothing wrong with books, you know!'

Something dripped from the ceiling and landed with a **PLOP!** beside the toe of his boot. It glistened like a spot of ink. Jones bent down to have a look and then stood up quickly when he saw that it was blood. 'We have to go—'

Another few drops came through the ceiling, spotting the floor like raindrops.

'Jones, what's happening?'

'A pregnant *ælwiht* will usually band together with others to make a nest.' He pointed up at the ceiling. 'And I think we now know where one might be, and where the horses' legs are too, what's left of them.'

He was about to say something else but a large creature burst through the ceiling and he was smashed to the floor.

TWO

Time paused for Ruby, like watching a shooting
star, as an *ælwiht* came through the ceiling and
landed on Jones.

And then she was aiming the gun at the creature which
was still struggling to stand up, one leg having plunged
through the rotten floor up to the knee.

'Aim, squeeze, shoot!' announced the gun as Ruby glanced
at the pale-faced Jones, so white, in fact, the blood on his
forehead looked black.

Ruby pulled the trigger but the bullet pinged into the
wall behind the *ælwiht* as the creature lost its balance and
toppled over.

Ruby felt the chamber spin as the gun locked and
loaded again.

'Ready!'

Ruby took a step back to steady herself as the *ælwiht* reared
up in front of her. She immediately wished she hadn't because
this time *her* foot went through the rotten floor and she fired
into the ceiling, bringing down more dust and plaster.

'What are you doing?' shouted the gun.

'Sorry, I—'

Ruby didn't have time to finish as she heard the window pane shatter behind her and a long rangy arm reached in and wrapped around her waist. She was yanked backwards, through the window, and out of the house into the cold dark night, the gun dropping out of her hand into the long grass as she was hoisted up onto a hairy blue shoulder.

The nest was cobbled together from furniture. Old wardrobes and chests of drawers had been broken up along with tables and chairs, the splintered pieces of wood jammed together to make a shallow saucer-shaped structure. Metal bedsteads had been bent around the outside to keep it all together.

The *ælwiht*, perched on the edge of the nest, growled its displeasure every time Ruby even thought about moving. Finally, when she had no option but to shift her legs because they were turning numb, the creature lunged forward and snapped its toothy mouth inches from her nose. She stared into the red eyes and saw nothing in them that gave her any hope. It was large and powerful and she was powerless, given her magic was useless against it. She was sure the creature smiled at her before glancing over at the other *ælwiht* which was pacing around the room, agitated for some reason.

Ruby had no idea why she and Jones were still alive. She was sure Jones would know but he was still out cold beside her, a dull red crust around the cut on his forehead. Ruby wondered if she would get the chance to apologize for getting them into this mess.

When the other creature gave a sharp yelp, Ruby's eyes darted to their corners to see what was happening. The *ælwiht* had slumped to the floor and rolled into a ball, its cries growing louder as its whole body spasmed. Suddenly it opened its arms wide and threw back its head. Ruby saw the belly start to swell. The bulge grew quickly, like a balloon being blown up, and then detached itself neatly from the abdomen of the creature and rolled off, dropping to the floor.

Ruby guessed what was happening even before she saw the furry ball burst open. Out gushed a milky substance that ran across the floor and with it came a baby *ælwiht*, flip-flopping like a fish. The mother bent over its young, licking clean the dark fur on its face, as the baby took its first jerky breaths.

Ruby watched with a mix of fascination and disgust. Then a little spark fired in her brain as the fur on the female caught the moonlight. It was no longer shining blue but was dark, like its baby's. Ruby's first instinct was to raise her hand and conjure magic but the other *ælwiht* was in her face again, its hair still blue in the moonlight. Its eyes stared at her, bright with an intelligence that scared her much more than the teeth and the claws. It knew exactly what she was thinking.

The *ælwiht* took hold of her hands, smothering them inside its own, the tips of the long talons scratchy round her wrists. Its cold eyes blinked like a bird's as the new mother walked towards the nest with its young.

Now she knew why she and Jones hadn't been devoured. They were being kept as baby food.

Ruby started to panic but it was impossible to move because the *ælwiht* holding her hands was much stronger than her. Sparks of magic desperately popped out of her fingertips, but with her hands balled tight into fists they had nowhere to go and burnt a little before dying away.

As the other *ælwiht* climbed onto the edge of the nest, it held out its offspring. The little black button of a nose twitched and tiny red eyes blinked at Ruby. The baby snapped its mouth open and shut, revealing little rows of sharp teeth. The mother reached forwards and held it closer to Ruby. Fascinated by her, the baby *ælwiht* stretched out a hand to touch her face. The tips of the tiny talons were so needle sharp Ruby felt one puncture her skin without hurting.

'I'm the only Badlander girl,' she whispered as tears welled up in the corners of her eyes. 'I'm just getting started and there's so much I want to do. There's a vote soon. The whole Order might change because of me. I want to take on my own apprentice one day. A girl.' The baby seemed to be listening and although it couldn't possibly understand her, Ruby wondered if it had perhaps sensed the panic in her voice and felt sorry for her. Then it sneezed and licked its lips and opened its mouth as wide as it would go.

Ruby held her breath.

But the teeth bit down on clean air as the baby *ælwiht* was pulled away by its mother which then whirled round, growling and sniffing the air, clutching its young to its chest. The other *ælwiht* was becoming agitated too, glancing towards the same dark corner of the room. Ruby looked but there was nothing there.

She heard voices before she saw anything.

And then the outline of a boy appeared.

Like an etching, at first, before rapidly being filled in. He was about Ruby's height and smartly presented in a brown tweed suit and red tie. He looked scared as he raised a bolas and started trying to swing it round above his head. But he was so tucked in to the corner, the two wooden balls at the ends of the cords clacked against the wall and the bolas collapsed and whirred around his arm in a tangle.

With its baby tucked securely into its chest, the *ælwiht* charged at the boy as a man appeared beside him, white sparks of magic dancing around his fingertips. He shouted a spell that Ruby didn't recognize and the magic formed a golden disc in his hand which he hurled at the creature. The *ælwiht* was struck on the shoulder, turning its back to protect its young. The disc sliced into the dark fur and the creature screamed in pain. Ruby heard the baby screaming too and then in one brief shudder both creatures were vaporized. The disc dropped to the floor. It rolled back to the man, who picked it up, and then it disappeared.

The *ælwiht* holding Ruby's hands pushed her hard back

into the nest. By the time she'd scrambled to look up she saw the bolas whirling through the air again. It caught the creature around the legs, bringing it crashing to the floor. The two Badlanders advanced. But the *ælwiht* was strong and it ripped the bolas cords from its legs and stood up, forcing the man and the boy to retreat.

'We have to save our skins without using magic,' shouted the man. 'I can't protect us. Think, Aldwyn!'

'I ... uh, I—'

'Think harder, boy!' thundered the man. 'Our lives depend on you for once, not my magic.'

Aldwyn plunged his hands into the pockets of his suit jacket. He drew out a small jar that glowed with a green phosphorescence and dropped it to the floor in frustration. His other hand drew out a small bug-eyed creature which yawned and then curled up and started to snore in his palm.

'Think clearly, for goodness' sake!' shouted the man. 'This is a test for you. Not only to save us. But that girl.'

Aldwyn was starting to shake.

Ruby moved fast. Sparks of magic already lit the ends of her fingers as she whispered a word, '*áhierde*'. She flashed the sparks at one of the bed frames around the edge of the nest. It juddered and then wrenched itself free, rising into the air as Ruby flung her hand up. When she threw it forward, the frame flew towards the *ælwiht* and as it hit the creature, Ruby clenched her fist. The metal groaned as it curled around the *ælwiht*, trapping it arms to its sides.

Ruby squeezed her fist harder, until the nails were digging into her palms.

There was a short cry followed by a series of popping sounds as ribs broke and then the spine. The *ælwiht* fell forward, wrapped in the metal, and landed with a clang at the feet of the boy Aldwyn.

Ruby opened her hand. She had squeezed so hard there were tiny red crescent moons in her palm.

The man looked up from the dead creature at Ruby and his face tightened into a scowl before he proceeded to berate his cowering apprentice for almost getting them killed.

Jones was alive. Ruby watched, with a great sense of relief, as he coughed and spluttered at the dose of smelling salts the man held under his nose.

'The name's Sloop,' said the man as Jones blinked up at him. 'Simon Sloop. You've received a nasty blow to the head so you need to take it slowly. I'm guessing you're Jones, because you –' he stood up – 'must be Ruby Jenkins.' He stretched out a large hand and Ruby shook it. 'We've been observing these pregnant females for a couple of days now. The gestational period of the *ælwiht* is most interesting. I thought my apprentice would find the experience invaluable. Aldwyn, this is the famous Ruby Jenkins. The first girl Badlander. Ever. And her companion, Jones, an ordinary boy as well as a Badlander. A curious duo.'

Aldwyn stared at Ruby. She guessed he wasn't used to girls. So she held out her hand and smiled.

'Be polite,' growled Sloop, and the boy shook Ruby's hand.

'Thank you,' said Aldwyn, 'for saving our lives. I hope I can repay you one day.' He smiled. 'I've heard lots about you.' Sloop growled and the boy looked down at the floor and stepped back.

'And thank you for saving our lives, Aldwyn. At least, I think so.' Ruby glared at Sloop, which seemed to set something flickering in the corner of his jaw. 'Because as far as I can remember, I'd have been baby food if that *ælwiht* hadn't sniffed you out in time.'

Sloop cleared his throat. 'Indeed, you would have met your end. But . . .' he paused and waggled his finger, 'I didn't intervene because I wanted to see if it was true.'

'If what was true?'

'That a girl really can be considered worthy of being a Badlander.'

'You mean you were testing me? You—'

Jones grabbed her arm as he hauled himself up, a bluish tinge to his pale face.

'What Ruby means, Mr Sloop, is that she's already proved herself in front of the High Council by passing their magical test. She *is* a Badlander.'

'Yes, I know.'

'Then, you've got no business testing me,' said Ruby. 'The *Ordnung* says a Badlander should always do their utmost to save another Badlander in trouble.'

'I wasn't testing you,' replied Sloop, grinning like a fox. 'I was testing the *wyrd*. Although some Badlanders support having a girl in our ranks, I, like many others, am undecided. There's a big question over whether Randall Givens even has the authority to appoint a girl in the Order, despite being Head of the High Council. I thought I'd see if the *wyrd* might speak and show me the truth. And it did.' He smiled. 'Ruby Jenkins, the universe decreed you should live and continue your journey as a Badlander. You can't be upset at that. All Badlanders trust in the *wyrd*, as I'm sure you know.'

Little red sparks fizzed in front of Ruby's eyes as something inside her glowed hotter and hotter.

'So you'd have been quite happy to see me eaten? You'd have done nothing to stop it?'

Sloop chewed on something inside his mouth for a moment.

'I quite understand how you're feeling.'

'Really?'

'Of course. I'm angry too, having an apprentice who skimped on the masking potion we've been taking to enable our observations here, simply because he doesn't like the taste.' Sloop paused for a moment and allowed himself a thin smile. 'But clearly his actions were all part of a bigger plan. So how can I be upset at him for that?' He gave Aldwyn a friendly pat on the head. 'How can any of us be angry at the way things have turned out? We should be celebrating.'

Ruby stared at Sloop, unsure.

'Well, then, Mr Sloop, given what you're saying, I've got a brilliant idea.'

'Oh, yes?'

'Let's write our names together to mark the kills we've made so other Badlanders will know what we did here tonight. To celebrate the *wyrd*.' Ruby watched Sloop's jaw tick in the corner again, and she knew then that the man was lying about everything, and that he'd been hoping to see her eaten or at the very least witness his apprentice saving her rather than the other way around. 'What could be better than you, a man, making a mark with the first girl Badlander there's ever been? It'll be an important moment in the Order's history. The first time I've done that with someone other than Jones.'

Sloop forced his face tight into a gracious smile.

'I'm not sure myself or Aldwyn deserve any credit.'

'No, fair's fair. We should claim the kills together. Let everyone know how well we worked together. When you tell others in the Order about what you saw tonight, if they don't believe you, then you'll be able to tell them about the marks.'

Sloop looked at the floor for a moment, his brain ticking over.

'Why not? It's a splendid idea.' His green eyes glittered.

After disposing of the second body, dissolving it in the usual way with a brown dust, Sloop and Ruby agreed on a place to put their marks. Sloop carved his name into a corner of the wooden floor with a sharp paring knife along with the type of creature and the date on which it had been killed.

Rather than using a knife in the traditional manner, Ruby

had thought long and hard about how to make her mark stand out and had settled on using magic. Every *mearcunge* she made was now written in special ink using a charmed fountain pen.

She wrote down the type of creature she had killed and the date beside Sloop's mark before adding her own name:

Ruby Jenkins

The letters sparkled and then flashed brightly before vanishing, leaving Sloop's drab carving.

'My mark only lights up when a Badlander comes near it,' said Ruby.

'How lovely,' said Sloop. The man bent closer and Ruby's name lit up again along with the other details, the light playing across his face. 'Aldwyn, we'll have to get used to more innovations like these if the vote to have girls in the Order passes.' He watched Ruby's name fade away. 'Of course, if the Order decide to stick to their traditions, then all we'll be left with in the future will be the usual marks men make. You'll be able to make a *mearcunge* like my one, won't you, Aldwyn?'

'Of course, sir.'

'Excellent, because when old traditions survive it's usually for a good reason.' He stood up and straightened his jacket and looked at Ruby. For a moment, the air between them crackled with things unsaid, and then Sloop yawned.

'I think we should all be getting back to wherever we're

from, don't you? It's been a rather long and exciting night.'
Sloop turned to leave and then looked back at Ruby.
'Aldwyn and I will be seeing you at Givens's party tomorrow
night, I believe. I very much look forward to resuming our
acquaintance.' He clicked his fingers and his apprentice
trotted after him, the young boy turning round and nodding
a smile before his Master cuffed him round the ear.

THREE

Over the course of the next day, Ruby tried not to worry about the party. She had been dreading it for weeks and it loomed over her like a dark thundercloud wherever she went. Givens had wanted to hold the party on the eve of the vote as a last chance to make a good impression. Ruby was to be guest of honour and Givens was hoping she might settle the nerves of some important Badlanders who were still undecided about which way to cast their vote and, in turn, influence others.

To pass the time, Ruby did as much reading as she could bear about different types of monsters, and even herbs and gardening, until her brain complained and she was just staring at the pages. She sat back in the chair and sighed, looking around the study which had once been Maitland's, the Badlander to whom Jones had been an apprentice before he had died. All of Maitland's journals were still on a long shelf, black books containing pages and pages of descriptions and facts documenting the various hunting trips the man had made during his career. Ruby had one small notebook in comparison, which sat on the desk beside her. Only the first few pages of it were full. She thought about all the Badlanders who would be at the party later, scrutinizing her and asking about her achievements. A dull weight dropped down her throat into her guts. She closed the book she'd been reading and left the study.

To cheer herself up she set about learning some new spells from *The Black Book of Magical Instruction*, practising her Anglo-Saxon pronunciation. It felt good to be wielding magic and she cast her spells with a flourish, imagining Sloop on the receiving end of a particularly nasty exploding fireball she had perfected. But *The Black Book of Magical Instruction* wasn't in a particularly complimentary mood as it sat on the grass, calling her out on her Anglo-Saxon and complaining about the stability and quality of the spells she'd cast. Eventually she gave up and slammed the book shut, only for it to spring open again and reprimand her for being so unruly and lacking focus.

Finally, after eating and trying to nap – impossible with all the thoughts rattling around in her head like stones in a bottle – Ruby did some work with the gun, shooting at tin cans lined up along a wall. The idea was to try and improve her aim and technique but the late afternoon air was so cold her fingers were stiff and she kept missing. The gun grumbled about her aim more than usual, but she stuck at it until she started to improve and the cans began pinging onto the grass.

'You know what?' said the gun. 'You're not a bad shot when you put your mind to it.'

'Thanks,' replied Ruby as she pinged another can off the wall, sending it up into a satisfyingly high somersault before it landed on the grass.

'As well as being a first-rate scryer and the first girl ever to do magic. Not to mention being the bravest girl I've ever met.'

'I'm the *only* girl you've ever met,' said Ruby, her brow wrinkled in concentration. She eased her finger off the trigger. 'Why are you being so nice?'

'Just trying to reassure you about tonight.'

'I'm fine about it.'

'Really?'

'All right, I'm nervous.'

'Then why don't you take me along? I can sing your praises. I've been around for many of your bravest moments, from taking out a Witch, to a *Scucca* hound and even a Vampire.'

'No,' said Ruby and aimed and fired at the last tin can on the wall.

Ruby knew the gun would want to be the centre of attention. The truth was, it had a big mouth and she didn't want it making a scene. It would only reflect badly on her. There was too much riding on the evening for anything to go wrong.

Even so, she felt a little guilty as she put the gun back in its box because spending time with it was the only thing that had made her feel good all day. She decided she'd make it up to the gun some other way. Perhaps by giving it a holster to sit in rather than being pushed down her waistband all the time. It was always complaining about that.

Ruby changed quickly, putting on a white dress with red piping around the V-shaped neckline. The sleeves were embroidered with blue lace. She had seen one like it in a shop window on the high street of a small market town one night and asked Jones's mother to buy one for her in London. Givens had warned Ruby she needed something smart to wear for various functions if she was going to be a Badlander.

Ruby admired herself in the mirror. The dress fitted perfectly. The tiny gemstones glued on the blue lace caught the light and winked at her like friends telling her she would be okay.

Jones was getting ready too. He'd smoothed down his hair, and had decided on a jacket and tie – a black one with the Badlander crest in yellow and the motto 'Be Prepared' in red beneath it – that had belonged to his Master, Maitland. Maitland had been in his thoughts a lot over the past few weeks for he'd started appearing in Jones's dreams, angry at him for not continuing the life of a traditional Badlander, and for giving up the gift of magic. In the dreams that stayed with Jones, Maitland raged at him for rejecting Commencement, a great honour for any apprentice. Jones had always presumed these dreams were just his guilty feelings about disobeying his Master lurking deep inside him that came out when he was asleep. But lately the dreams felt so real he had started to wonder if the man was communicating with him from somewhere he couldn't see. He thought he could feel a presence around him when he was awake and he would glance up sometimes, thinking he'd heard Maitland's gruff voice. The feeling was particularly strong now and he looked around his bedroom. Was that his name being called? There it was again. Louder. Surely it couldn't be. The man was dead. Gone forever.

'Jones! Jones! You complete and utter disappointment.'

Jones pinched himself but he knew he wasn't dreaming. As he blinked he saw his Master beside him and he stepped back in horror, before the man vanished, as though Jones had hit the TV remote to turn him off. He turned to leave, but Maitland was in front of him again and Jones found himself looking up into his Master's face, the old baseball cap he usually wore pulled down towards his eyes.

Jones stumbled back with a cry and tripped, collapsing onto his bed. Maitland was glaring down at him. His body was shimmering, fizzing like static on a dead TV screen.

'You're ... you're dead,' muttered the boy. 'You're gone. I can do what I want now. I'm only imagining this.' But Jones knew he wasn't as he felt a force pushing down on his chest and keeping him stuck to the bed.

'I might be dead. But I'm not gone,' said the man. 'As you can very much see, boy.' He pointed at the tie Jones was wearing. 'Like our motto says, you should always "Be Prepared" for anything. A Badlander should never, ever, forget that.'

*

Givens's house was full of Badlanders accompanied by their boy apprentices. When Ruby walked into the drawing room, conversations stopped and the guests began to stare. Givens excused himself from the balding old man he was talking to and clapped his hands sharply.

'Gentlemen,' he announced. 'The star of the show has arrived.' Ruby tried her best to smile. 'You all know who Ruby Jenkins is, and why she's here among us. Not only has she proved her worth as a Badlander by despatching various creatures, but she's saved my life, for which I am eternally grateful. As Head of the High Council, I value her highly and I know others on the Council have been impressed by her. Just as the people of the ordinary world we have sworn to protect adjust and change their ways through history, so perhaps should we. The vote I'm proposing on establishing girl apprentices is for the good of the Order. To make it, and us, more relevant than ever before. Tonight, gentlemen, all I ask is that you keep your minds open to the new possibilities that come with change.'

For a few embarrassing moments it seemed as though Givens's speech would be met only by a deafening silence, until a single pair of hands started clapping politely. Others followed. It was hardly a hearty round of applause, and as people went back to their conversations, Givens raised his eyebrows at Ruby.

'Seems like we've got some work to do tonight,' he whispered. 'Let's see if we can make a difference to some hearts and minds.' He put out his arm and Ruby took it and he swept her towards a group of Badlanders, some of whom raised their eyebrows at Ruby as if she was a creature they would normally be hunting.

'I'm all for progress, Givens, if it helps the Order,' said an elderly gentleman with strands of white hair combed across his head. 'But you'll never alter the *Ordnung* when it comes to apprentices in our lifetimes. People will need a lot longer to be persuaded about a change of such magnitude.' He looked at Ruby and frowned.

'Hear, hear,' said a younger man. 'The Order have survived for centuries without women, so why change now?'

Givens opened his mouth but Ruby opened hers quicker.

'Maybe it would have worked even better if women had been part of it for all those centuries.'

Everyone looked rather shocked. One man stared through his monocle at her and scowled.

'And what do you base that theory on, exactly?' asked the young man.

The group seemed to lean in towards Ruby. Givens watched her too and she knew he was hoping for a good answer.

'Well, like Mr Givens said, the ordinary world has changed through history. Women are just as important as men in Great Britain – and in lots of countries actually – for coming up with ideas. There's scientists and inventors and writers. All sorts of women have made the world better.' Everyone kept staring, expecting to hear some examples and Ruby squeezed her brain to try and think of some she had learnt at school. 'What about Marie Curie, or Mary Shelley? Or the Queen?' She clicked her fingers. 'I know, how about J. K. Rowling?' There wasn't a flicker of acknowledgement from anyone. Ruby cleared her throat and stared defiantly back at the faces around her. 'If you're protecting the world where women are capable of doing whatever men can do, then surely you're already admitting you respect them.'

'That's in the ordinary world. *We're* in the Badlands.'

Ruby pointed at the young man's apprentice, a boy of no more than six or seven. The boy blushed and looked down at his feet. 'Where'd he come from? All of you were born as ordinary people, weren't you? You weren't just magicked out of thin air. You all became Badlanders, like I did. I think you should all remember you've come from the world you've sworn to protect.'

Givens beamed at her as a murmur went around the group. 'I'd say she's got a point, Beaufort.'

A thin-lipped man with a chin like a trout raised his glass. 'Yes, she has.'

Beaufort managed a gracious smile. But Ruby saw in his eyes that he was just playing along. She recognized the same look in the eyes of others she met during the course of the night, dragged around by Givens and forced to stand up for herself as she was challenged about her role in the Order. She did her best not to shout and be rude because she knew it wouldn't help. But it made her prickle on the inside.

Simon Sloop seemed to slip around the room with his apprentice like a snake, avoiding her, talking and laughing in groups, while looking over at Ruby. At one point it seemed as though their orbit around each other was going to bring them together, until Ruby decided she couldn't bear it and whirled away, heading for a tall man standing on his own.

'Samuel Raynham,' said the man, introducing himself with a nod. He was wearing a red velvet jacket and sporting a short white beard cut precisely into an upside-down triangle. Ruby managed a smile and took a sip of the rosehip drink she'd been given.

'Can't be easy being in the spotlight tonight.'

Ruby sighed and her body sagged more than she expected it to and she almost dropped her drink. 'I'm not sure there'll ever be enough votes to change the *Ordnung* in the way Mr Givens is proposing. Everything I've done in the Badlands doesn't seem to matter at all for some people.'

Ruby downed her drink and banged the empty glass on the table beside her. A few faces looked round, none of them friendly, and she glared back. She wondered where Jones was and cursed at him under her breath for not coming. *He's probably still sore about last night in Wighton and making a point about it*, she thought.

'My advice,' said Raynham, 'is to carry on with what you've been doing. You've impressed me. And I bet you've made an impression on others. Perhaps they just don't want to admit it in front of other Badlanders?'

'Maybe,' sighed Ruby as she looked around. 'Where's your apprentice?'

'I don't work with one. My work doesn't lend itself

to training up a boy, or a girl, for that matter,' he added with a smile.

'What sort of work's that?'

'Cold cases. I follow up unsolved mysteries. They're all compiled in this.' He took a large red book out of his pocket and held it up so Ruby could see the title written in silver lettering:

The Book of Mysteries

'If I solve a case it's struck out from the book.'

'How many are you working on?'

'Seven hundred and sixty-five, at the last count.' Raynham smiled rather weakly. 'I know,' he said, sighing. 'It's slow work. A lot of the cases are decades old. Some have remained unsolved for centuries. I spend time researching them, looking for clues in old books or going back to places where events are said to have happened. It's not often that something turns up. The cases are all mysteries for one reason or another. That's why it's not considered suitable work for apprentices who need to be taught the basic knowledge they require to survive as a Badlander.'

'How many cases have you solved?'

'Five in thirty years.'

'Wow. I mean ... well, is that good or bad?' Ruby cocked her head to one side like a doctor trying to sound sympathetic and enquiring.

'I like to think it's not bad. But most other Badlanders

look down their noses at me so I can certainly relate to how you're feeling tonight. I enjoy my job, though. I like solving puzzles. When a mystery disappears from this book there's no better feeling. Of course, it's not so good when a new one appears.' He cleared his throat. 'I'm glad we got to meet. I'm interested in talking to you about the Black Amulet and the boy Thomas Gabriel. You were the last person to see him. The case has been entered in *The Book of Mysteries* and officially handed over to me.'

'I told Givens and the High Council everything I know,' said Ruby. 'I'd try and help if I knew any more.'

'I know. But I'd still like to sit down with you and go over your testimony again, if you can spare the time. Details can be very useful in my line of work.'

'If you think it'll help.'

'Thank you.' Raynham finished his drink and placed the glass on the table as Givens arrived beside them.

'Ruby, I'd like you to meet someone else. Simon Sloop. He's important.'

'Because of those damned Lucky Drops of his,' whispered Raynham, raising his eyes at Ruby who just smiled politely because she wasn't sure what he meant.

'Precisely,' said Givens.

'Knock 'em dead,' smiled Raynham, as Givens turned Ruby round and steered her towards Sloop.

The man smiled graciously as the others around him fell silent.

'Sloop, I'd like you to meet—'

'Good grief, I know who she is, Givens, you've already introduced her to the whole room.' A couple of men laughed into their drinks. 'And, in fact, we've already met. Just last night.'

Givens looked at Ruby, who nodded.

'Mr Sloop's right,' she said. 'We crossed paths after Jones and I went on a hunting trip. We tracked an *ælwiht* to a nest and found two pregnant females. Mr Sloop was already there. He and I each took out a creature, which his apprentice, Aldwyn here, will back up.' The young boy smiled at Ruby.

'Impressive,' said a man with thick, woolly sideburns, wearing a crumpled black suit. 'They're damned difficult creatures to despatch.'

'Well, Sloop,' said Givens, 'I'm relieved to hear you've had the chance to work with Ruby. You must be *tempted* to vote for my motion, at the very least, now that you've seen how talented she is.'

Sloop looked as if he'd bitten into a lemon. 'Actually, Ruby's mistaken. There were two creatures, that's true, but I despatched them both, saving Miss Jenkins and her partner, Jones.'

'That's a lie!' shouted Ruby, making some of the men take a step back.

'I think Miss Jenkins has been on the champagne. I can assure you it's true, gentlemen. Ruby and her partner got into trouble and it was only by great good fortune that myself and my apprentice, observing the pregnant females for study, managed to step in and save the day.'

Ruby could feel her spine tingling.

'We each made a *mearcunge* for the kill we made.'

Sloop produced a small scrying mirror and conjured an image of the nest in it, holding it up for all to see. 'I'm afraid you're mistaken, Miss Jenkins. As we can see here, this is the nest and over here – ' he pointed into one corner – 'are my *mearcunga* for the two kills I made.' Everyone crowded round to look and nodded as they saw the two marks scratched on the wooden floor, both of them bearing Sloop's name, the date and the type of creature killed.

'Liar!' shouted Ruby. 'Aldwyn, tell them what really happened!'

'Young lady, I'm the only one who can order my apprentice what to do and say, according to the *Ordnung*.' There was a murmur of approval from various onlookers. 'And isn't my word enough? As well as the evidence, there for all to see? Persist with your tone and things won't go well for you. There's no shame in being rescued by a man, is there? Don't all fairy tales in the world of ordinary people we're sworn to protect play out to the same story?' He grinned at Ruby's ever-reddening face.

The laughter rang around the room and it flicked a switch in Ruby. Sparks of magic flickered around her fingers and the laughter turned to murmurs. Sloop eyed her like a fox about to go in for the kill.

'You see, gentlemen, although Miss Jenkins is undoubtedly an able Badlander, she allows her emotions to get the better of her. There have been studies in the past suggesting that magic and women don't mix, that it brings out the worst in them. This is what the *Ordnung* undoubtedly took into account many centuries ago when it was decided magic wasn't for women.' Ruby heard the anger ticking like a bomb inside her. She was looking down a dark tunnel at Sloop and there was only one thing on her mind. Before she blew up, a hand landed on her shoulder. Givens. Ruby remembered the other Badlanders in the room. It was like waking up from a dream.

Sloop was still staring as Ruby felt Givens's hand tighten even more on her shoulder.

'I can assure any man here,' continued Sloop, 'that if they go to the location of the *ælwiht* nest they will see only my *mearcunga*.' Ruby knew then that he must have gone back and erased her mark somehow, no doubt with magic. Sloop had been planning to embarrass her tonight as soon as they'd met in the farmhouse. She wanted to make him pay for what he had done. But she let the magic around her fingers disappear because now was not the time or place. It would only make things worse. She cursed silently at Jones for not being there at the party to back her up, even though he was clearly still angry at her for going after the *ælwiht* in the first place. Hanging her head in front of everyone else, Ruby wished she could melt into the carpet beneath her smart black shoes.

FOUR

Jones didn't go to school the next day. He stayed at home under his duvet but he wouldn't tell his parents why.

'If you're not ill, you're fine to go,' said his father.

Jones rolled over and stared at the wall. 'You can't make me,' he said. He felt the duvet being pulled away and tightened himself into a ball.

'Darling, what's wrong?' his mother asked, sitting beside him and stroking his hair. 'What's happened?'

'It's the Badlands,' said Jones. 'I can't tell you anything else.'

'But we can't help you if you don't tell us what's wrong.'

Jones felt something trembling inside him. He wanted to explain about Maitland appearing to him the night before, but the man had sworn him to secrecy and Jones knew he was listening. He still couldn't understand how his Master could appear to him, despite being dead. Now all the guilt he'd hidden away about disobeying Maitland's dying wishes was swilling around inside like a poison. Maitland had made it clear that Jones was not to go to the party and lend his support to Ruby and Givens's vote. He had magically controlled the boy like a puppet on strings when Jones had tried to leave, forcing him to listen. His Master, it seemed, was able to make him do whatever he wanted.

Jones's life, of being an ordinary boy and living with his parents yet still hunting monsters in the Badlands with Ruby, was over. Maitland had instructed him to bid his parents farewell and return to the house in which he had lived with his Master to carry on his instruction.

'I'm more important than your parents, boy,' Maitland had said. 'I saved you from the Witch and brought you up. You owe me a debt and that's to continue my legacy. Your life will be a misery if you don't. I'll make sure of it. Together, we'll find a way to sort out your Commencement.'

The words were like thorns pricking Jones's heart. Now, he looked past his mother and father and saw the vague shape of Maitland, visible only to him, lurking in the corner of the room.

Jones's jaw tightened as he stared at the man's blurry shape. He would find a way to keep the life he'd built for himself. But as he rubbed his tired eyes and stared at his parents' questioning faces, he had no idea how to do it.

Ruby had not slept well either. Every time she'd closed her eyes, she'd seen the Badlanders and their apprentices at the party staring at her. When she did finally fall asleep, she dreamt about Sloop making everyone laugh at her until he changed into an *ælwiht* with blue hair, rendering her magic useless against him, as he came at her with his sly, toothy smile and talons instead of fingers. Ruby woke with a scream, then hurled off the covers.

She spent the next few hours in the forest near the cottage, pretending that various trees and bushes were Sloop, hurling every magical spell she could at them, making them fizz and burn, crumble and disintegrate. By the time her arms were sore and her fingers felt singed with all the magic she'd conjured, it was past midday and she trudged back to the cottage. The vote was tonight, and in all likelihood she had blown any chance there might have been of it going in her favour. Givens had warned her as much, saying that news would travel about her row with Sloop, raising questions about women and magic.

Ruby knew that Jones would be at school until later in the day so she couldn't talk to him. She wasn't sure he'd listen anyway, since he hadn't turned up to the party or been in touch at all since the hunt for the *ælwiht* which had almost ended in disaster. The only company she had was the gun. It listened sagely to her story of the party and then sighed.

'Well, I suppose if you'd taken me, I could have stopped you whirling into such a rage. And I could have told some of my finest stories about the Badlands to keep everyone occupied, for example that time I—'

'Any ideas about what to do *now*?'

'Nope.'

'You're a great help.' Ruby sat back in her chair. She looked around the study, at all the books in their shelves, and then stood up. She ran her finger down the various spines, thinking.

'You'd have to hunt down the most difficult creature in the Badlands before tonight's vote to make any sort of difference, and that isn't going to happen,' said the gun, as if reading her mind.

'I know.' Ruby's voice sounded dreamy and distant to her. Someone else could have been talking. Her finger stopped at a book, its title embossed in gold:

The Training Manual for Scucca Hounds
by Severin Lafour

Ruby had flicked through the pages when Jones had first given her the *Scucca* egg that he and Maitland had hoped to hatch. It had been a thank-you present for helping him. Although Ruby had inspected the egg a couple of times she hadn't plucked up the courage to hatch it. In truth, it was because she was scared. Ruby had seen a fully grown *Scucca* hound in the wild, in its natural habitat of a graveyard. The creature had been extremely aggressive, not to mention large, at least as tall as she was. Such memories seemed at odds with being able to train an animal that could help her in the Badlands. Indeed, the opening pages of Lafour's book, which she looked at again now, made it quite clear just how difficult it might be:

Training a Scucca hound is no task for an ordinary Badlander. It requires the skill of a supreme man, not only to find the ægg and hatch it, but also to retain the hound

40

after it is born and train it to be obedient. This manual aims
to unlock the secrets of success for a truly special Badlander
to control such a great and fearsome animal. Many have
tried but few have ever succeeded.

Ruby flipped through more pages, scanning the words, and a plan slowly began to form. *What have I got to lose?* she thought. When she had read enough she turned to the gun.

'Want to help me train up a *Scucca*?'

'You've got to be kidding!' replied the weapon, before it burst out laughing so hard that Ruby thought it might fire a shot by accident.

'You might laugh now, but just think if I turn up to the vote tonight with a *Scucca* hatched and ready to be trained.' The gun laughed even harder.

Ruby slammed the book shut and walked out of the study.

When she opened the black tin box, she saw the egg lying on its bed of shredded paper. It looked exactly the same as when she had first come across it, a small black oval stone with tiny silver veins running over the surface. This time she knew better than to pick it up. She still had a nasty scar on her forefinger from the last time she'd tried.

She leafed through the pages of the manual again, reading carefully the paragraph about hatching:

An ægg must be handled carefully using the appropriate
tongs since the slightest warmth from human hands

41

will trigger a hatching. In the wild, a gradual rise in the
temperature of the soil during spring and through the
summer incubates the ægg until it is ready to hatch.

A Badlander must be ready to replicate the generous
food source left for the newborn pup by its mother. The
appetite of the young creature will be voracious. This is an
instinctive trait designed to improve the pup's chances of
survival because if it has enough food it will grow rapidly
in size in order to be able to defend itself. The question
a Badlander needs to ask is: How big do you want your
hound to grow in its first few hours, if you want it to stay?

Ruby eyed the sides of cooked beef and ham and strings
of sausages placed on the counters around the kitchen.
Although the meat had been ordered a long time ago by
Maitland in preparation for taming the *Scucca*, it had been
kept in cold storage under a charm. Ruby was hoping, no
doubt as Maitland had, that this would convince the tiny
pup to stay, instead of instinctively returning to its 'deadland',
a small graveyard in a village in Yorkshire, from which Jones
and Maitland had originally dug up the egg.

Ruby had also uncorked a bottle of imps and stationed
them around the kitchen to help her ensure the pup could
not escape. According to the manual, it was imperative to
keep the creature close in the first hours after hatching. The
pup had to be exposed to the prospective owner's smell and
voice, as well as their body movements and facial expressions.
It was this degree of initial contact that would affect how

loyal a *Scucca* might become. The large amount of food would keep it around long enough to bond. At least, that was the idea.

Ruby was curious to know if the pup might remember her. Having hatched it accidentally the first time around, just after meeting Jones, it had bitten her, leaving the scar on her finger. Jones had quickly stowed the tiny creature away in the box in time to allow it to re-form its egg casing, but would it remember the taste of her blood? Ruby rubbed her scar as she thought about that.

The manual made mention of some Badlanders having experimented by giving pups their own blood after hatching them, in an effort to try and create a tighter bond. This had only worked once. The majority of other times had ended in serious injuries, even death, as the animal had grown, driven by a greed for more human blood. The history of such stories fluttered through the space of Ruby's mind as she eyed the imps around the room.

'Here goes then,' she announced. 'Remember to do exactly as I say.'

And then she picked up the egg.

The heat in her hand caused an immediate reaction and the black egg changed to a dark red that made it look like a ripe plum. The tiny silver veins vanished and the top half of the egg cracked, then lifted a little. A pair of red eyes peered out through the gap. A black dot of a nose sniffed the air. Then a little mouth went to work on the egg, tearing it apart until a tiny black dog stood on Ruby's hand, pieces of shell all around it and caught in its wiry hair. Ruby's scarred finger twitched as if remembering just how sharp the creature's teeth had been. As quickly and carefully as she could, Ruby placed the creature on the floor and presented it with a sausage, far longer than the tiny *Scucca*.

As it took a sniff, Ruby wondered if the sausage might be too big to start with, but then the pup lunged and took as big a mouthful as it could. It seemed to like the taste of the sausage meat and took another bite. Its eyes darted round the room as it chewed. The imps looked nervous, despite being far bigger than the *Scucca*, because Ruby had briefed them about the creature growing rapidly the more it ate.

'Stay sharp,' she announced to them because the tiny black hound had gulped down the last of the sausage already and was glancing around the kitchen, eyeing the nearest imp. Ruby thrust another sausage in front of its nose. This one went just as quickly. Ruby held out one more, and the *Scucca* grabbed it, shaking it round like it was playing with a stick, until it stopped, dropped what was left, plopped down on its backside and gave a little burp.

The sound acted like a warning for what happened next. Every bit of the tiny hound grew at once: the muzzle lengthened, the shoulders bulked out and the legs extended, ending in bigger paws with claws that curled a little tighter and looked a little more lethal. Suddenly, the pup was about the size of a large rat but leaner and stronger, its black fur lustrous and rich, as if it was wrapped up in a little piece of night. Ruby heard a collective gasp from the imps.

The *Scucca* pricked its ears and growled. Then, it stretched and yawned and returned to the remains of the sausage.

'There, it's not that bad, is it?' Ruby felt as though she was saying it as much to herself as to the tiny dog.

The *Scucca* gave a little bark in response, tail wagging. It sniffed the air, eyeing the large ham high above it on the counter, then barked again before trying to jump up and clattering into the cupboard door in front of it. When Ruby laid the meat on the floor, in its foil tray, the *Scucca* tore off chunks, fat and all, its muzzle glistening with the ham's juices.

When Ruby realized it might be getting thirsty, she offered it some water, pushing the bowl across the floor that she'd filled earlier, according to the manual's instructions. The little pink tongue lapped steadily until the creature paused and burped again, rounding it off with a low growl as it grew once more, more than doubling in size.

It looked like a proper dog now, albeit a small one, and it tore into the remains of the ham again.

By the time Ruby had retrieved a piece of beef from the counter, the *Scucca* had finished and was eyeing up an imp guarding the door out of the kitchen.

'Come on . . .' she said, her voice faltering because she was unsure how to address it. She waggled the beef but the *Scucca* was more interested in the living, breathing imp.

'Steady,' commanded Ruby as the imp raised a foot and looked ready to run. 'Give it something to chase and it'll go for you.'

But as the *Scucca* stepped closer, the imp panicked and started backing away. The *Scucca* moved fast, as if attached to the imp by a piece of elastic, and pounced on the poor creature.

'No!' shouted Ruby. 'Get off!' The *Scucca* turned and growled, sniffing the air, one paw planted on the imp's chest as Ruby waggled the piece of beef again. 'Come on,' she said. 'This is the *good* stuff. Much nicer than a chewy imp.'

The *Scucca* sniffed the imp and growled, turning up its nose, and then padded towards Ruby. It stopped about halfway, its ears pricking, and turned to look through the doorway out of the kitchen, beyond the cowering imp still lying on the floor.

Ruby couldn't hear anything as the *Scucca*'s ears swivelled, trying to locate the source of a sound. She wondered if this was the moment she had read about in the manual, that the *Scucca* was hearing its 'deadland' calling to it. The book had warned her the call would come soon after hatching. If the *Scucca* returned to Yorkshire there'd be no chance of taking it to the vote later, or of ever training it up, because the connection with the earth in which the egg had been laid would be too strong to break.

Ruby thanked her lucky stars that the dog was not yet very big as she reached for the collar and leash that Maitland had bought in preparation, along with all the food, sliding it quietly off the counter top.

Suddenly, the *Scucca* bolted for the doorway. Ruby whirled the leash and sent it sailing through the air, the line of leather extending, snaking longer and longer as she held the other end, the power of Maitland's charm thrumming through it. The collar at the other end opened and closed neatly around the *Scucca's* neck. The leash went taut, but Ruby managed to cling on and pulled up the dog inches short of the doorway, yanking it back.

It fell back in a furry black heap on the floor. But the *Scucca* was up in an instant, hackles raised, its red eyes burning fiercely. It jerked like a fish on the end of a line but the collar wouldn't budge. When the hound tried biting the leash, there was clearly something about the leather that didn't taste good and it stopped immediately, coughing and spitting onto the floor.

Then it growled and charged at Ruby. The *Scucca* barrelled into her shins and Ruby landed with a loud *oomph*. When she opened her eyes, the *Scucca* was standing over her, teeth frosty with spit. Its little red eyes were burning and she thought it smiled before it turned and trotted off. She reached for the loose leash but missed and hit the floor.

Ruby heard a fizz of Slap Dust, followed by footsteps.

'Ruby?' It was Jones.

He emerged from the hallway and stopped by the door to the kitchen. He looked down at the small black dog which was staring up at him.

'Jones! Don't let it out.' Ruby could see Jones wasn't sure as the creature growled. 'It's not that big,' she said, scrambling to her feet. 'It won't try going for you.'

The *Scucca* burped and doubled in size.

47

It was a reasonable-sized dog now, one that could easily do some damage. And it seemed to know it as it glared up at Jones. Carefully, the boy reached into his overcoat pocket and drew out his catapult.

'Don't hurt it,' hissed Ruby as Jones slotted a silver ball bearing into the sling. 'I'm going to take it to the vote tonight. To show everyone just how special I am.'

'It's a *Scucca*, Ruby,' said Jones as calmly as possible. 'It can take weeks to get anywhere training a creature like this, if you can do anything at all. Take it tonight and you might as well kiss any chance of winning the vote goodbye.'

'Jones, I pretty much kissed it goodbye last night. You'd have known if you'd been there. Sloop made sure I embarrassed myself in front of everyone. You'd have stopped me. Everything might have been all right if you'd turned up.'

'I couldn't come.' Ruby opened her mouth but Jones got there first. 'Ruby, you shouldn't have hatched this hound. Training it up is going to be impossible.' The creature bared its teeth and growled. It raked the floor with its claws, drawing bright lines in the wooden floorboards. Jones pulled back the sling of the catapult. 'You're only a girl! I should never have given you the egg. I should have kept it and hatched the pup out myself and done it properly.'

'Jones, what are you talking about? Why on earth would you say that?' But the boy just grunted. Ruby heard a click in her brain and then she was marching towards the *Scucca*, determined to show Jones he was wrong, whatever he thought of her. *Who cares if he's still sore about the other*

48

night, she thought as she picked up the end of the leash. *I'll show him ...*

'Jones, sit!'

'What?'

'SIT!'

'You've got to be jok—'

'Sit down, Jones!' said Ruby in a firm and controlled voice, sparks of magic at the fingertips of her free hand.

'But—'

'SIT!' she yelled at the boy, the sparks snaking out towards him. 'I'll show you just how good girls are.'

Jones's nose twitched and he grumbled something under his breath before sitting down slowly, the catapult still aimed at the dog.

'And, you,' she said, glaring at the *Scucca*, 'you're staying here!'

Ruby remembered what the training manual had said. A Badlander had to be dominant enough for the *Scucca* to follow its Master. But the creature didn't seem to want to believe that she was the one that mattered most in the room.

'Sit!' Ruby ordered the imps and they immediately did as they were told. She stepped closer to the *Scucca*. 'And, you, sit down too.' The red eyes stared back and the dog bared its teeth. 'Sit down.' Ruby watched the magical sparks at the ends of her fingers dancing in the *Scucca*'s eyes. It glanced round at the others in the room, everyone sitting except for her.

And then it seemed to understand. With a brief whine

it slumped to the floor, yawned and started panting. Ruby took a step closer and then another until she was standing over the *Scucca*.

'Good boy,' she said quietly. 'Good boy.' Slowly, she reached out a hand, inching it closer and closer until she rubbed the creature's head and she felt her heart fizzing in her chest.

'You see? It just needs someone to be firm with it.' She glared at Jones. The boy scowled and seemed to glance beyond her at something. 'What is it? What are you looking at?'

'I need to tell you something.'

'So tell me.'

'I'm instructing you to leave this house. It's no longer yours. Read this letter,' he said, taking an envelope out of his coat pocket and laying it on the floor. 'It'll explain everything because I haven't got time to hang around with a girl any more.'

'Jones, what's got—'

'Just read the bloomin' letter! Read it and do exactly as I ask. No questions.' And then Jones walked out of the room without another word.

Moments later Ruby heard a fizz of Slap Dust as he left.

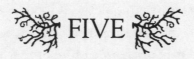

FIVE

The *Scucca* seemed quite happy to sleep after its eventful birth and lay stretched out on the kitchen floor, legs twitching. Ruby had tied the leash to the silver bar that ran along the front of the range oven in case the creature made a bolt for it again. But it looked so content it was hard to believe it might want to do so. Ruby had to manoeuvre around the creature, careful not to step on the tail as she sat down to read Jones's letter.

Dear Ruby

EVERYTHING I SAID WAS AN ACT
  I can't tell you anything but I can write it down.
Maitland has come back. I don't know how, but
he's haunting me like a *Gást* – only worse cos he
can control me too. That's why I didn't come to the
party. He's watching me practically all the time
(I'm writing this letter on the toilet!), telling me to
give up my parents and go back to being a normal

Badlander. He's angry at what I've done and he's angry at you too. He doesn't think girls should be Badlanders. We're not supposed to speak to each other any more.

I need you to make me a potion. It's the one on page 356 of *Potions and Lotions Vol 1*. I'm hoping it'll get rid of him for a while so I can think about how to sort this all out. Make the potion as soon as you read this letter. It's the only way I'll be able to get away from him to vote tonight.

Send me the potion at 9 p.m. I'll be in the bathroom at home. Don't try to contact me, or Maitland'll know I'm up to something and he'll stop me. Everything you need is in the house.

Jones x

Ruby read the letter twice and the same chill crept up her spine each time. When she heard a creak from somewhere in the kitchen she looked up, expecting to see Maitland scowling at her, but there was no one there. Even so, she couldn't shake off the uncomfortable feeling of sitting in what had once been Maitland's cottage. She had loved the house ever since Jones had given it to her because it had been the first time she'd ever felt she belonged somewhere after being a foster child. It had rooted her like a little oak tree ready to grow. Now, she felt that same uneasy sense of needing to move on again, of not being able to call the house 'home'.

She found *Potions and Lotions Vol 1* on a shelf in the study and followed all the instructions for 'The Basic Banishment of Unruly Spirits', mixing the various ingredients in their correct proportions, stirring and shaking when required. By the time she'd finished, the mixture smelt like the pile of compost kept warm under a tarpaulin in the garden, and she held her breath as she poured it into a glass vial and popped in the cork.

Her work done, her thoughts started to curdle again as she thought ahead to later that night. She hoped the potion she'd made was strong enough to help Jones because every 'yes' in favour of Givens's vote really counted now after what had happened at the party. Without enough votes in favour of having girls in the Order there'd be no one else to carry on after her. She'd be the first and last female Badlander.

After placing the vial inside a small ring of Slap Dust, Ruby sent it to Jones at exactly 9 p.m. It vanished, leaving her staring into space. She imagined in its place a small apprentice standing there, looking up at her. A girl. Someone who had always wanted to be extraordinary and make a difference to the world, without knowing how to do it before. Ruby closed her eyes and made a secret wish.

Jones had never been to the *mótbeorh*, but he knew it was a sacred place where Badlanders met at times of great importance for the Order. The special packet of red Slap Dust required to take him there had arrived a week earlier, appearing on his pillow one night as he'd been getting ready for bed. The brief instructions had informed him of the exact time to arrive – 1.05 a.m. on the specified date. If he was late, he would miss his opportunity to vote.

Standing in his bedroom, watching the seconds tick down on his smartwatch, Jones tried not to worry about Maitland. Ruby's potion had reduced the *Gást* to a dark blur, just visible out the corner of his eye. Now he could not hear Maitland, or feel any of the controlling power the man had used the night before. Jones had no idea how long the potion would last, though, and he knew at some point he was going to have to face Maitland's wrath, unless he could figure out how to banish him for ever.

For Jones, voting to have girl apprentices in the Order was the right thing to do, and he didn't care what Maitland thought. He only had to remember all the things he and Ruby had achieved since they'd met: taking on a No-Thing; meeting Charles Du Clement and learning how to make gravestones whisper; defeating Mrs Easton the Witch with the Dark Bottle; recovering the Black Amulet, and overcoming all manner of monsters that would strike fear into the hearts of ordinary people. Out of every man and boy voting tonight he alone knew how much Ruby had done to prove that girls were just as good as boys in the Badlands. He would vote for what he believed in.

He said a little prayer to the *wyrd* as his watch ticked over to 1.05am then slapped his hands together. The last thing he saw was a strong red spark zigzag into the air before he felt the air whoosh up all around him.

He arrived on a hilltop, in the middle of a long stone slab, a sea of dark countryside below. An eerie white glow shone down, making it light enough to see everything around him. He thought he must be one of the first to vote because only a few other boys were there, standing to one side, huddled together like birds in the cold.

Givens and the rest of the High Council were standing in a line watching him. Ruby was with them, the *Scucca* sitting obediently beside her on the leash. Jones felt a great sense of pride at seeing her with the hound. He understood just why she had wanted to hatch it. It was the last thing each Badlander would see before they cast their vote. He smiled at her, to make sure she knew he'd been putting on a show when he'd last seen her at the cottage, and she winked back, but didn't move another muscle.

A man in front of Jones held up a large book, nodding at him to come forward. Jones stepped into two grooves worn into the stone slab where many pairs of feet must have stood before him. Standing there made him realize just how far back in time the Order reached and how much he was now a part of its history. As the burden of tradition and expectation weighed heavily inside him, he wondered if the stone was charmed to make him consider the importance of his vote so as not to take it lightly.

The man cleared his throat and Jones felt a prickle of embarrassment as he looked up at the open book in front of him.

'What am I supposed to do?' he asked.

'Cast your vote, of course.' Jones stared at the blank pages and opened his mouth because he still wasn't sure what to do. 'Point and use your magic, boy.'

'I don't have no magic.'

The man frowned at him over the top of the book. 'So you're the one called Jones. Most irregular.' The man nodded at a small apprentice, who handed Jones a pen. 'Randall Givens, the Head of the High Council, has made a provision for you. You're to make your mark with this pen.'

'What do I write?'

The man sighed as if the book was heavy. 'Yes or No. "Yes" if you want the Order to admit girls or "No" if that is what you don't want.'

Jones scribbled YES on one of the blank pages facing him and the word faded into the paper. The pen vanished from his hand too.

'Right, hurry up and join the others,' said the man. 'The next one's already coming through.'

Jones turned to see a boy not much older than him emerging out of thin air exactly where he'd appeared. Quickly, he stepped out of the grooves in the stone slab and joined the other boys on the grass.

They stood in silence, watching Badlander after Badlander appear in the same spot, then step forward to log their vote in the book with a single spark of white magic.

He recognized a few of the men from his time with Maitland. Some of them gave him disapproving looks as they passed him. No doubt they thought the same as Maitland himself, and Jones did his best to ignore the odd angry whisper as the dark blur beside him roiled and raged.

Soon the hilltop was packed with Badlanders and a murmur of voices filled the air. Jones had never been sure how many Badlanders were in the Order but it seemed to be in the hundreds.

Catching snippets of conversation, he heard phrases like 'core values' and 'no need for change'. He also heard other people talking about 'modernizing' and mentioning Ruby, how gifted she was at scrying and that she'd been accepted by magic, which the *Ordnung* had claimed to be impossible. There was a lot of talk and raised eyebrows about the *Scucca* too.

'What's she like, this girl?' asked the boy beside Jones in a low voice as those around him stared, waiting to hear what he had to say. 'Is it true you lost your magic because of her?'

'No,' said Jones. 'I didn't want no magic inside me to start with.' A great deal of whispering went up and down the line of boys. But Jones didn't care what they thought. 'You en't let stories like that affect your votes, have you? You should each go and cast your vote again if you have.' His voice rose in panic. 'You ain't all voted against girls, have you?' Blank faces looked back at him.

'She lost the Black Amulet,' said one boy, wearing a dark overcoat and a long red scarf. 'That's one reason not to vote for her.'

Jones opened his mouth but the man holding the book slammed it shut with a great **BANG** that echoed round the hilltop.

The High Council came forward and stepped up in a line along the long stone slab to address the Order. Ruby came with them, the *Scucca* straining at the leash, as if it knew something was about to happen. The white light made Ruby look pale and Jones found himself crossing his fingers. For the first time since meeting her, Jones wished he had magic to be able to cast a spell to make her feel better.

Ruby did her best not to look at the Badlanders lined up in front of her and see all the pairs of eyes staring back. Although the strange light that silvered the air lit up everyone, she felt as though she was standing under a spotlight. After all, everyone was here because of her.

She placed a calming hand on the head of the *Scucca*, then stood up straight, pulling her shoulders back, and aimed her eyes over the tops of the heads in front of her to the black sky beyond.

'Friends and colleagues,' announced Givens in a clear voice that was somehow magnified by the light around them. 'The *mótbeorh* holds great significance for us because we only meet here together at times of great crisis or celebration, or of potential change to the Order. As Head of the High Council, I acknowledge in front of you all, as is the custom, that I have chosen to hold a vote on the matter of introducing girl apprentices into the Order, potentially altering the course of our founding fathers and of our future. I hereby proclaim the result is to be accepted by the High Council now and for all time. Gentlemen, I trust you have voted with your hearts and minds in good working order and my proposal will be carried. But I accept, as is the custom on a night like this, I must step down from the High Council if the vote does not fall in my favour, allowing another to take my place.'

A murmur rippled through the crowd.

As the stillness settled again, Ruby realized that nothing in her life had ever mattered so much as now. As a foster child, constantly moved from one home to another, she had always believed she was meant for something other than the life destiny seemed to have chosen for her. The idea that she mattered and was meant to make a difference had always fizzed secretly in her blood. It was what had made her so determined to run away and seek out a new life. If she hadn't crept out of her foster parents' house that night, over a year ago, she might never have arrived at this moment. Because most vital of all had been meeting Jones. Without him none of this would have been possible. She sought him out in the crowd.

He was staring back at her as if he knew exactly what she was thinking. She smiled back as everyone on the slab shuffled closer to allow the Badlander with the large book to stand beside them. He cleared his throat as he found the correct page.

'I hereby announce the result of the vote as follows. The number for "No", two hundred and fifty. The number of votes for "Yes" . . .' The man paused and Ruby watched him peering closer at the page as if not quite sure what he was seeing. Her heart trembled as she hoped for history to happen. The man looked around at the others on the stone plinth, his face suggesting he wanted someone to help him with an unexpected problem. 'The number of votes for "Yes": two hundred and fifty, also. It would appear the vote is tied – the first time such a thing has happened.'

Something stretched, but didn't break, inside Ruby. It wasn't the result she'd been hoping for but it wasn't the one she'd feared either.

Givens raised his arms and the whispers and murmurs died away.

'Let us hear what the appropriate course of action is in such circumstances.'

The man with the book was leafing rapidly through the pages and when he found the text he wanted, he cleared his throat.

'Although there is deadlock, the vote may not be cast again. In such circumstances a compromise must be reached that will lead to a clear decision. As Badlanders we are resourceful and fair and we all trust in the *wyrd*. And this will be our guide for agreeing on a most suitable course of action. Anyone can suggest how to proceed, and when a suitable suggestion is made the light upon this sacred place will rise brightly again.'

As the white light woven into the air dimmed, various hands shot into the air and some men pushed eagerly towards the front. But everyone stopped as one Badlander started to walk between them, the lines of men parting for him. It was Sloop.

'I'd like to speak,' announced Sloop, uncorking a small

glass vial. Ruby watched him pause to tip the small bottle towards his open mouth; a single green drop fell onto his tongue, bright as a glow worm. Like a bird swallowing a grub.

'It's those damned Lucky Drops of his,' Givens hissed into Ruby's ear.

Sloop squeezed the cork back into the vial. When he reached the front he stepped up onto the stone slab as if he should have been there all along with the High Council.

'I have a suggestion,' he announced. 'One that I hope will work – we may be standing here a very long time if we have listen to everyone else's ideas, and I'd like to get to bed.' This drew a laugh, and Sloop surveyed the Order like a king basking in the adoration of his subjects. 'And of course, no one else has the Lucky Drops bequeathed to me, as we all know, by my Master on his death.' Sloop grinned and the dull white light made his teeth blue.

'What's your suggestion, Sloop?' asked Givens.

'Oh, I think you'll like it,' he said.

'It doesn't matter what I, or anyone else thinks, it's up to the *wyrd*.'

'Then let's get to it,' said Sloop. 'I propose that you, Ruby Jenkins, solve a case from *The Book of Mysteries*, to decide the question of women being in the Order once and for all. For are not all the cases in the book ones that have stumped Badlanders for years, making any of them a suitable test?' There were murmurs of agreement from the crowd. 'I propose not just any case, but one befitting the importance of this vote – for Ruby Jenkins must prove her worth beyond all doubt in order to demonstrate the value of girls to the Order. The case I propose, therefore, is the Mystery of Great Walsingham.'

Ruby heard a sharp intake of breath among the High Council. The rows of men below were full of noise too as people talked and shook their heads. The white light above pulsed, as if thinking through Sloop's suggestion. Before she could ask any questions, Givens spoke.

'Is there any Badlander who wishes to challenge this proposal before the *wyrd* decides?' he asked, his eyes flicking towards Ruby.

Jones stepped forward immediately from the front and half-turned to address those behind him as well as those on the stone slab. He didn't care about everyone watching him; there was only one man he was interested in. He had been aware of Maitland's form starting to materialize more fully over the last few minutes and knew the potion was starting to wear off. It had made him scared. But here was a moment now, when he could make clear to his Master what he wanted. Maybe then he would leave him alone.

'I want you to know,' he said in a voice that first wavered and then grew stronger, 'that Ruby is better than any other Badlander I've ever met. She's saved lives and been brave. Not only that, she's shown me what I thought already – that the Order are too proud and selfish, that lots of Badlanders think they're superior to ordinary people cos of what they can do with magic. But we en't better than the people we protect. We need to change and that's what this vote

62

is all about, making the Order better than it is. Than it's ever been.'

Sniggers started in the front row among the boys that had been standing with Jones. Someone shouted out that he wasn't a true Badlander any more because he lived with his parents. Jones ignored them. He could see Maitland more clearly now as if his words had brought the figure of his old Master into focus. He tried not to wilt under the man's hard stare as he continued.

'Ruby's already proved girls are worthy of being in the Order. It's not fair to send her to Great Walsingham. That's not a test. It's a punishment. And it only shows why the Order are so rotten and need changing, because there are some of you here that are scared of a girl like she's the most terrible monster in the world. And I'm talking about all of you what voted against Mr Givens's proposal tonight, or wanted to.' He glared at Maitland. 'It means you're scared of people for who they are and not able to accept 'em for what they can do. I'd leave the Order if it wasn't cos of being with Ruby and making a difference to the world by protecting people. She's taught me more than any *Ordnung* ever can. And anyone here who don't believe what I'm saying can stuff it, even my old Master Maitland what was kind and looked after me. People like him don't count no more.'

As Jones stared at the flickering, grainy figure of Maitland he gradually became aware of the silence, wrapped tight like a blanket around him. Everyone was staring. Some with faces aghast, others shaking their heads. Maitland was deathly quiet. Jones shivered. All the fire and rage that had been keeping him warm was gone. Maitland didn't seem to be going anywhere. He just kept staring at Jones.

Sloop raised his arms as the white light pulsed and addressed the crowds below. 'Isn't this boy the real reason this vote has come about? Didn't he rescue Miss Jenkins and tell her about the Order and their secrets after they met? Surely it's their partnership that should be judged too, in all of this? That boys and girls, men and women can work together?' Sloop looked at Jones as he played with the bottle of Lucky Drops in his hand, removing the cork again. 'So what better outcome, then, if I were to propose that you, boy, take on the mystery in Great Walsingham with your partner Miss Jenkins?'

Sloop raised the bottle to take another Lucky Drop and something toppled over inside Jones, because he knew just how powerful the drops were, having read about them as part of his studies when living as an apprentice with Maitland. And now that Sloop was prepared to use his drops to stop the Order from changing, and to punish him and Ruby too, Jones was filled with rage all over again.

'You don't need to drink any of your stupid drops, Sloop. I'll go if the *wyrd* says Ruby should go. Cos she's my friend.' Sloop stopped short of taking another drop and looked at the boy.

'As you wish.' The man grinned.

'Let the *wyrd* decide,' announced Givens as the light began to quicken and blip. It flared brighter, drawing out shadows across the grass, and Jones's heart shrank as he realized what he had agreed to do.

'The *wyrd* approves,' announced Givens as the bright light settled, shining clear and true on everyone. 'The task proposed by Simon Sloop befits the magnitude of what is being decided here tonight.' He turned to look at Ruby. 'Now, Ruby Jenkins, it is up to you to accept the proposal or else go against the *wyrd*.' He hung his head for a moment as he thought about what to say next, hands clasped except for his thumbs turning over and over each other. 'And going against the *wyrd* is something a true Badlander would never do.'

Ruby knew that everybody was looking at her. It made her wonder just what sort of a mystery there was in Great Walsingham. But it didn't scare her as much as not being able to prove men like Sloop wrong. Her need to fight for what she thought was right and fair was a feeling inside her that she trusted more than any other part of herself.

'Well, Miss Jenkins?' asked Sloop.

Ruby heard a little click inside her, like a key had turned in a lock, and then she was speaking out loud so every man and boy there on the hill could hear.

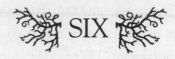

SIX

The following morning, while Jones was at school, Ruby visited Samuel Raynham, at the behest of Givens and the High Council, to learn all she could about the Mystery of Great Walsingham. Ruby hoped to find out something from Raynham and *The Book of Mysteries* that might convince Jones their task was not as impossible as he'd described it.

Jones had looked small and pale in his overcoat as he'd poured some Slap Dust into his shaking hands, after the *mótbeorh* had started to empty. Ruby had hugged him close, whispering everything would be okay. But he'd whispered back that it wouldn't, refusing to say any more when she asked why. It had unnerved her to hear him sound so terrified. His voice had crept into what little sleep she'd managed, conjuring terrible imaginings of what waited for them in Great Walsingham. Now, on the morning of a new day, the sun warming her face, she was filled with a greater sense of hope. Together, she and Jones would solve the mystery. Together, they could do anything.

Raynham's cottage was set deep in the countryside at the end of a quiet lane. The stonework glowed like honey where the rays of warm autumn sunshine touched it. A large hill rose up behind the house and, from a distance, it looked like a giant green wave was about to come crashing down upon the dark slate roof.

Raynham was waiting for Ruby beside the edge of a pond to the right of the house, fed by a small burbling stream. He put a finger to his lips when he saw her as he lobbed bread into the water, trying to tempt a group of ducks down from the bank. They didn't take much convincing, waddling noisily into the water to scoop up the bread. As they fought among themselves, they didn't see something swimming towards them. A black snake of a body slipped in and out of the water, appearing and disappearing, barely making a ripple. Raynham threw more bread and didn't flinch when there was suddenly a great splashing and terrible quacking as the ducks flew up into the air . . . except for one. Clamped between a pair of long jaws it was dragged below the surface, disappearing as a single feather landed on the water and was left to ride the ripples.

Raynham shrugged as Ruby stepped back from the bank. 'Don't worry, the Lesser-Sized Water Wyrm only lives in water.' He brushed his hands clean and breadcrumbs speckled the grass. 'I adopted a creature or two to keep me company since I don't have an apprentice.'

'Can you train them?'

'No, I don't think so.' He smiled. 'Not like your *Scucca* hound. Very impressive.' His smile quickly bloomed and died. 'Not impressive enough, though, I suppose.'

'Do you think the *Scucca* could be useful in Great Walsingham? I've got a copy of the Lafour book on his particular training methods.'

Raynham grunted and started walking back to the cottage. 'Ruby, I'm not sure how much I can really help you and Jones when it comes to Great Walsingham. Come inside and I'll show you why.'

In the house, books were stacked in the hallway in large towers, many of them draped with dusty cobwebs, and they had to pick their way around them. With no apprentice to set an example for, Raynham seemed to have fallen into his own way of living, unencumbered by the strict codes of discipline and cleanliness other Badlanders always seemed to strive for. Ruby remembered how Raynham had been standing on his own for most of the evening at Givens's party and decided she understood him a little more, knowing what it was like not to fit in.

As she was led through the house she noticed almost all the doors had a small white card stuck to them, with a title written on it in black ink. Each name, she realized, was a specific case taken from *The Book of Mysteries*. Some rooms were dedicated to one case while others were linked to three or four. Ruby paused in front of one door to read down the list:

The Vampire Imps
The Golden Spot
The Ruins of Grant Castle

'All very interesting cases,' said Raynham.

'Why are these ones in the same room?'

'Sometimes I put cases together for the sake of space, especially if I've only just started working on them and there's not much evidence to go on. But sometimes it's to help my thinking. If I'm working on one case that's not going anywhere it can be refreshing to switch to a different one. Occasionally, something in one case makes me think about something in another and I find they can help unlock each other.'

'It sounds like you spend a lot of time thinking,' said Ruby as she opened the door and saw pieces of red string connected to various notes and papers pinned to the walls.

'Well, I spend a lot of time on my own, as you can probably tell.'

Ruby paused at another door. The title on the card had sent a small shiver fizzing up and down her spine as soon as she'd seen it. Peeking inside the room she saw a lifelike drawing of Thomas Gabriel pasted on the wall. The back of her neck prickled as she remembered the look of hatred in the boy's eyes the last time she'd seen him. He'd wanted nothing but to harm her for outwitting him with her scrying skills.

'Is there anything in this room that speaks to you, in any way?' asked Raynham as he pushed open the door further.

Ruby saw various maps of the river islands she had visited with Jones and Thomas Gabriel. There was a picture of St Anselm's Abbey too. But her eyes were drawn back to the picture of Thomas Gabriel.

'He was so angry,' she whispered. 'The Black Amulet changed him.'

'Not so angry he's been reckless. He's hidden himself away completely.'

'I know, I've tried scrying for him but I can't find him anywhere.'

'Do you remember anything he told you? Something that might provide a clue about where he is?'

Ruby shook her head. 'I never knew Thomas Gabriel as well as I know Jones. But I think he must feel very alone. Maybe that helps?' Raynham nodded and then scribbled something on a piece of paper and stuck it on the wall. The word he'd written was 'Alone?' He stared at it for a moment. Then he sighed and showed her out. Ruby couldn't help taking a last glance at the picture of Thomas Gabriel before she left. *Where was he?* she thought.

'There's one other thing,' she said. 'If you do ever find him, then I never want to see him again. Ever. Not after what he tried to do to me and Jones. I don't know what I'd do if we ever met again. But it wouldn't be pretty.'

Raynham thought about that and then nodded and pointed down the hallway. 'My study's this way. I've taken the liberty of preparing all I have on Great Walsingham for you.'

The grey manila folder on the desk in his study only had one scrap of paper in it. It was a section torn from an Ordnance Survey map, with the town of Great Walsingham circled in red. Ruby could vaguely remember some of the meanings of the various map symbols she'd learnt in school, which seemed a lifetime ago now, and managed to work out that Great Walsingham was in a flat part of the country. The river running past the town looped like a snake slithering across the page.

'Is it near the sea?' she asked.

'I believe so. I've never been there. No point, really.' He sighed.

'What's so terrible about this place?'

'Ruby, Great Walsingham is the most mysterious and dangerous town in the country as far as the Order are concerned. More Badlanders have gone missing there than anywhere else. And ordinary people too. Nobody in the Order has come close to explaining why. My predecessor vanished there one night and he was an excellent Badlander. He solved over twenty cases from *The Book of Mysteries* before disappearing, more than anyone else.'

Ruby stared at the map and tried to imagine what the town might be like in real life, conjuring up dark alleyways and abandoned buildings. 'There must be something to go on, some clues about what's happening.'

'Various details have been compiled in *The Book of Mysteries* and I can show them to you, of course.' Raynham tutted and gave a great sigh as he drew out the book from his jacket pocket. 'But there's not too much in here, except a list of the Badlanders who've gone missing.'

'Why did they all go there if it's so dangerous?' asked Ruby as Raynham flipped through page after page.

'To try their luck. The mystery whipped people into a frenzy in the early days. Most Badlanders went to try and carve out a place in history by attempting to become the first one to solve what was happening. But the novelty wore off as more and more people disappeared. Eventually, the mystery went into the book, and became a case for my predecessors – until it became mine. Nowadays, Great Walsingham's a place for only two types of Badlanders: reckless or stupid ones.'

Raynham licked the tip of his finger and turned more pages, stopping when he found the one he wanted.

'There is one fragment of an account.' He held up the book for Ruby to see a picture of a man with a black moustache, his hair combed into a neat parting. 'It's the diary of a Badlander called Oliver Fredericks. He went there not long before the case was placed in *The Book of Mysteries*. Fredericks wasn't a Badlander of note, as far as I know. His casebooks revealed an average career. So it may well have been that he was seeking glory like all the others. He was different in one regard, though, in that he was generous-spirited. Being aware of the dangers he decided to leave his journal on his desk at home, in case he disappeared, as a document to help others.'

'I suppose no one else had ever thought of that.'

Raynham smiled. 'You know how Badlanders are, all fiercely ambitious. Leaving clues for others to follow would have meant handing the chance to solve the mystery to someone else.'

'Being so ambitious isn't one of the good things about the Order, is it?' said Ruby.

'That depends on your point of view. Ambition encourages competition, which leads to bravery and good work being done. But in the case of Great Walsingham then it does perhaps show up the perils of individual greed over what's best for the Order.'

'So what's in the journal?'

'Every night after exploring Great Walsingham, Fredericks would return home and record his experiences. Over the course of the first week nothing of any note occurred to him or his apprentice. But on the eighth night, Fredericks and his boy disappeared, never to be seen again. The final entry in the journal from the day before revealed that he and his apprentice were planning to visit a churchyard on the outskirts of the town. His disappearance reignited some interest for a few months. But no one found anything at the graveyard and Badlanders started going missing again. As I said, not long afterwards the case was placed in *The Book of Mysteries*, making it officially illegal for anyone other than the holder of the book to pursue the case. So I'm the only one who's allowed to investigate, or should I say I *was*, until last night.' Raynham sighed. 'I'm truly sorry it's come to this. I voted for changing the Order. But that chance seems to have gone, unless you and your partner Jones can successfully solve a mystery that has claimed the lives of so many Badlanders.'

'You've really cheered me up,' Ruby said.

'There's one silver lining, I suppose. There's no record of any girl Badlander ever going missing in the town.'

Ruby managed a smile but something clicked and tightened in her chest, making it difficult to breathe for a moment. She tapped on the picture of Fredericks in *The Book of Mysteries*.

'Does the journal say what time he was planning on going to the churchyard?'

'He left every night around ten o'clock to visit the town, according to the previous entries. There's no way of knowing what time he went to the churchyard precisely.' Raynham shook his head. 'I know what you're thinking, but scrying doesn't work. The town doesn't come up in the mirror. Various predecessors of mine have tried. So if that's the case then I'm not sure trying to go back in time will work either.' Raynham cleared his throat. 'I've heard of your scrying ability. Most remarkable.'

'Do you mind if I try with your mirror?'

'Be my guest.'

Sure enough, when Ruby attempted it, listening to a description of the church at Great Walsingham and its graveyard, read out to her by Raynham from the *Badlander Guide to the Churches of Great Britain*, all that appeared in the mirror was a blur. When she tried again the only thing she could muster in the glass was a strange kaleidoscope of colours and shapes moving in a clockwise motion. Even when she put her hand on the glass it was cold and hard, like a normal mirror should be. There was no way through.

'Don't lose heart,' said Raynham as Ruby watched the shapes moving in the mirror. 'At least it's a new finding to go in *The Book of Mysteries*.'

When Ruby left Raynham's cottage, he gave her the scrap of Ordnance Survey map and a long list of items he thought might be useful to take to Great Walsingham. Then, he held up his finger as he remembered something else and darted back into the house. Ruby folded up the piece of map and put it in her pocket as she waited by the pond in the weak sunshine. She hadn't heard of many of the items on the list Raynham had given her, which didn't help her mood. Her hopes of finding out something useful here had been dashed, and now there was something even more dark and foreboding about Great Walsingham, like the Lesser-Sized Water Wyrm lurking somewhere below the surface of the pond.

'Here we go,' said Raynham, making Ruby jump. It took her a moment to work out what he was holding up. It was a leather harness attached to a leash. 'I thought it might help if your *Scucca* pup hears its deadland calling. It's specifically charmed to help with training, more so than the simple leash I noticed you were using last night. My Master once had a similar idea to train up a hound a long time ago. It's only gathering dust here.' He held out the harness and she took it. The rich brown leather smelt peppery and it was light and supple in her hands. 'It'll change size to fit the hound as the beast grows. If you *can* carry on training that *Scucca* of yours it might be useful in Great Walsingham, especially given Fredericks was last seen in a churchyard.'

'Thank you,' said Ruby, her spirits lifting a little. She gave the man a hug as though she might never see him again, the harness hanging from her hand, the leash attached to it making it look like Raynham had grown a thin brown tail.

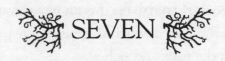

SEVEN

J ones studied Raynham's list as he sat at the kitchen table in Ruby's cottage. It was difficult to concentrate because of Maitland's presence. The effects of the potion had waned, resulting in a strange state of affairs. His Master was visible like a *Gást*, and could be heard, but he was unable to control Jones as he had done before. For now, Maitland had given up saying much and lingered with all the brooding of an angry thundercloud. From time to time he would shout a furious stream of words at the boy as though the frustration of being unable to do anything was too much to bear. All Jones could do was ignore the man as best he could.

'A silver cage for the *Scucca* is going to cost,' said Jones, tapping the item at the top of the list and looking at Ruby, while avoiding any eye contact with the spectral Maitland. 'I'm sure there's a set of Boom Balls here at the cottage. I know there's enough salt and rosemary in the van along with Buttress Beetles, copper flakes and iron filings, but some of these potions are very rare; they won't come cheap.' Jones ran his finger further down the list. 'A Rhapsody Flute?' He purred like a propeller and shook his head. 'Raynham's written down enough to take on practically everything in the Pocket Book Bestiary.' He drew a line through the item on the list as Ruby sat down and sipped her tea, then tapped his pencil on the page and sighed.

'Didn't he tell you *anything* useful about Great Walsingham?'

'He gave me a piece of a map.'

'Let's see.'

Ruby unfolded the scrap and placed it on the table.

'And?'

Ruby pointed a finger at Great Walsingham.

'Right there.'

'So the map doesn't do anything? It's not charmed? No hidden markings or places? Nothing out of the ordinary?'

Ruby shook her head as Jones puffed out his cheeks.

'At least we know how to get there,' she said.

'It'd be better if we didn't.' He glanced across as he heard a sarcastic chuckle from Maitland.

'I'm sorry it worked out like this,' said Ruby. Jones ran a finger around the rim of his mug. 'Jones, I know how hard this mystery is going to be to solve, Raynham's already made that clear. But we're good. We've got each other, your brains and my magic. And then there's the gun. And all the other things Badlanders use. And there's the books . . . the van . . . we've even got a *Scucca*.'

'One that isn't trained yet . . .'

'It will be, now I've got Raynham's harness. And think about all the things we've already done. No one else ever got close to finding the Black Amulet.'

'Great Walsingham is different, Ruby ...' Jones paused, thinking about all the things he'd ever heard about it. 'No one comes back from there.'

'It's not like you to be scared.'

'I en't scared. I like to be prepared for anything.'

'You mean follow the Badlander motto?'

'Yes, that's how to stay alive. But Great Walsingham's different to any normal monster hunt. You can't prepare for it. Not when no one knows anything about it or what's there.'

'This is about the other night with the *ælwiht*, isn't it?' Jones took a sip of his tea, looking at her over the top of the mug. 'We're different, Jones. You like to plan and prepare. I ... well, I just like to get things done.'

'In your own particular way, I s'pose.' Jones leant forward and looked into Ruby's eyes, at the little flecks of gold around each blue iris. 'I need you to promise to follow my lead once we get there.'

'But we're a team.'

'Do you want to make it back from Great Walsingham alive? I know I do. Better Badlanders than us have disappeared there.' Jones stabbed a finger at the piece of map. 'It's like the town just swallows them up.' He sat back in his chair. Maitland was watching on in silence. 'Ruby, it's got nothing to do with you being a girl, if that's what you think.' Maitland tutted and grumbled something under his breath. 'I just think we need a careful approach, at least to start with.'

He took another sip of tea and Ruby could feel him watching her, waiting to see what she'd say. She liked being who she was. *It's got me this far, hasn't it?* she thought. But she knew that Jones was only asking to take the lead on this case because he wanted to help them stay safe. So she took a breath and waited for her head to cool down a couple of degrees. There was something inside her that always made her want to leap into things and take charge. It had been a part of her for as long as she could remember but she wasn't sure why she was made that way. It was a private thing that she'd never discussed with Jones and she wondered if she should one day. But now didn't feel like the time to do it.

'Okay, you're in charge, to start with anyway.' She drained the rest of her tea and wiped her lips. 'Now we've agreed on that, we have more important things to do. If there's any upside to this situation then it's retail therapy.' Jones looked at her, not quite understanding what she meant. 'Shopping! I've booked us a slot at Deschamps & Sons this evening.'

Ruby had not been to Deschamps & Sons before. She was excited about finally getting to see the place where Badlanders shopped, having heard so much about it. The trip to Great Walsingham provided the perfect reason since it required the purchase of a great many items according to Raynham's list, and not everything could be found around the cottage, or stored in the van that she and Jones used.

They appeared in one of the special cubicles at the store, reserved for arrival by Slap Dust, and consulted the list again, laying it out on the small desk. A frosted door with tiny five-pointed stars arranged in a beautiful pattern on the glass separated them from the shop floor. A small alarm clock warned them that the next arrival booked into the cubicle was in five minutes' time.

'How much of Maitland's money have you got left?' asked Jones, and Ruby could see him looking up nervously at a corner so she knew Maitland must still be there with them, even though she couldn't see him.

'Not enough for everything.'

'But there was a lot of money left over.'

'So we need to prioritize.' Ruby plucked a pencil out of the pot on the small desk and handed it to Jones. He scratched his chin and looked at the list and started drawing a line through even more things he didn't think they needed to buy.

'Where did all the money go?' he asked as he tapped the pencil on the page.

'Food, for a start. I'm using the same suppliers you and Maitland did, but it's expensive. The prices have gone up. And I'm not great at gardening, as you know; I'm not growing all the vegetables you did, so that's an extra cost. And now I've got the *Scucca*, I've got to feed him too. I can't just magic food out of thin air. But the Badlander Tax took the biggest chunk of the money.'

'What's that?'

There was a sharp knock on the other side of the door

as a silhouette of a figure loomed in the glass. 'Is there a problem?' said a muffled voice. 'The cubicle will be required in a few minutes.'

'We're just coming,' shouted Jones, putting a line through *Silver Knuckleduster (pair)* on the list. 'What's this tax, then?'

'Every time a Badlander takes on a house, say an apprentice takes over one from their Master, there's a tax to pay to the Order. That's why they're so keen on the death of every Badlander being reported. I had to pay a tax for Maitland and then for *you*. They said you were a special case because even though you were no longer living in the house, technically, it passed to you because of Maitland's death before you gave it to me.'

Jones glanced up at the corner again as if he he'd heard something.

'Isn't any of this getting through to him?' Ruby asked, tilting her head towards where Jones had looked. 'Doesn't he realize life's moved on and he should too?' Jones shook his head.

'I don't know how he's still here,' he said quietly, almost in a whisper. 'There's nothing in any book I've ever read about it. But he en't going away. Maitland's angry. And he's stubborn. It en't a great combinatio—'

Jones sat sharply back in the chair and Ruby could only imagine that the man had shouted something at the boy that had cut him off. By the look on his shocked, pale face, Ruby could see that Jones was still scared of his Master, having learnt to be obedient to him for so much of his life.

She tapped the list. 'Just try and ignore him for now,' she said. 'Focus on the list. I lost a lot of money with the house tax thing so we've got to make sure every penny counts. Did you know there's a *mearcunge* tax as well?'

'You're joking,' said Jones as he crossed out *Slurp Slime*. 'A Badlander has to pay for every creature they kill?'

'Hurry up, please,' said the voice through the glass again, clearly more agitated than before.

'We're just coming,' shouted Ruby, before turning to Jones. 'The *mearcunge* tax isn't much,' said Ruby, 'but it adds up. The Order send out teams to check on marks made by Badlanders. So, if you don't want to pay you don't make a mark.'

'But then you don't get the credit for a kill.'

'Exactly. So either you pay up or no one knows what you've done and your legacy suffers. I've covered all the ones we've made, by the way.'

'Oh, right.' Jones looked a little uncomfortable.

'Jones, you've given me so much. I didn't mean—'

There was another sharp knock and this time the door opened. A smart-looking man in a red bow tie, white wing-collar shirt and a particularly pink waistcoat, cleared his throat.

'You need to vacate this arrival room, please.' He motioned for them to get out as the alarm clock rang and he smacked the top to stop it, then pointed through the open doorway. 'My name's Minks. How may I be of service to you today?'

Ruby had never seen such a place. There were floors and

floors of things to buy. Many of them were devoted to clothes from jumpers to trousers, overcoats to capes and hats and scarves and gloves. There was nothing for girls, of course, and she imagined floors of clothing stocked for female Badlanders one day, all because of her and the vote.

When Ruby dipped her hands into the pockets of a row of black leather jackets she felt the space from the limitless charm in all of them. Another row of jackets came with items pre-packed in the pockets, a long menu beside them detailing what one could expect to find. A large sign floated in the air that read:

For the Discerning Badlander who wants to be Prepared!

Jones had been to the store a few times before and wasn't as easily distracted or overawed. So, while Ruby walked behind, her mouth open wide, he chatted with Minks, consulting him about the list and asking about special prices and discounts. Even so, when they walked into the horticultural section, Jones stopped and whistled, nodding at the rows and rows of plants.

'You've made it bigger since I was here last.'

'Monsieur Deschamps wanted to expand this section because it was proving so popular.'

Minks wheeled the trolley past a row of small blue bushes that whispered to them about the weather, warning of rain over the next few days. Jones scooted on, pausing to inspect the bright red apples on a young tree growing in a tub.

'It's a Death Apple tree,' said Minks, and Jones nodded.

'I en't ever seen one before,' said Jones. 'Supposed to have the shiniest apples ever. Maitland made me learn all about them!'

'What's so special about it?' asked Ruby but Jones had already moved on to a line of red roses in pots, the thorns hooked like scimitars.

'Fighting roses,' Jones informed Ruby, with a huge grin. 'They're brilliant at keeping out anything unfriendly. Useful in the garden.' When he walked on to look at something else, Ruby motioned to Minks to put one in the trolley and he did so, avoiding the thorns with great dexterity, as they stabbed at the air. Ruby was so impressed, she nodded at Minks to choose another one too.

'Ruby, we can't afford them!' said Jones, when he realized. 'And they're not on the list.'

'I said it was retail therapy, Jones. That means it's good for you.' She winked at Minks, who winked back and nodded.

Minks, they learnt, had grown up as a Whelp, someone who had not been considered suitable for Commencement yet deemed useful and loyal enough to have been retained in the Badlander community. At first he had worked for his Master, running the household, and after the man's untimely death, had moved to the store. There seemed to be no hard feelings at having to move on.

'I never thought I'd get to meet you,' Minks whispered to

Ruby. 'But after the vote and what happened, we were told you might come and pay us a visit because of where you're going.' Minks's voice tailed off at the end and he gave Ruby a pitiful look. 'I think you're very brave to fight for what you believe in.'

'Thank you, Minks. But I'm also pretty poor. So let us know if there's anything on our list we can substitute with something cheaper that still does the job.'

'I'd be happy to.'

Minks advised them about alternative items that were just as suitable, picking out own-label potions and lotions and traps and devices that were not always the ones being advertised as the newest and the best. He also informed them that if Ruby set up an account it would give them a special discount since it was her first visit. Ruby picked out a smart leather holster, made from soft black leather, to carry the gun around in on her hunting trips.

After so much browsing and shopping she had sore feet and was growing tired of the glances she kept receiving from other customers. At first she had ignored them but now they were getting on her nerves. When one man cuffed his apprentice around the ear for smiling at Ruby she stopped and glared.

'And that's why I'm going to Great Walsingham,' she said under her breath, but just loud enough for the man to hear, before walking on.

Once they decided they had enough items and estimated they couldn't afford anything else, they followed the signs for the counter, weaving through the corridors with the trolley. Ruby stopped when she saw a sign over a doorway, which read:

The Rare and the Wonderful

She opened the door and saw finely wrought glass cases in which vials full of coloured liquids lay on velvet cushions.

'I don't suppose we could get a bottle of Lucky Drops in here, like Mr Sloop's, could we?' she asked Minks. The man laughed and shook his head. Jones snorted too.

'No one can *buy* Lucky Drops,' Minks told her. 'Only a few batches of them were ever created, some decades ago, before the Badlander who made them, the great "mixer", Mr Cornelius Louchette, was killed in an accident trying to create a new detonation mixture. The Lucky Drops were handed out to certain Badlanders by lottery, such was the decision of the *wyrd*. They've either been used up since or handed down to their apprentices. It's considered a very rare honour to own a vial of them. In fact, Simon Sloop is the only known owner left of such a prized possession.'

'That's a shame. We could do with some of our own.'

'Why don't you ask Sloop to loan us his?' said Jones, half-jokingly.

Ruby gave him one of her particular looks that could burn off a nose. 'Why's life so unfair?' she asked, tailing off into a sigh, as she closed the door. Jones and Minks just looked at each other and raised their eyebrows.

A little further on, Ruby saw another sign. It was much bigger this time and stuck to the wall beside a smart glass door.

The Deschamps Clinic

She paused as something occurred to her. 'Do they see you for any illness or problem?' she asked Minks as she scanned a panel of information hanging in a glass frame.

'Yes, do you have something you need diagnosing?'

'No, but Jones does.'

'They're very good. But very busy. It's hard to get an appointment at short notice.'

'Let's see, shall we?' Ruby opened the door and beckoned Jones in after her.

The reception area was painted in such a way that the walls changed from one calming colour to another. Soft music ebbed and flowed, and it filled Ruby with a golden warmth that made her feel like she was floating up to the counter rather than walking.

'I feel so much better just standing here,' she said, addressing a young man who nodded at Minks. 'My friend here,' she said, clapping her hands on Jones's shoulders, 'has a problem with a dead person.'

The man behind the counter licked the tip of his index finger and proceeded to turn over the pages in a large diary. 'We don't have any openings for three weeks.'

'We can't wait that long.'

'Unfortunately, it's all down to the quality of our professional staff here. It makes them so very popular.'

'But this is a very peculiar problem.'

'All our clients' problems are special and unique.'

'Not like this one.'

The receptionist smiled and was about to say something else when a man opened a door and peered through the crack he'd made. The name on the door said, *Gillespie, J* in red lettering. 'Malcolm, I'll see Miss Jenkins and her colleague. Just get them to fill out the usual forms.'

Malcolm cleared his throat and sat up in his chair. 'Of course, Mr Gillespie. I'll send them right in once we're finished.' But he shot a vicious look at Ruby as the door closed again.

'Let's get those forms sorted out, shall we, Malcolm?' said Ruby with a twinkle in her eye.

Gillespie prodded and poked Jones, inspecting his eyes and ears and teeth. He used small doses of various dusts and potions on the boy's skin and made a note of the reactions, most notably a green vapour that emerged from Jones's nostrils that smelt like rotten eggs. Finally, he applied a small Wurm to the inside of the boy's forearm which bit him, although he was amazed not to feel a thing.

'There's a natural anaesthetic in the Wurm's teeth,' said Gillespie, without looking up from his books. He waited patiently for the Wurm to bloat up with Jones's blood, and smiled at Ruby. 'I voted in favour of changing the Order,' he said. 'You can appreciate that change is important in my line of work, where we're discovering so many new things all the time. But of course, the *Ordnung* doesn't keep up with innovation nearly as much as we need it to.' He detached the Wurm with a pair of pincers and held its distended body up to a gas lantern on his desk, turning the flame higher. As it shrank down to a sharp blue point, he whispered, 'You're brave, both of you.'

The Wurm screeched suddenly and Gillespie held it close to his ear to listen and nodded. He dropped it into a glass vial and banged in a cork as the Wurm slithered and stretched, flattening like a fat finger against the inside.

'Your Master was a very clever man. Or should I say *is*, given your situation,' said Gillespie, addressing Jones.

'What's he done?'

'He's tied your energies together. Bound your spirits using a complicated and ancient ritual. It's very much on the cusp of what's allowed by the *Ordnung*. But it is considered legal.'

'How does it work?'

'The role of any Master is to guide his apprentice, and that's what your Mr Maitland is doing, even after death. He allowed himself to be caught in limbo, held in the space between life and death, by an attachment to you. It's an act of great sacrifice to give up the prospect of peace in death. The magic that he used to make it happen is questionable. Some might say it tips over into the realm of Dark Magic. The key that he gave you for your Commencement, did it whisper to you? Tell you to carry out the rite?'

90

'It spoke to me, yes.'

'And me,' said Ruby.

'Would it be fair, Jones, to say that your Master was concerned you might not want to Commence?' Jones nodded. 'His worries about you not carrying out his wishes must have been weighing heavily on his mind to have created this attachment to you before death. Why would he be so desperate for you to carry on as a Badlander and receive the gift of magic?'

Jones drummed his fingers on his knees as he thought about that. 'He always said I was destined to be a great Badlander. At least that's what he believed.'

'There are many Badlanders who hope that to be true of their apprentices.' Gillespie stroked his chin as he stared at the boy. 'Well, whatever the reason, the attachment he fashioned between the two of you whilst he was alive called him back from a strange place that wasn't death as soon as you Commenced. However,' Gillespie raised a finger like he was conducting an orchestra, 'given the unique situation between yourself and Ruby and your Commencement together, it took a lot longer than it should have done for your Master to reappear to you.'

'But I don't have no magic in me now. How come it's still working?'

'The attachment Maitland made to you doesn't depend on your magic – only the act of Commencement to enforce it. The effect of the ritual is to draw on the magic all around us that we harness as Badlanders.'

'So how's it broken, this bond?'

'Normally you'd be the one to sever it using your own magic once you felt confident enough to let your Master go and allow him eternal peace.'

'But I can't use magic.'

Gillespie raised his eyebrows. 'And therein lies the problem of any cure. You can't do anything without magic. The only other way is to reason with your Master and ask him to release himself from you.' Jones stared at the floor as his black boots tapped up and down.

'So there's nothing I can do?'

'Potions can lessen the effect of the attachment as you've already discovered. In terms of an overall resolution to the situation, then, no, I'm afraid not. The only course of action open to you is to reason with your Master.'

Jones bowed his head and sighed as Ruby patted him on the shoulder.

'Well, at least we know the problem and one way to solve it,' she said. But Jones found it hard to be cheerful.

'I en't sure Maitland can be reasoned with, not now he's so disappointed in me.' The boy heard something tear a little inside because in life he'd been nothing but respectful of his Master and had never wanted to hurt him by letting him down.

'Jones, if we solve the mystery of Great Walsingham, Maitland's legacy will be assured for ever. Imagine how it would make him feel, his apprentice solving the most notorious case in *The Book of Mysteries*.' Ruby looked around the room, trying to guess where Maitland might be. 'Why doesn't he have a think about that?' she said loudly. 'Helping us could be the best thing he ever does. That way we all get what we want.'

'As ever, Miss Jenkins,' said Gillespie. 'I believe you may be right.'

When they reached the counter, every item was double-checked for any damage, passing through a quality control test, and then the price written down on a piece of paper that added up the ongoing total. When the final item, a small bag of silver nuggets that Jones had assured her could come in very handy, had been added, Ruby looked at the total: £12,154.23, even with the first-time visit discount.

'That pretty much clears out the account,' said Ruby.

'It's worth it, even if one thing we've bought helps keep us safe,' whispered Jones.

Each item was despatched to Ruby's cottage from a special plinth with a small hammer attached to the side that clanged down onto a metal plate holding a grain or two of Slap Dust. When a red button was pressed, the hammer came crashing down, igniting the dust, and the item vanished.

When everything had been sent, Minks gave them a receipt in a smart embossed envelope and shook their hands. 'I added something extra in,' he whispered to Ruby as he pulled her close. 'I have a discount I've never used. You'll know what it is, when you see it. Good luck with everything,

Ruby.' And then he was letting her go, bowing and clicking his heels together and leading them back to a cubicle.

When they arrived back at the cottage, Ruby found Minks's present easily because he'd tied a red ribbon around the small blue box. After prising off the lid, she heard herself gasp. The silver whistle sat on a green velvet inlay. It looked like a normal dog whistle but there was an exterior ring fixed around it halfway down that could be clicked round to different settings. A wrist strap, made from supple brown leather and studded with tiny copper rivets, was attached to one end. The pamphlet that came in the box revealed the whistle was charmed, designed to help train *Scucca* hounds. The ring around the middle adjusted the frequency of the whistle's sound, enabling Badlanders to hear the whistle in the early stages of training and practise different notes for various commands. The pamphlet made it very clear that only Badlanders who had the approval of the Order and the accompanying paperwork for their *Scucca* would be allowed to purchase the whistle. Minks had stamped the relevant box saying that Ruby had all the necessary documents.

'He must have liked you,' said Jones, as Ruby turned the whistle through her fingers and put it to her lips to see how it felt.

'I think we're just quite similar. Outsiders with something to prove, sticking it to the Order because of what they think of us.' She looked at all the things they'd bought. 'Do you think we've got everything we need?'

Jones crossed his arms. 'We won't know till we get there,

will we? It'll take a miracle to fit it all in the van, so we might have to leave a few things behind.'

'Let's get started and see, then.' Ruby paused as she made for the door. 'Has Maitland said anything yet about helping us?'

Jones shook his head.

'Well, if he doesn't want to be a part of history like we're going to be that's his call,' she said, hoping the man had heard her.

They worked for an hour or so, carrying the smaller items out to the van first. When they started opening drawers and cupboards, spiders were disturbed and crept out of the light. Earwigs skittered for cover.

'The whole thing needs a spring clean,' said Jones. But they both knew there was no time for that. They managed to find spaces for brown packets filled with various coloured dusts, squashing them in among glass jars packed with seeds or amber liquids in which fruits, beetles and fungi were preserved. When they ran out of room for the little glass vials, cloth pouches and twists of paper they had bought, Jones and Ruby stashed them inside pots and pans and mugs. All the expensive potions were slotted securely into a wooden holder that Jones remembered Maitland had made to fit above the counter top. It was clipped onto three hooks and then each vial was placed in its own slot.

'I hope you're pleased we're finally using it,' said Jones to

Maitland, who was floating in a corner like a phantom. But the man didn't say a word.

The largest item, the silver cage, they discovered in the instructions was designed to fold flat so it was slotted into a small gap between two units, ready for the *Scucca* to use.

But there were still two cardboard boxes full of purchases from the store that left Jones shaking his head.

'We'll have to leave them behind. The van's jammed. It's a wonder it en't burst.'

Ruby clicked her fingers. 'I know how we can fit them in,' and she went back into the house as Jones sat down for a breather.

The familiar smells of engine oil and the spicy odours of the jars full of their preserves set his mind drifting to the hunting trips he'd made with his Master. Before Maitland's reappearance, Jones had had moments when he used to feel a shiver, imagining Maitland was watching from somewhere, tutting in disappointment about how he was living. Now he knew he must have been picking up on something for real.

'I did my best for you, you know,' he said, looking at Maitland. 'I loved you like a dad. I know all that discipline was kindness cos you wanted me to do well. I reckon you loved me too. In fact, I know you do, otherwise you wouldn't have left yourself in that place between life and death for me.'

He waited for Maitland to shout some gruff words or laugh sarcastically. When he didn't, Jones felt brave enough to carry on.

'I en't got no choice now but to go to Great Walsingham,

and you know what that means, most likely.' He paused as he swallowed and thought about that. 'So I'm glad you're here. Cos I couldn't think of no better person to have with me. I'll do my best, sir, because I want to leave a legacy for you. And I want to come back alive so I can carry on living with my parents and doing things ordinary boys do, however much you don't understand it. People have to be who they want to be. There en't no other way or else a person en't true to themselves and how they were made.' His throat was dry as he tried to swallow. 'Ruby's right, you know, we can help each other get what we want if we work together. Then maybe you'll be proud of me like you want to be.'

He realized he was looking down as his voice tailed off so he glanced up to see if the man was still there ... straight into the face of Maitland. His head rocked back with the shock of seeing him up close. The man's eyes were burning a hole right through him.

'Okay,' said the man, his voice wispy and faint. 'You solve that mystery and I'll go to the place I'm supposed to be. And if you don't, you'll be in that place with me anyway.' Maitland smirked. 'Call me when you need me and I'll do my best to help.' And then he vanished as if someone had snuffed him out. Jones felt a weight lift off his chest. Not only had he plucked up the courage to reason with Maitland, he remembered the glow of how it used to feel to make his Master proud. Going to Great Walsingham felt a little less scary now than before, with the prospect of having his Master to call on giving him a tiny flicker of hope.

'Are you okay?' Jones looked up to see Ruby with a bundle of coats and jackets draped over her arms.

'Maitland's gonna help us,' he said.

'Good.' Ruby dumped the coats on the table. 'I can't wait to work with him. And I'm sure he'll say the same about me.' She raised her eyebrows and smiled. 'In the meantime, let's stuff what's left over into these limitless pockets.'

'Clever clogs,' said Jones, and Ruby twirled her arm and bowed extravagantly.

When they were done filling up the pockets, although everything was put away, there were now a lot of coats and jackets lying on top of one another, cluttering up the van.

'We can do something about that,' said Jones as he rummaged through the cupboards and produced a glass jar of reddish dust and another one full of black dust. After popping the lids off each he took a pinch of the red dust and sprinkled it over one of the coats and then did the same with the black dust. The coat shrank to the size of a doll's jacket immediately. 'Maitland's special shrinking fungal powder,' he said, picking up the tiny coat. 'Shrinks anything to a sixteenth of its size when you use the two mixtures together. You just reverse the combination to change things back to normal.'

'I'm sure there's a spell for that,' said Ruby, her plan for using the jackets and their limitless pockets losing a bit of its sheen now Jones had improved it. 'And it's not that practical. Look how big the jars are.'

'Maybe,' said Jones, putting the tiny jacket on the counter. 'But you can't rely on magic for everything.'

'Because it's dangerous, I know,' sighed Ruby.

'Maitland used to say there's so much in the world around us that's special, all you need to do is look for it. For nature's secrets.'

'Well, let's hope he's got more lessons he can teach us,' said Ruby.

When they had packed away all the tiny jackets the van was far less cluttered and Ruby grudgingly admitted it had been a stroke of good thinking on Jones's part.

'When do we leave?'

Jones tapped his fingers on his chest as he thought about that. 'Tomorrow night. That means I've got the weekend and the whole of the half-term week after it too. That should give us enough time to figure out things, one way or another.' He paused, and time seemed to stop for a moment because they both knew what he was really saying. And then Ruby was reaching out and giving Jones a hug.

Ruby was restless, unable to sleep that night, her mind turning over and over. *This might be the last night I ever spend here.* Eventually, she got up and walked about. She found herself sitting on the floor, rubbing polish into her scrying mirror because mundane tasks often allowed her mind to drift off elsewhere. But this time was different, she couldn't help thinking about the upcoming trip to Great Walsingham and why Sloop had suggested it. She wished she'd never tried to show him up in the farmhouse. If she'd listened to Jones and not gone after the *ælwiht*, she would never have had the opportunity to try and get one over on him with the *mearcunge*. It felt as though everything that had happened since was because of her recklessness. No wonder Jones wanted to be in charge once they arrived in Great Walsingham.

The mirror flickered like a television coming to life and Ruby found herself looking at Sloop, the connection between her and the glass so strong it had picked up on her thinking and created a picture for her. Sloop was talking to Givens and some other members of the High Council. As they got up to arrange themselves at a round table to inspect a large book, pointing and debating the pages, Ruby realized they were in Givens's sitting room, a place she had been many times. Sloop's voice pricked her mind like a needle as it rose above the murmur of everyone else. His smile made her heart fold into tight, painful creases. She thought about his Lucky Drops and how unfair it was he had them and then her eyes darted to Sloop's jacket which was hanging off the back of the chair he'd been sitting on. Something tingled in her brain and then in her fingers, and she reached out her arm towards the mirror and pushed it through.

EIGHT

The journey to Great Walsingham only took a couple of hours because the roads were so quiet at night. As he did before any drive, Jones had checked the van over to ensure it was roadworthy, even though it had been recently serviced and passed its MOT. Living with his parents meant he knew about things like car tax and servicing and insurance, which all cars on the road were supposed to have.

He wasn't sure how Maitland had signed them off before and he'd been wary of contacting the garage his Master had used because he was only a boy and he wasn't sure if he was even allowed to own a vehicle at his age, let alone drive one. So he had asked his father to help and they had signed the van into his name before taking it to the garage for the MOT, which it had passed, and then buying insurance and tax online.

As he drove through the night, following the Sat Nav instructions on his phone, he knew how lucky he was to have a mother and father who were so generous. But as the journey wore on, the thread between him and his family seemed to stretch more and more and he was worried it would snap the longer he drove on.

Finally, he took a left turn and brought the van to a halt as he looked at the sign welcoming them to Great Walsingham. Next to him, Ruby stirred. She rubbed her eyes and peered through the windscreen.

'Just remember what I asked,' said Jones in barely more than a whisper. 'We take things carefully and you follow my lead. Especially now that Maitland's helping us.' Then, over the grumble of the engine, 'Ready?'

'Yes.' Ruby could tell by the tone of his voice that he was focused now, what Badlanders called *tyhtnes*, when they were in that space of thinking clearly and calmly.

'Right.' As Jones stared down the road, the darkness seemed to be trying to suck the van towards the town, and he reassured himself it was his mind playing tricks.

The gun was lying in a string basket that Ruby had hooked inside the passenger-side door and it tutted.

'Come on, boy, let's go and see what's what. I'm ready to take this town apart to find what we're looking for.'

Jones chose first gear and accelerated gently.

Behind them, the *Scucca* whimpered in its cage and growled at something neither Ruby nor Jones could see. Ruby shushed it and the creature pricked its ears and seemed to understand her, lowering its head.

Jones turned down a residential street, the houses set back from the road, half-lit by an orange glow from the lights as he followed the Sat Nav.

'So what do we do first?' asked Ruby.

'Keep your eyes peeled for anything. A flickering street lamp. A cat looking at a house. And open your window.'

'Are you sure?'

'It'll be easier to listen out for anything.'

When the window went down, chilly air rushed in.

Jones pushed aside all his thoughts about his parents. He was a Badlander now and that was all that mattered if they were going to survive this trip. He had made that shift in himself as he always did when he came to the Badlands to do a job. But even with all his skills and knowledge he had never felt quite this scared. He tried to own his fear by remembering it was good to feel afraid because it kept his mind sharp. He eased his foot off the accelerator to make a point to anything that might be watching, hidden in the dark, that he wasn't scared at all. But most of all, he was trying to convince himself too.

The churchyard that Oliver Fredericks had been planning to visit, as mentioned in *The Book of Mysteries*, looked like any other. But Ruby and Jones were cautious. They stood in the road and watched for anything moving among the gravestones. Ruby held tight to the leash, the *Scucca* straining at the other end, clearly excited by the idea of being so close to a patch of deadland, its nose twitching, ears standing up.

'I said not to bring it out till it's trained up a bit,' Jones said in a gruff voice.

'It can't stay cooped up in the cage all the time,' replied Ruby.

'Keep it quiet, will you? It'll give us away. And we have no idea what's out there,' he said, pointing to the churchyard.

'I'm doing my best.'

Jones sighed as he went back to using his smartphone, shooting some video footage. He focused on the church, panning across the stained-glass windows and the roof, the gravestones and the dark spaces between the trees and bushes.

'What are you doing?' Ruby asked, as she tried to stop the *Scucca* whirling round on the end of the leash.

'I saw a show on the television about what ordinary people do when they're hunting for ghosts and the like. With all the technology they've got, sometimes they can spot things Badlanders don't, like strange images or noises. Badlanders won't have used anything like this,' he said, pointing at the phone. 'Perhaps what we're looking for knows how the Order work so can't be seen by them.'

'If you say so,' said Ruby, not terribly convinced, but remembering that she was supposed to be letting Jones take the lead.

When Jones decided he had enough footage, they crept up to the low stone wall running round the graveyard. The top of the wall was triangular, sloping on either side, the stone mossy and mottled with lichen, and they peered over it.

Ruby wrapped the *Scucca*'s lead tightly around her hand. It was becoming even more excited about the deadland beyond the wall. Jones shot her one of his *'I told you so'* looks.

'Shh,' she said when the *Scucca* began to whine. She stroked the top of its head, the rough black fur leaving an oily residue on her hands. 'What do you want to do, Jones?' she whispered.

Jones nibbled the insides of his cheeks. He couldn't sense anything out of the ordinary. But it was too dark to see much and even on a normal night he would think carefully about strolling into any graveyard.

'What are we waiting for?' groaned the gun in Ruby's holster. 'We aren't going to learn anything by standing around.'

'Since it's our first time here,' said Jones, 'we should come back during the day. The night's against us so we can't see much. There's got to be a *Scucca* guarding this deadland and who-knows-what-else in there. I don't know about you, but I can't tell if there's something different about this place or if my mind's playing tricks because of what we already know about Great Walsingham. Daylight will help us think more clearly.'

'Agreed,' said Ruby as she watched a white mist creep out of the dark, licking round the gravestones. An owl hooted. Bats chittered as they came looping overhead and then vanished as if attached to elastic that pinged them back into the dark.

Suddenly, her arm jerked forward as the *Scucca* lurched to scramble up and over the wall. Ruby's hand crashed against the stone and she cried out, the leash slithering out of her fingers. The hound was over the wall before she could stop it, disappearing among the gravestones, the leash flying behind it. Jones cursed.

'It's making too much noise,' he hissed as the creature raced around on the turf, playing some sort of game with itself. Suddenly, it appeared on the top of the wall, panting hard and looking down at them, then thundered off again before either of them had time to catch it.

The *Scucca* started barking and Jones put his head in his hands. When he looked up at Ruby, she was thumbing through the pages of the training manual, the torch on her phone aimed at the text. She turned the book and pointed at a paragraph for Jones to read.

A young Scucca *needs plenty of exercise. It is recommended to run it at night in a large field or on a moor but be wary of livestock. If the initial bonding has worked then the* Scucca *is unlikely to run off but it is advised to keep food close to hand to ensure the creature does not stray. A training collar, or preferably a harness, may be used. If available, a deadland of some sort is the best place for exercising. A* Scucca *will benefit from the deadland's properties and keep it healthy and happy. A* Scucca *will not enter the territory of a rival hound so a Badlander must find an unoccupied piece of deadland.*

Ruby shut the book and smiled. 'At least we know something about this churchyard now.' As the young *Scucca* appeared on the top of the wall again, panting hard, its pink tongue dripped onto the pavement below and Jones was hit by a big drop as he tried to move out of the way.

'Good!' said Ruby. But the creature was still in a playful mood and raced off again before Ruby could catch the leash. 'Let's go and get it,' she said, trying to clamber over the wall. Jones pointed at the entrance into the churchyard further along and started walking, hands in his pockets and shaking his head.

'Just cos there's no other *Scucca* living here it don't mean it's safe,' he said. 'Remember what you promised about letting me lead.'

'I didn't exactly promise, Jones. I just said you were in charge to start with.' The boy grumbled and tutted and shoved his hands deeper into his pockets.

'En't you wondering why this en't a *Scucca*'s territory? It's not that often you find a deadland without a hound living in it.'

'No. I've got you to worry about that for me, haven't I?'

The Lych Gate was different to all the others Jones had ever seen. Instead of being a wooden porch with a pitched roof, it was built from stone and looked like a gatehouse to a small castle. But rather than a drawbridge or portcullis there was just a gate held shut by a latch that opened into an archway. As they approached, Jones could see through the vertical wooden bars of the gate. A wooden bench ran down either side of the structure. Beyond it was a gravel path that wound through the gravestones towards the church.

Ruby lifted the latch and ran through, glancing up at the archway. Her feet crunched on the gravel when she stepped onto the path, stopping when Jones cleared his throat loudly and waved her back. So she beckoned the *Scucca* towards her, slapping her thighs to tell it to come and it came trotting back, clearly exhausted from running around. As Ruby grabbed hold of the leash she could see that the hound's muzzle was caked in earth, its front paws too. It had been digging a hole.

'Bad dog,' she said in a stern voice. The animal flipped over onto its back and started rolling around in the grass. Its fur was giving off a smell like a burning tyre. Ruby wondered if it was marking the territory as its own and decided to read more about it in the manual later.

Jones stood beneath the archway of the Lych Gate, scanning the graveyard for anything suspicious, catapult in his hand. He was expecting some creature to come running out of the mist towards them, teeth bared. But the longer he waited for something to happen, the louder the silence grew.

'I'm surprised this deadland doesn't belong to no *Scucca*,' he said. 'It feels like it should.' He was about to step through the rest of the Lych Gate onto the path when he felt a draught lick the back of his neck and whirled round, catapult raised, expecting to see something behind him.

There was nothing there, just a view through the gate back to the road.

'Jones?'

Jones turned to look at Ruby again.

'I thought I felt something.'

'What?'

'Hard to say exactly.' He rubbed the back of his neck and inspected his fingers as if expecting them to be covered in something.

'Some sort of presence, I think. A *Gást* maybe? Or a *Gliderunge*.' Jones studied the vaulted ceiling, shining the torch on his phone into the nooks and crannies. Dark spaces appeared and vanished as he moved the light around. The faces carved into the stone looked down at him. Some seemed to wink, while others mouthed words as the torchlight passed back and forth. But however much he wanted to believe the carvings were alive he knew it was just a trick of the light.

'A Lych Gate can be a hiding place for a Demon too. There's all different sorts. Diabolical, Greater, Lesser ... there's even minor ones what can do you damage –' He paused when he thought he saw one of the stone faces moving again and held the light on it. 'They can hide in the stone,' he whispered. 'And when your back's turned they slither out and claw through your skin to eat your heart.' He cleared his throat.

'Oh Demon in the stone I see
Come show your head and teeth to me,
For with this rhyme I force you out
To see your form and have no doubt
That I'm the one to cut you down

109

And so increase my bright renown
As hunter of the base and foul
What creep and crawl and hide and prowl
Through shadows and the world at night,
Where I am too, prepared to fight.'

But the stone face just kept staring back at him, the grinning mouth not moving nor the eyes blinking.

The *Scucca* whined as if bored and looked around as if there had to be something else more interesting to do.

'The rhyme's only one way of forcing 'em out.' Jones pressed a finger to the stone wall, as if testing the temperature, before going closer and giving it a sniff. Suddenly, he gave it a big lick, leaving a wet stripe glistening in the torchlight.

'Eww, Jones.'

'Sometimes a Demon'll leave a taste in the place it's hiding or even turn the tip of your tongue black depending on what sort it is.' He wiped his mouth and inspected his tongue, which was still pink, using the little mirror he kept in the limitless pockets of his overcoat. Finally, he gave up, tapping his foot for a moment until he clicked his fingers and beamed a smile.

'Maitland?' he said quietly. 'You could help.' Ruby watched the boy looking around until he peered forward in the beam of the torch at something she couldn't see. He nodded and Ruby presumed he was listening to his old Master before he said, *yes, yes, that's right, of course*, and slapped his hand on his forehead, as if he'd forgotten something of great importance.

'A Lych Gate is an in-between place,' he said to Ruby. 'A border between the living and the dead that we can't see. Maitland's gonna have a look around in it to see if there's anything there because he can. While we're waiting, let's see if that *Scucca* can sniff out anything. There's got to be something here, I'm sure of it.'

Ruby dragged the hound down the path and walked it into the Lych Gate, playing out the leash and allowing it to sniff about. It rooted around on the floor and then hopped up onto one of the wooden benches. Jones watched it carefully. But it did very little except stop to sniff the wall a couple of times before jumping down.

'Make it check the other one.'

Ruby dragged the *Scucca* up onto the opposite bench and the creature walked down it without pausing. When it reached the end it sat down on its haunches and stared at Jones with its head cocked.

'Well, I'm not—' Ruby paused as Jones raised a hand, leaning forwards as he studied the hound, which was looking at a spot on the floor, nose twitching.

'It's found something,' whispered Jones, barely able to contain his excitement.

The *Scucca* leapt from the bench as a mouse shot out from a hole in the opposite wall and scuttled over the floor. The *Scucca* landed in a black furry heap but the mouse squeezed out from underneath it, making it safely to a hole the other side and vanishing.

Jones grumbled under his breath as the *Scucca* sniffed the

floor, tail wagging, whining as it tried to figure out where the mouse had gone.

'Maybe there's nothing here, Jones.'

'It's a churchyard, Ruby. A deadland. There's supposed to be all sorts of creatures hiding here. And a Lych Gate's a prime place to find something.' He looked up at the ceiling again and frowned before marching up the gravel path. 'This en't right,' he said, shaking his head. 'It en't right at all.'

The mist was growing thicker, curdling like cream around the gravestones.

Ruby appeared beside him as he folded his arms. 'What do you want to do?'

'There's something odd about this place.'

'I think we knew that before we got here.'

'But we didn't expect *not* to find anything. It's night-time. We're in a churchyard.'

'Jones, there could be all sorts of creatures hiding here.'

Jones shook his head. 'No, I don't think so. I'd know. Can't you feel it?'

'What?'

'It's so quiet. Maitland used to say he could sense things, that Badlanders get a feeling. Sometimes it's the hairs on the back of your neck or your heart going faster. The more time you spend in the Badlands you start to know when something's not right. You get a feeling. Maitland called it *inbryrdniss*. But here, there's nothing. I don't feel it.' He looked at the *Scucca* sitting beside them. 'It's not just me. That *Scucca* should naturally be sensing things even though it en't trained.'

112

'So how do you explain it?'

'I don't know.'

'We could check some gravestones, make them whisper to us. They'd tell us if anything's here.'

'Good idea.'

They worked on some of the nearest stones, drawing on the symbols they knew with pieces of chalk that Ruby kept in her pockets. But the only whispers they heard from the gravestones were about the corpses buried beneath. There was no mention of a single creature, or of any special object hidden in the earth. By the time they had worked the sticks of chalk down to stubs, an early morning light was starting to turn the sky grey and the air even chillier. Their mouths were like the spouts of boiling kettles as they breathed out. Ruby was tired and cold, especially her fingers because she'd forgotten to bring any gloves. Jones was determined to check the church before they left, though. They let themselves in through the big wooden door and walked the *Scucca* up and down the nave, letting it have a good sniff between the pews.

But they discovered nothing out of the ordinary.

It was a beautiful church and Ruby felt a sense of peace as she stood watching the early daylight filter through the stained-glass windows and seem to catch fire. When Jones started talking into an empty space by a wall, she knew Maitland had to be there. The boy hung his head and nodded and then looked at Ruby who knew what was coming before he even said it.

'Not a sausage,' he grunted.

They left before anyone saw them and walked back to the van which was parked in a lay-by. They sat facing each other across the small drop-down table and drank some tea, ate some toast with butter and jam, and didn't say much because they were tired. Jones's mind kept churning. Ruby could tell because despite the dark rings under his eyes they were burning and he kept tutting and rubbing the back of his neck and jiggling his foot. He started leafing through his copy of the Pocket Book Bestiary.

'We know there's something wrong with this place,' she said, 'otherwise we wouldn't be here. We need to take a break.'

Jones yawned and closed the book. 'Let's sleep on it,' he agreed and they made sure the curtains were closed tight to keep out the daylight and went to bed, Ruby on the pull-down seats and Jones in his normal place on the front seats. The *Scucca* was put in its cage, snoring the moment it laid down its head.

Jones took a long time to fall asleep, even though he was tired. His head was full of questions, scattered inside him like jigsaw pieces that wouldn't fit together. When he did eventually slip into a deep sleep, he dreamt that Maitland was standing with him at the edge of the churchyard, warning him to be careful. When the man patted him on the shoulder and walked off down the path between the gravestones, Jones felt the soles of his boots sticking to the ground. He couldn't move. He cried out to Maitland. But the man just kept on walking, disappearing among the gravestones until he was swallowed up by the dark.

When Jones woke with a start, he was clutching his blanket and Ruby was peering in at him, her worried face blinking as she tried to reassure him he'd only been having a dream. But it didn't feel like one to Jones.

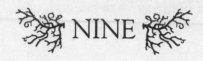

NINE

The video footage on Jones's smartphone was grainy but the night setting on the camera had picked up a fairly decent image. Jones tutted and sighed as they watched it because there were none of the moving lights or strange patches of shimmering air that he'd seen people on television programmes talking about in relation to their paranormal experiences.

'Nothing,' he said, his face melting into a frown. 'Those programmes must be a con. Maybe technology en't as useful as I thought.'

After closing his phone, he spent the next hour or so consulting the Pocket Book Bestiary for information about the most difficult creatures to find in the Badlands. But they were all very small and it didn't seem likely that the Jumping Brownie, the Thumb-Sized Goblin or the Pebble Elf (only found under pebbles of a particular shape and colour) could be responsible for the disappearance of so many Badlanders. So he moved onto the specialized books they had bought from Deschamps & Sons. He found very

116

little there either, although he did make a note about the *wælgæst*.

Finally, he went back through his Learning Book, full of interesting tips and insights he'd learnt when working with Maitland, in case there was something in it that might give him a clue. He paused at a page filled with curious diagrams, most of them fairly rudimentary, of types of traps, which were labelled with various names. He cupped his chin in one hand as he leant forward on an elbow to study them a little more, scanning the notes he had written in his spidery handwriting.

In the meantime, Ruby gave up listening to his tutting and bad-tempered slamming of books, deciding she could make better use of her time by trying to train the *Scucca* with the silver whistle and the training harness that Raynham had given her.

To start with, she sat on a blanket on her own in the sunshine and practised making different notes, twisting the dial in the middle so she could hear them. The whistle was a little longer than her middle finger and made a very pure chime, rather as if she was hitting a triangle dangling from a piece of string. She found that she could change notes by adjusting the shape of her mouth, squeezing it tighter for the higher ones. She had tried playing the recorder once at school and hadn't been very good at it, so producing a clean sound from the whistle consistently was quite hard. Not only did she have to master making a pure sound, she had to create a different sequence of notes for each command.

117

Although she couldn't read music, it didn't matter because the pamphlet that had come in the box made an allowance for that. As long as it was laid flat on the grass, the notes jumped off the page whenever she hit the correct pitch and held them for the right duration, after which they would drop back down. It meant she could tell when she had played each note correctly and could learn the various sequences off by heart.

She went slowly at first, squawking and screeching, making some horrible sounds. Jones banged on the window to let her know just how bad she was. But she persevered. Eventually, her lips sore and her cheeks aching, she'd managed to memorize three commands.

Ruby let the *Scucca* out of its silver cage and slipped on the training harness Raynham had given her. Although the hound had heard her practising with the whistle, it hadn't reacted to any of the sounds she'd made. The whistle only worked on an animal that had been fed the potion that came in the box with it, which Ruby had found under the green velvet inlay.

Ruby poured the gloopy red liquid onto a piece of meat that had been stored in the cold compartment of the van and fed it to the *Scucca*. She waited for a few minutes for the potion to take effect, playing through the sequences of notes in her head as she walked the creature round the field beside the van. Eventually, she summoned the courage to let the animal off the leash.

Once released, the *Scucca* tore off, eager to stretch its

legs, and Ruby blew the first command. The dial was turned up high enough to allow her to hear the sequence of notes. They sounded good to her, but the *Scucca* kept racing further away, growing smaller and smaller until it reached the far left corner and then trotted beside the hedgerow that bordered the top of the field. Ruby blew the whistle again, the pamphlet open this time, making sure she made every note jump high off the page.

As soon as the notes pinged out of the whistle, the creature stopped and sat down.

When she blew the whistle again, using a different sequence of notes, the *Scucca* bounded back towards her, its great loping strides swallowing up the ground. When it reached her, it sat down beside her, its big red tongue dangling out of the corner of its mouth and great gobs of spittle dripping from its jaws.

'Good boy,' said Ruby softly, stroking the creature's head. A thrill fizzed around her body as the *Scucca* thumped its tail on the ground. Some faint connection seemed to crackle between them. Ruby realized that it was not only the harness but the potion that made the creature more tuned-in to her than before. With each blast of the whistle she sent it scurrying off to sit obediently some distance away, before bringing it back to the exact spot it had started from. Ruby also taught it to retrieve sticks which she flung as far as she could into the field. It brought them back in its mouth and dropped them at her feet.

When they had finished, Ruby gave it food and water and

the *Scucca* burped and grew again, the torso and shoulders beefing up, the legs extending so that its head ended up at her chest height. The power wired through its body would have scared her but for the silver whistle she clutched tightly. She tried not to show any fear as she scratched it behind its ears. The training manual had warned her that any weakness would be sensed. Ruby made sure she stood tall and spoke to it in a firm voice, trying not to betray the awe tingling in her bones.

Later, Jones decided they should walk around the town in what was left of the daylight and wait for the *æfenglóm*.

'The time between day and night can be good for seeing things out of the corners of your eyes that other people don't see,' he told Ruby as they sat in the van, looking out at the deepening gloom.

Ruby knew about the power of the twilight to tempt creatures out and agreed it was a good idea.

'Can we bring the *Scucca*?'

'No.'

'But I've trained it.'

'You've done *some* training. Ruby, we're going round the town. People'll see it. Who knows what'll happen if it gets excited and you can't control it?' Jones pointed at the hound, snoring heavily on the floor. 'It's tired anyway.'

They made sure the *Scucca* was shut in its silver cage in the van with the curtains drawn. Ruby had to admit that it did seem tired, falling asleep again even before the van door had been shut and locked. She couldn't help being annoyed at not being able to bring it, though. She was beginning to regret agreeing to Jones being in charge. But she held her tongue and didn't say anything.

Great Walsingham had an old centre with newer buildings, in particular a housing estate and an industrial park built around its outskirts. As they walked down the various residential streets, wending their way into the town, Ruby and Jones had the sense that they were stepping into the past. By the time they reached the high street, Ruby felt as though she had come through a scrying mirror into a different century. The buildings rose crookedly from the ground. Many of them were whitewashed with black timbering on the outside. The leaded windows in lots of them made it difficult to see in without making it obvious.

Ruby and Jones wandered among the shoppers and tourists, listening to snippets of conversation, trying to pick up any hints of strange occurrences. But they heard nothing of importance. Ruby kept a cap pulled down over her eyes, wary of being recognized by someone as a runaway. Having been missing for over a year, she hoped she was just another statistic now, another missing person, vanished like others around the country. As the sun began to set, they turned off the main street and walked down a cobbled alley, small gift shops dotted on either side, and eventually came to a park bordered on the right by a murky green river containing the odd duck.

A humpbacked stone bridge sat over the water and Jones

peered over the balustrade to try and inspect what was underneath it, while Ruby kept watch for anything moving in the shadows or emerging onto the bank. When they were satisfied nothing was there, they walked on to the park.

It was dark enough now that the lamps along the path cast an orange glow on the grass below.

'Now's a good time to see something,' whispered Jones. Ruby barely nodded, keen to stay focused and alert.

Jones led Ruby along the path, sniffing the air, telling her to listen out for anything odd. Eventually, they struck out over the grass and headed for a small copse of spindly trees. The dry leaf litter was ankle-deep and hissed as they walked through it. Jones inspected some tree trunks, peeling back the bark and poking his fingers into the soil at their base, while Ruby explored a group of large stones for signs of a burrow.

'What now?' she asked as they stood in the cold, hands in their pockets. 'There's nothing here. There's nothing anywhere. This town is so normal, it can't be normal.' She held up her hands in exasperation and dropped them with a loud slap onto her legs. 'I bet the *Scucca* would have found something.'

'Do you?'

'Most likely.'

Jones pulled up the collar of his overcoat. 'Ruby, whatever's wrong with this place we need to agree that it won't make us argue all the time. We'll lose our focus and that could be dangerous.' Ruby blew out a big breath. She nodded.

'So what now?'

Jones opened his mouth and then shut it as they heard a rustling sound somewhere off between the trees. He raised a finger like a periscope and pointed it in the direction of the noise. They moved as quietly as they could, creeping between the trees. But the rustling stopped as they got closer and Ruby knew that whatever was rooting around in the leaves had heard them. She stuck close to a tree and peered round. The creature was about three feet tall with a rat-like snout and scimitar-shaped canines poking down over its bottom lip. From its wide eyes and short, jabby breathing she could tell it was listening. Its nose twitched as it tried to catch a scent. The triangular green pupils flicked from side to side. A black tail swished like it belonged to a giant cat.

Jones already had his catapult out, a silver ball bearing locked and loaded. But before he could fire, the creature set off, sending the leaves whirling around it, grabbing something off the ground as it fled.

'It's a Lesser Gobbolin,' shouted Jones as he set off after it, and Ruby detected a trace of excitement in his voice. The creature slipped between the trees ahead of them and it was difficult to keep track of it. There was no way Jones could hit it using his catapult and Ruby could not aim her magic either. By the time they reached the edge of the treeline the creature was halfway over the park and then it stopped and looked back at them, as if playing a game and waiting for them to catch up, before turning and running on towards a group of houses on the far side of the grass.

Jones paused, hands on his knees, blowing hard.

123

'If we can catch it, maybe we can start to find out what's really going on in this town.' Jones pointed at the houses on the other side of the park. 'Can you stop it before it reaches those houses?'

'I'll try.'

Ruby was aware that they were in a public space and that anyone might see them. Even so, various possible spells ran through her mind. Deciding on something appropriate, Ruby threw her hands forward, pushing out a spray of white sparks that hurtled low over the grass. Although the Lesser Gobbolin was some distance away, the small figure was struck in the back. It seemed to split into two pieces as it fell until Ruby realized it had been carrying something over its shoulder which had made the creature look a bit bigger than it actually was. The Lesser Gobbolin was up fast and didn't hang around, leaving whatever it had been carrying steaming on the grass. It didn't look back as it disappeared between two rows of houses.

Ruby and Jones raced on and discovered that the creature had dropped a sack, but Jones didn't stop. 'We'll come back for it,' he shouted. 'We need that Gobbolin.'

But by the time they reached the street, there was no sign of the Lesser Gobbolin. They walked on quickly down the path on one side of the street, looking for where the creature might be hiding, peering into dark corners and stopping every now and then. When they came to a dead end, they strode back up the other side of the road. Jones kicked at the ground.

'We've lost it,' he said. 'I don't know how. They en't much

good at climbing or hiding. And a creature like that normally sticks around and fights. They're nasty buggers. It has to be here.' They stayed for a few more moments, looking into dustbins, under parked cars and in the front gardens of the houses. 'It just don't make sense,' said Jones, shaking his head. 'I never seen one run away like that. And why do you think it stopped like it was trying to get us to chase it?'

Ruby figured that Jones was thinking out loud rather than asking her, because she had no idea.

They headed back the way they had come and when they reached the sack, Jones picked up a stick and lifted open the mouth to see inside. A child's teddy bear peered up at him with glassy amber eyes, one ear missing. There were other bits and pieces inside the sack too: scraps of silver foil, sweets in golden wrappers, some loose change.

'Let's go back to the van,' he said. 'I want to look through some books.' They walked through the town, neither of them talking much. Any strange sound made them look up and listen. Ruby felt a fizz in her blood now they had finally seen a creature but she could tell that Jones wasn't as excited as her. In fact, he was brooding as he muttered and shook his head.

'What's wrong? It's a start, Jones,' she said.

'Yeah, but the start of what exactly? First we don't find anything and when we do, that Lesser Gobbolin doesn't act normal for a creature like that. In fact, it just vanishes.' He stopped and then walked on more quickly than before. 'It's given me an idea, though.'

*

125

Tired and cold, they ate tomato soup for their supper, dipping slices of buttered toast into the steaming bowls. Ruby tried to talk but she could tell Jones wasn't in the mood for conversation. He was busy looking through books and making notes as he ate.

'I need a couple of hours to make what we need,' he told her, scraping his bowl clean with a piece of bread. 'And then we'll go back to where we last saw that creature.'

'What are you making?' Ruby asked, as Jones cleared the table and started taking things from the cupboards.

'Silvereen,' he said, without bothering to look up at her. He placed a large silver mixing bowl in the centre of the table. As he started emptying various liquids and pastes into it, fretting like a chef about the consistency and colour of what he was making, a nasty smell filled the van, the mixture bubbling like hot mud. Even with the windows open, it was too much for Ruby, and the *Scucca* sneezed and whined in its cage.

Ruby took it for a walk in the fields and tried practising new commands with the whistle. On her way back to the van, the *Scucca* stopped and burped and then grew. Its red eyes shone in the dark, almost level with Ruby's face now. She felt the creature's power on the end of the leash and her legs had to tick over a little faster as it padded in front of her. She felt around in her jacket pocket for the whistle and held it tight, grateful for Minks's generosity.

Ruby found Jones dozing, his face pressed against the window like it was made of putty. The van was tidy but there was still a lingering odour that made Ruby wrinkle her nose.

Jones was dreaming, his body twitching. When the *Scucca* sneezed, he woke with a start. His tired eyes blazed wide and he looked about him, before remembering where he was. He pointed at the vial on the table.

'Told you I'd make Silvereen,' he said proudly.

The vial was full of a silver dust and he shook it hard enough to make the contents fizz, each granule moving like a tiny fish.

'What does it do?'

'You'll see. Ready to go?'

'Jones, can we take the *Scucca*?' Jones's face started to melt.

'But, Ruby—'

'It's trained up pretty well now with the whistle. And look at the size of it. It's got to be useful if we run into anything bigger than a Lesser Gobbolin.'

Jones waggled the vial, making the silver dust flutter against the glass.

'Okay,' he said. 'But you'd better be right about being able to control it.' He stood and started putting on his overcoat. Then he looked at his smartwatch. It was some way past eleven o'clock. 'Let's get going, it's a fair walk back.'

'We could use Slap Dust.'

Jones paused. 'You mean on the *Scucca* too?'

'Oh, yeah,' said Ruby. 'It's ready for that.'

'You're sure?'

Ruby nodded. 'Just give me a moment to give it some water and make sure the harness is tight and get myself ready too.'

Jones grunted a reply and checked his overcoat pocket

for a vial of Slap Dust and then headed for the door. 'Five minutes,' he said.

After Jones shut the door behind him, Ruby waited a moment before reaching into her pocket. Rooting around she drew out Sloop's vial of green Lucky Drops and unscrewed the top.

'It's for luck,' whispered Ruby to the *Scucca*. 'They've worked once already. We got a lead in this stupid town so why not use them again.' She tipped back her head and allowed a single drop to land on her tongue. The *Scucca* whimpered.

'Not for *Scucca* hounds like you,' said Ruby, putting the vial back in her pocket. 'And don't tell Jones,' she said, wiggling her eyebrows. 'He doesn't know I took them from the great Simon Sloop.' She could barely say the name without smirking.

'Oh, boy,' said the gun as she strapped on the holster. 'You are in so much trouble if Jones finds out, let alone this man Sloop.'

'And so are we if I don't use them,' hissed Ruby. 'Or hadn't you noticed that we're in Great Walsingham?'

The door opened and Jones stuck his head in. 'What's going on?'

'Just nattering to the gun. It won't stop saying thank you for the new holster.' The gun grumbled something as she marched towards the door with the *Scucca* on its leash.

The hound's red eyes burnt like jack-o'-lanterns as Jones poured out a ring of Slap Dust around the three of them. The animal seemed excited and kept trying to lurch forward and sniff the brown dust, its big tongue unfurling to try and take a lick. It was difficult to control such a strong animal, and it managed to lick up a section of Slap Dust, before spitting it out.

'Make it behave, will you, otherwise it's going back in the cage,' grumbled Jones, pouring out some more of the dust to make the ring complete again. Ruby blew a command on the whistle and the *Scucca* sat, still licking its gums to try and get rid of the dust in its mouth.

When the Slap Dust fizzed, Ruby held on tight to the leash and almost immediately she was standing in the copse of trees where they had spotted the Lesser Gobbolin earlier in the evening. The *Scucca* was beside her, wagging its tail as it looked around, intrigued by suddenly having somewhere different to have a sniff, and apparently none the worse for magical travel.

'Come on,' said Jones, who was already walking towards the treeline and the park ahead.

When they arrived in the street where the Lesser Gobbolin had vanished, the street lights were casting a bright orange glow now it was the middle of the night, doing their best to hold the dark back. All the windows of the houses were covered with curtains or blinds as everyone slept. In the quiet, Ruby felt bigger and more clumsy than normal as she tried not to make a noise. Even the *Scucca* seemed quieter.

Jones popped the cork from the vial and poured out a handful of Silvereen which fluttered up and down in his palm.

'Pop the cork back in for me, will you?' instructed Jones,

and Ruby took the cork out of his fingers and pushed it in as the remaining silver dust threatened to float up and out of the neck of the vial. Looking around to check no one else was about, Jones threw the Silvereen up into the air. It moved in a cloud, zigzagging like a shoal of brightly coloured fish.

'What does it do?' whispered Ruby as the *Scucca* leapt up to try and catch the sparkling stuff in its paws.

'Well, what if there's a secret door and the Gobbolin went through that to escape?'

'What sort of a secret door? To where?'

'Maybe we'll find out.' Jones folded his arms and watched the Silvereen shimmering as it moved. 'Silvereen can find lots of unusual things. Especially anything strange like a secret doorway or a portal. Don't you think it's odd we've only seen one creature since we got here, given what we know about the place? Perhaps Great Walsingham is one big portal to somewhere else.' He paused as the dust gathered itself into a small pulsing ball in front of the wall that brought the street to a dead end. Then, quite suddenly, the Silvereen dropped to the ground and lost its colour, turning into something grey that resembled ash.

'Is that supposed to happen?' asked Ruby as the *Scucca* gave a whine at the lack of sparkles in the air.

'No.' Jones kicked through the Silvereen, but it seemed to have lost all life and floated back down to the tarmac like tiny grey feathers. 'All the books say how temperamental it is. Even the best-made mixture doesn't work all the time. It's got a mind of its own.' Jones popped out the cork and sprinkled some more Silvereen into his hand, Ruby replacing the cork as before.

After Jones had thrown the mixture into the air again, the Silvereen raced around and the *Scucca* watched it, even more excited. Ruby did her best to hold on but the creature dragged her forwards as the Silvereen formed another ball in front of the wall. Then, just like before, it lost all its colour and dropped to the tarmac in a pile of feathery grey ash.

Jones grumbled something under his breath. But Ruby wasn't listening. She was watching the *Scucca* as it sniffed at the spot in front of the wall where the Silvereen had gathered before falling to the ground.

'Jones, look.'

The *Scucca* seemed fascinated by something Ruby couldn't see, and she allowed the creature closer, unwrapping the leash from her fist. The *Scucca* cocked its head to one side and whined, then sat back on its haunches and pawed at the air.

'What's it doing?' asked Ruby. Jones shook his head.

Faster and faster the *Scucca* pawed until suddenly it seemed to catch hold of something and tore a little jagged rip in the air in front of it. The untidy slit was blue and it looked to Ruby like a narrow view through to a bright, sunny sky.

As the *Scucca* tried to make the gap wider, Ruby felt a force pulling her towards the opening.

'Ruby! Get it away!' shouted Jones and she turned to see him struggling to step back as the force pulled him too. The

Scucca just sat happily on the ground, tail wagging, pawing at the hole.

Now Ruby could see not only blue sky but white fluffy clouds too.

The force pulling on her made it impossible to haul the hound back. She grabbed the silver whistle from her pocket and blew a command. Immediately, the *Scucca* lay down, retreating from the opening, which rapidly started to close. As Ruby and Jones were pulled forwards, the hole in the air vanished and their momentum took them crashing into the wall beyond it with such force that they collapsed in a heap together.

The *Scucca* watched them, tail wagging, and barked as if they were playing a game. Then it lurched forwards and gave Ruby a big lick on the face.

By the time she'd stood up and pulled her jacket back down, Jones was inspecting the spot where the narrow opening had been, walking around it and reaching out a hand, waggling his fingers.

He shook his head, looking at the *Scucca* and back again at where the rip in the air had been.

'I don't get it,' he said. 'That *Scucca* opened something we can't. A doorway the Silvereen couldn't find either.'

'A doorway to where?' asked Ruby. Jones made the sort of face that meant he didn't know. 'I'm sure I saw blue sky and clouds.'

'We know it's a doorway that creatures can open cos we've seen what the *Scucca* can do. That Gobbolin must have done

132

the same thing. Only by the time we got here it must have gone through and shut it otherwise we'd have got sucked towards it.'

'What do you think would have happened if the *Scucca* hadn't stopped?'

'I en't sure. Maybe we'd have got squished getting sucked through it. Maybe it's got something to do with no Badlander ever coming back from Great Walsingham?' They both looked at the space where the gap had been and thought about that.

'Jones, maybe we should call it a night. Aren't there some books you can read up on this stuff? You could ask Maitland what he knows.'

'Yeah, but we're gonna walk back.'

'Why?'

Jones was already heading off, waving at her to follow him. 'Keep that whistle handy,' he said, looking over his shoulder. 'I reckon we might need it before we get back.'

Jones was right.

On their journey back to the van, they allowed the *Scucca* to sniff wherever it wanted, stopping when it seemed interested in the air around it. They allowed it to swipe a paw through the air wherever it liked and they made a note of five other openings it found. Jones recorded the location of each one by dropping a pin onto the map on his smartwatch screen.

Neither Jones nor Ruby had an opportunity to look through any of the openings because they had no choice but to let each small slit the *Scucca* made close up before they were sucked too near it. It meant they had no idea what sort of place lay beyond each opening or 'doorway' as Jones had started to call them.

'I wonder how many there are around the town,' asked Ruby. 'And how they were made.' Jones just shrugged.

'Seems like lots of mysteries all rolled up in one,' he said. 'I en't sure what we're gonna do about 'em. Do you want to risk being sucked through?'

As the *Scucca* walked on, Ruby paused and held it back.

'Jones, I've got to tell you something because I think it might be helpful.'

'What?'

'Don't get angry.'

'Ruby, what have you done?' asked Jones.

'You're still in charge, don't worry. I just thought we could do with some help with these "doorways".'

'Ruby?!'

Ruby took a deep breath. 'I borrowed Sloop's Lucky Drops.' Jones looked at her. His mouth was open and his tongue was moving but no sound was coming out, as though it was impossible for him to find the words he needed. But then he did.

'Ruby! You didn't borrow 'em, you stole 'em. I can't use 'em. And you can't either.'

'Well, I can, because I have. Which proves there's no such thing as "can't". We've had some luck already, haven't we? Found something out? I thought maybe you should take a Lucky Drop, too.'

Jones placed his hands on his head, a look of sheer terror appearing on his face. 'We'll be slung out of the Order if Sloop doesn't come after us first.'

'He won't find out. I'll put them back without him knowing, just like I took them . . . to *borrow* them.'

'Of course he'll find out. Do you think something as valuable as that en't surrounded by various charms that'll tell him exactly where they are if he's lost 'em? I bet he knows exactly what you've done, that you've swallowed a Lucky Drop. He's probably on his way here right now.'

'Really? He'll come to Great Walsingham, the most dangerous place for Badlanders there is? Well, he's not here yet, is he? And for the record, I've actually swallowed two Lucky Drops.' Jones cursed under his breath and crouched down, as if the weight of what Ruby was saying was crushing him. 'Even if he does know, do you think he'll tell anyone? It'll mean admitting I've got the best of him. That a *girl* took his Lucky Drops from him. There's no way he'd admit that. As long as I put them back there'll be no damage done.'

'Ruby, those drops can change a person. They can have side effects. You've seen what Sloop's like.'

'I feel fine. You will too.'

'No way am I taking one!'

'But they work best on someone who's never used them before. The lucky effect gets less each time you take a drop, I read up on them. So since I've taken two, we'll get better results if you take one. I mean, my luck hasn't been great, but maybe it's because I'm a girl? We know some things in the Badlands don't work as well for me as they do for boys and other things work better. If you take a Lucky Drop, then who knows what'll happen? We might crack this mystery and be able to go home.'

'Ruby, listen to yourself. You've stolen from Sloop. Those Lucky Drops are his. He—'

Jones paused as the *Scucca* started sniffing the air again. 'Don't let it open another doorway, we've got to talk abou—'

'Jones, I don't think it's a doorway.' Ruby pointed to the creature's tail which was pointing straight up. '*That* didn't happen before.'

'What's up with it, then?' asked Jones.

Ruby studied the hound's posture, trying to remember what the manual had said and then she remembered.

'A *Scucca* can get excited by all sorts of other creatures in the Badlands. Something's coming,' she hissed.

Jones's eyes scanned the dark for a sign of something moving. 'What sort of something?'

'Could be anything.'

'Can't you be a bit more specific?'

'I'm not a mind reader,' said Ruby as she tried to control the increasingly excited *Scucca*.

'En't you read the whole manual?'

'No! So remember what you're always telling me and *Be Prepared*,' said Ruby.

'Well, why don't you swallow another Lucky Drop and we'll be just fine!'

Ruby opened her mouth, but didn't manage to shout a

136

word as she felt a gentle thudding coming up from the tarmac through her feet and into her knees.

Then Jones's voice was lost as something thundered past the far end of the street. Ruby only caught a glimpse of the creature but she knew three things.

It was big.

It was surely an *Ent* of some sort.

And somebody was clutched between the fingers of one giant fist, legs dangling.

TEN

The creature was fast. Jones felt his heavy overcoat trying to lift behind him like a cape as he ran. His mind was whirring as he tried to assess what they were chasing. There was no time to stop and consult the Pocket Book Bestiary but he knew it was an *Ent*. By its speed he guessed it was a Spring-Heeled type.

'It's a rare one,' he gasped to Ruby. 'It's too fast to be anything common. Ones this quick come and hunt in towns more often because people can blink and miss 'em, thinking it's an earthquake or something.'

Ruby didn't bother replying. She was finding it hard to keep up and didn't want to waste her breath. And at the same time she was trying to make sure she didn't let go of the *Scucca* either. It was like trying to hold back a boulder rolling down a hill. Her legs were confused as she tried to run and haul back the creature at the same time. The *Scucca* was pulling so hard that all sense of feeling was draining from her fingers. When the creature took a corner sharply, all Ruby could do was hold on tight, skidding in her trainers. She barely had time to realize that they had left the residential streets and were in the greener outskirts of the town.

When the *Ent* veered off the road, the *Scucca* raced after it and Ruby found herself high-stepping across uneven, stony ground. It was impossible to keep up with the bounding *Scucca* and she brought it to a stop with a sharp blast of the whistle. It sat, panting beside her as Jones went on, turning round when he saw he was on his own.

'We'll lose it!' he shouted, waving an arm at them.

'No, we won't,' said Ruby. She gave another quick blast on the whistle, which prompted the *Scucca* to stand up. 'It's the only way to keep up,' she shouted as she clambered onto the creature's back, taking two big fistfuls of fur. She looked down at Jones. 'Hurry up, then, or you're right, we *will* lose it,' she barked.

Jones ran back and climbed onto the hound, wrapping one arm around Ruby's waist, and taking a fistful of fur in his other hand. Ruby blew the whistle and the *Scucca* leapt forwards.

They could feel the power beneath them as the creature bounded over the uneven ground. Despite the dark, the *Scucca* seemed to spot everything in its way, dodging mounds of earth and lumps of abandoned concrete that flashed by as they raced across the industrial wasteland. It wasn't long before they saw the *Ent* and Ruby urged on the *Scucca* hound, leaning into its ear and shouting at it to go faster. It was exhilarating to be travelling so fast, and Ruby's belly rose and fell into her mouth like she was riding a rollercoaster.

139

The *Ent* glanced back when it sensed them, its long nose swinging round like a rudder that made the rest of its head turn. It had a hooked jaw like a salmon and eyes sunk deep into its face under a heavy brow. The mouth was full of gnarled, higgledy-piggledy teeth that glinted like copper. Long strands of greasy grey hair were swept back across its head. Without stopping it scooped up a large piece of rock and hurled it at them. The *Scucca* swerved and the stone thudded into the ground behind. The *Ent* tried again with another larger rock but missed again. Whoever it was carrying in its other hand kicked their legs and thrashed about.

Ruby felt a tap on her shoulder and she half-turned to try and hear what Jones wanted to say.

'Magic . . . up.'

'What?'

'Can you trip it up? Give . . . chance against it.'

Ruby nodded. 'Hold on to me!' When Jones tightened his grip, she raised an arm and felt the magic at the ends of her fingers. She focused on the *Ent* and shouted the spell, sending a spray of light towards it that rotated faster and faster and became a swinging bolas which caught around the legs of the *Ent* below its knees and sent it crashing to the ground.

Its hand opened with the impact and Ruby saw a small child in a nightdress clamber out and sprint for safety behind a large piece of rock. The *Ent* roared and stretched out an arm, groping for the figure. Then it remembered the bolas around its legs as it tried to stand up and started working to rip it clear. Ruby blew the whistle, and the *Scucca* slowed and sat down as she and Jones jumped off.

The *Ent* had already scrambled to its feet, sweat glistening on its dirty legs and arms, its chest heaving. A roar came from its mouth and it charged at Jones. The boy aimed his catapult and shot a ball bearing that fizzed through a bicep, bringing a terrible scream and leaving a small, steaming hole. He dodged to avoid a sweeping arm and went to ground, scuttling among the scrub.

Ruby had already made a beeline for the child and found a girl of about six years old crouched behind the rock. She was terrified, her eyes bright and wide.

'What's your name?' asked Ruby.

'O Olive,' stuttered the little girl, her eyes glassy with tears.

'Well, Olive, you're safe now, I promise.' The little girl began to cry and Ruby squared her up by the shoulders and looked into her eyes. 'I'll get you home to your parents.'

'I don't have any,' spluttered Olive. 'I'm a foster kid. I don't have anyone.'

Ruby paused, having not anticipated such an answer or the effect it had on her. For a moment, all she could do was stare as thoughts clicked and ticked. Living in the Badlands, among men and boys, Ruby had become used to being different to everyone else. But here she was, face to face with someone who knew what it was like not to have anyone love you or miss you when you were gone. And it made Ruby realize how lonely she was, ever since she'd been living on her own in the cottage and Jones had been with his parents. But it unlocked something else much deeper inside her too. In that moment she knew exactly why she was so impatient and headstrong, always rushing into things and wanting to be in charge. It was because she'd only ever known that she could rely on one person: herself. Just like this little girl she'd found.

The roar of the *Ent* brought Ruby to her senses.

'Well, Olive, I know how that feels because I'm a foster kid too. And we may not have anyone we can depend on but that's okay, because kids like us are tough. And we're special too; I can prove it.'

She conjured some magic at her fingertips and Olive's mouth made an 'O' before Ruby sent a fireball fizzing through the air. The *Ent* dodged, and she cursed. The missile hit the ground, ploughing through the earth like a meteor, until it fizzed and died, leaving a deep, steaming furrow.

Olive was still staring. 'Was that . . . was that . . . magic?'

'Yes, and I'm going to use it to keep you safe. I promise. You can depend on me.'

Before Ruby could conjure another spell, Olive grabbed hold and clung on tight, burying her face in Ruby's neck. As the girl squeezed with her little arms, Ruby heard something around her heart cracking, then giving way. Olive had helped her understand a bit more about who she was. Not even Jones had ever done that. It made her special.

She hugged Olive back as hard as she could. Just for a second.

Then she heard a yell. Jones. There was barely time to look as a boulder came hurtling out of the sky towards them.

*

Jones shouted again as the boulder sailed noiselessly through the air, spinning like an asteroid.

It landed on the smaller rock behind Ruby's hiding place, making a terrible CRACK! Rocks exploded and a great cloud of dust mushroomed into the air. He ducked as a piece of stone spun past his ear and when he looked round again he saw the *Ent* rummaging in the rubble and picking up the little girl before setting off again.

Jones sprinted to where Ruby lay, her pale face covered in dust, and immediately thought she was dead. And then the *Scucca* was pushing past him and licking her face.

Ruby's eyes flickered. And then she moved, and Jones's heart leapt as the *Scucca* barked and then he was helping her up.

'I'm all right. I'm okay,' she said, waving him off. 'Where's Olive?' she asked, spotting a scrap of her nightdress in the dust.

'You mean the girl?' Jones asked. He pointed in the direction the *Ent* had taken.

And then Ruby was picking up the scrap of material and hauling herself up onto the *Scucca*. 'I made her a promise, Jones. I promised I'd keep her safe. I told her she could depend on me. And I'm not going to let her down like she's been let down by everyone else.' Ruby made sure she was set on top of the *Scucca*, the whistle already in her lips. It was dented but Jones knew she was going to blow it as she leant forward and held the material under the *Scucca*'s nose. Quickly, he clambered on as Ruby blew a command on the whistle and the hound took off.

The *Scucca* raced faster than before. Ruby felt her tired arms wanting to sag like they were made of wet cardboard. There was a pain in her shoulder too, which made it difficult to hold on. Her arms were about to give up when she heard Jones yell. The *Ent* was standing looking at Olive in its clenched hand, her head lolled to one side, her legs dangling and not kicking. Ruby felt a spike being driven through her heart as the *Ent* shook the little girl. Olive twitched like a fish, her head came up and she screamed into the startled face of the *Ent*, planting her hands on the giant fist around her and pushing down to try and free herself. Ruby's heart leapt and she urged the *Scucca* on.

But Jones was shouting at her.

'Stop,' he said. 'Stop! We need to turn back.'

Ruby looked to where he was pointing and saw the *Ent* looking at them. Its free hand had found something that it was using to unzip the air. It pulled the gap apart like a pair of curtains and stepped through into a sunny place, that looked to be full of trees.

'Ruby, turn round!' shouted Jones.

'I promised her, Jones,' shouted Ruby as she urged the *Scucca* towards the gap. As they got nearer to the doorway she felt the force of it sucking her on. 'We're going through!'

She felt Jones let go of her and jump off. But moments later he floated into the air in front of her. He cried out as he was dragged through the opening. And then Ruby was lifted off the *Scucca*'s back too and she hurtled through the opening after Jones.

*

144

Jones had landed awkwardly on the grass and he sat up carefully, his body crickling and crackling. But nothing seemed to be broken. His palms were grazed and he'd bitten the inside of his mouth. Ruby was lying nearby, an angry lump on her forehead, but at least she was breathing.

Jones tottered over and laid his overcoat across her.

'Ruby?' The *Scucca* wandered towards them and whined when Ruby didn't move. 'Ruby?' said Jones again, shaking her shoulder gently. Her eyes fluttered open and she licked her lips.

'Get off! I'm okay,' she said, sitting up and touching the bump on the front of her head. 'Oww.' She shielded her eyes in the bright sunlight as she looked about. 'Where'd the *Ent* go?'

'Who knows? Anyway I en't worried about that.'

Ruby blinked as she rubbed the back of her neck. 'Jones, that little girl—'

'We've got to think about ourselves first. We en't no good to anyone if we're stuck here, least of all that little girl.'

'Stuck here?'

Jones pointed in the general direction of where the opening had been that had sucked them through, because now there was no sign of it at all.

'What if every Badlander who came to Great Walsingham ended up in this place and couldn't get back? That would explain a lot about the mystery, wouldn't it? We couldn't find any opening in Great Walsingham so who's to say we can find one here?'

'We've got the *Scucca* for that.' Ruby wobbled to her feet as Jones helped her up. 'It found the doorways that creatures use to come and go in Great Walsingham. So why can't it do the same here?'

She picked up the leash and stood beside the hound, and mimed pawing at the air. The *Scucca* looked at her, not understanding, until she lifted its paw and then it got the idea. It sniffed the air and trotted over to roughly where the opening had been and started to feel for something unseen. It took a few moments but then its paw snagged and the *Scucca* made a small slit in the air as it had done in Great Walsingham. Through it, Ruby and Jones could see the part of the town they had come from, where it was still night, a cold breeze trickling in.

'Good boy!' Ruby beamed a big smile which seemed to encourage the *Scucca* to claw the opening wider, and stick its head through. Ruby blew on her battered-looking whistle and made the hound sit down on the grass in front of the hole, sniffing the air coming through from Great Walsingham. 'So you see, Jones? We're not stuck here after all.'

Jones inched his way forwards, wary of suddenly being sucked into the opening as before. But he didn't feel any force pulling on him, which set something ticking suspiciously in his brain, despite his eagerness to get out.

'We should go straight back to the van,' he said. 'Who knows what this place is and what we might need to help u—'

As he got closer to the opening, an invisible force smashed into him so hard it knocked the wind out of him and he

146

went hurtling backwards. He crashed to the ground and by the time he looked up the opening was starting to close. Something landed with a thud in his stomach as he started to understand the implications of what had just happened.

'Oh,' said Ruby as she realized it too.

'This place sucks you in and then doesn't let you out so, yeah, Ruby, *Oh*. In fact, I'd say it's a whole lot worse than that. Wherever we are it's one big trap set for Badlanders.' Jones looked so angry, Ruby thought he might bare his teeth like the *Scucca*. 'This is all your fault.'

'Mine?'

'You shouldn't have stolen those Lucky Drops. They bite you in the backside if you get too greedy with them. They turn on you to teach you a lesson. Any Badlander knows that. Even Sloop! I bet you took more than the two drops you said.' Ruby grumbled something and looked down. Jones had to wipe his mouth he was so angry, spit flying as he spoke. 'I was supposed to be the one in charge!'

Ruby kicked at the dirt, unsure what to say. And then she started marching towards what was left of the opening.

'Well, maybe it's different for gir—' She didn't have time to finish as she was sent hurtling backwards by the same force, collapsing onto the ground as she tripped over a rock. At least that's what she thought it was. But as she looked closer she saw it was a skull overgrown with moss and little green plants.

She saw other parts of a skeleton lying, disassembled, on the ground, the bones half-submerged in the dirt. Some of them had been gnawed and she ran her finger over the toothmarks, trying not to think about what sort of creature might have done such a thing. When she saw a scrap of material she pulled at it and up came a matting of roots and earth stuck to what she realized were the partial remains of a jacket.

As the dirt fell away, she saw a label embroidered on the silk lining. It was a name both Ruby and Jones recognized immediately: *Deschamps & Sons.*

ELEVEN

Jones's first idea was to sort through everything in their limitless pockets and work out what might be useful. They worked silently, laying out everything on the grass, the space between them crackling with unsaid words.

Ruby had no idea how a bag of pear drops, various pens and pencils and a book on fungi had made it into her jacket. That was one of the problems with limitless pockets: you could drop anything in and easily forget about it. After sorting through both pockets she found that she had: Sloop's Lucky Drops; vials of salt and rosemary; a pair of silver balls that could be hurled to create nets of finely spun silver; a pair of broken sunglasses; the Pocket Book Bestiary and some supplementary books about particular types of creatures (largely to please Jones) and some dog biscuits for the *Scucca*. Most important of all was the silver whistle and her tin of scrying polish as well as *The Black Book of Magical Instruction*.

Jones's collection consisted of: his Learning Book; vials

full of various coloured dusts; some small tubs of brown ointment; Maitland's jars of fungal shrinking dust; a couple of the expensive potions they had bought in Deschamps & Sons; Slap Dust; a little mirror; some Boom Balls; a large jar of salt and rosemary and some books which Ruby noted were collapsible into tiny squares, one of them springing open to reveal the title *Rare, Rarer and Rarest Horticultural Wonders* by P. L. Tierney. Jones also had his catapult and a number of silver ball bearings which sat on the grass and glinted in the sun. He found a bottle of tonic too, half of which he drained and then offered the rest to Ruby in moody silence. Ruby thought about refusing but because it was hot she drank it and set the empty bottle down.

'Right,' said Jones, picking up a Boom Ball. 'We need to know what we're dealing with. Can you get your *Scucca* to open the doorway?'

'I'm pretty sure I can.' Ruby acted out what she wanted the creature to do by raising its paw and scratching at the air as she had done before. It understood and duly obliged, creating a small opening through which they could see a small patch of cool night.

'Call it back.'

Ruby blew the whistle but the dog didn't seem to hear, being more interested in the opening, and Ruby had to blow the short tune more than a few times to encourage it back to her.

'Stand further back,' warned Jones as he pulled a small pin from the Boom Ball and hurled it at the opening and ran.

The Boom Ball exploded with a tiny *pop* that made Jones's shoulders droop as he frowned.

'That en't right,' he said. 'It's called a Boom Ball for a reason.'

He took a few tentative steps forward, watching the doorway disappear, and toe-poked the ashy remains of the Boom Ball. Bending down he took a sniff and shook his head.

'What's wrong?'

'Smells like it's gone off, like a rotten egg or something.' Tapping his finger on his chin for a moment he walked over to the other Boom Ball on the grass and looked it over in the sun. 'This one's gone all spongy,' he said, squeezing it like a tennis ball.

'So?'

'So that en't right. It weren't like that when I took it out of my pocket.' Without any warning, he pulled the pin and hurled the Boom Ball into the trees. It hit the nearest trunk and slid down the bark like wax, dropping to the ground in spits and spots. 'Oh, no,' said Jones, running over to all the various items laid out on the grass. 'No, no, no, no, no.'

'Jones, what's wrong?' Ruby asked again.

'Feel any different after the tonic?' he asked, as he inspected the various things he'd taken from his pockets.

'Not really.'

'Like the tonic didn't quite hit the spot?'

'Maybe. I suppose it didn't have its usual fizz.' Ruby stood blinking at him. 'So?'

'Don't you see? The tonic didn't work and the Boom Balls

151

didn't either and they're all charmed with magic, or at least the ingredients in them are. Everything that uses magic is turning rotten.' Jones uncorked a vial and emptied the bright red dust into his hands, which rapidly turned black and he threw it to the ground in disgust.

'You mean magic doesn't work here?'

'I'm afraid so.' Jones waited for Ruby's brain to tick through the gears. She looked at her hands. The sparks that she conjured around her fingers were droopy and yellow, falling to the ground where they hissed and melted away.

She cursed and tried again, and something whirred inside her like a wheel spinning on its own. This time no sparks appeared at all. As the sensation of panic died away, Ruby was left feeling hollow inside until a sense of great shock and sadness began trickling into her. It was as though a very close friend had suddenly died.

The two expensive potions from Deschamps & Sons curdled as Jones studied them in their bottles and when he popped the stopper from one, he gave a sniff and turned up his nose.

'All gone,' he grunted, opening the other vial and discovering it had gone off too. 'What a waste of money.' He sprinkled a ring of salt and rosemary around himself and stood up. 'Bring the *Scucca* over here.'

Ruby led the hound to him and it sniffed the mixture on the ground, then snorted as its nose tickled. It stepped across the ring and proceeded to lick Jones's face as Ruby held the leash. 'Geroff,' he shouted and pushed the creature away. He kicked at the salt and rosemary on the ground. 'Nothing that's charmed bloomin' works.'

Ruby plucked the gun out of its holster. There was no wisecracking voice now. When she aimed and tried to pull the trigger, nothing happened.

'Try pulling back the hammer first,' suggested Jones. 'If the charm isn't working, it's just an ordinary revolver again.' Ruby did her best to pull back the hammer and cock the gun, which took some effort because the mechanism was heavy.

When the gun was primed, she aimed and fired. A shot whipcracked around the trees and a branch collapsed to the ground, severed in two. It was impossible to shoot again without pulling back the hammer once more.

'I bet the chamber hasn't refilled like it normally should, has it?' said Jones, showing her how to open the cylinder. An empty casing dropped out, leaving only five bullets.

Jones reached out and touched the gun, wary of the charm Maitland had placed on it to prevent him from using it. But when nothing happened, he wrapped the rest of his hand around the weapon. 'It's definitely not charmed any more,' he said.

Jones and Ruby decided to check through everything to figure out which of their things might still be useful. Jones ended up with his Learning Book, his little mirror, catapult and silver ball bearings and his small collapsible books, as well as a few items that were plant based and worked without needing to be charmed. This included the two jars of Maitland's fungal shrinking dust and the small tubs of brown ointment, one of which had the name *Smellies* scrawled on the lid. After trying out the jars of dust on a flower and shrinking it down, Jones divided it up between them, pouring out some of the red and black dust into separate vials for Ruby.

'Remember, it's red first and then black to shrink something down, anything you want. Even creatures, if it comes to it. All you do is reverse the order to make something big again. Only use it if you have to, mind, as there isn't a whole lot.' Ruby nodded and stowed the vials of dust in her pockets. They bulged now that the limitless charm no longer worked. There was barely any room after she'd pocketed the silver whistle (which she couldn't bear to leave behind), the dog biscuits, her tin of scrying polish and the Pocket Book Bestiary. There was no point in keeping anything else, not least Sloop's Lucky Drops, which had turned a nasty brown colour and stank of manure.

But it was the loss of her own magic that she really cared about. She could barely bring herself to speak since discovering it was gone. The lightness she had felt in her stomach had risen into her head and made her dizzy. The feeling had got worse after opening *The Black Book of Magical Instruction*. The words had been unreadable, lines of letters jumbled into no particular order. It was as if she had never been given the gift of magic at all.

Jones could tell she was shaken up. He looked her in the eyes.

'I know losing magic must feel strange, like you're missing

154

a piece of you, cos it's wound into your spirit. It was inside me once, remember? But there was a time before you were a Badlander and didn't have magic. You were fine then. And you'll be fine again now.'

'But how are we going to protect ourselves? What are we going to do? It must have happened to every other Badlander who ended up in this place.' She tried not to look at what was left of the old raggedy coat on the ground.

'That's one of the problems with the Order. Being able to do magic makes people forget they've still got their brains cos they feel invincible.' Jones tapped his head. 'We'll be fine if we stick together and use our noggins. I've got my catapult. And we've got the *Scucca*.'

'But the whistle doesn't work any more. Or the harness it's wearing.'

'That don't matter. The creature's bonded to you, Ruby. It knows you're in charge. Or else it would've run off already. It'll protect you from anything.' As they talked the *Scucca* seemed to understand they were referring to it and its tail thumped the ground.

Ruby sniffed. 'What about that little girl? I said I'd save her.'

'And we will. We've just got to figure out this place first.' Jones smiled. Though deep inside he wasn't smiling. He knew that every Spring-Heeled *Ent* was keen on eating little boys and girls. 'I'm sure we'll find her,' he said. His priority now was to keep Ruby calm and full of enough hope to stay alive so they could find a way out of this place. *Something*, the little voice inside him whispered, *that no other Badlander has ever done before.*

155

Suddenly, the *Scucca* stood up, its tail erect, and sniffed the air.

'A creature, do you think?' asked Jones.

'I think so, yes.'

'Let's go. That gunshot's probably attracted something and I don't want to hang around to see what it is.'

'Fine by me.' Ruby grabbed the leash and dragged the *Scucca* around. It trotted beside her as she walked quickly after Jones.

They walked for some time, neither of them saying much. The sun pierced the branches of the trees with golden rays that were filled with insects fizzing and whirring like tiny clockwork creations. Birds twittered and chirruped. Little scuttering sounds erupted in the undergrowth as tiny animals skittered away from their approaching footsteps. The *Scucca* pounced into a bush at one point and Ruby saw the brown tail of what she thought was a mouse slip away.

But there were other, louder scuttering sounds too and Jones reached for his catapult when he saw two orange eyes peeping out from a patch of scrub, and sharp teeth glinting between a pair of bulbous lips which he recognized as belonging to an Eelax.

He saw burrows in the leaf litter too, which he thought might have been made by Teeny Trolls, and he held his nose as they passed a foul-smelling pile of colourful dung which he informed Ruby was made by a Purpleback Ogre.

The further they walked through the trees, the more

Jones realized there were signs of creatures everywhere. When he heard a flapping of leathery wings above the canopy he crouched and pulled Ruby down with him as a large Snarl flew overhead, head bobbing at the end of its long neck.

Jones wiped his brow and looked around at the trees. They were covered in green leaves, their great trunks twisted round like rope. He knew they were old oak trees.

'Wherever we are, it's not autumn like it was in Great Walsingham,' he said. 'What do you think this place is?'

'I was hoping you'd know.' Ruby tapped her head. 'You're the brainy one.' As they stood up, Jones heard a voice.

'*There's no way out of here,*' it hissed. Jones looked about, catapult raised, expecting to aim at something. But there was no one else except for Ruby. She was looking around as though she'd heard the voice as well.

'Did you hear that?' she whispered. Jones nodded and then he heard the voice again.

'*This place was made by a No-Thing with Dark Magic for all the creatures that live here, and there's no escape for Badlanders,*' it hissed again. Jones sensed that the voice was inside him, somehow, sounding like it was his own thinking, rather than outside his body. '*You'll get all the answers you want about this place, I'll make sure of it.*'

'Jones, what is it? Who's speaking?' Ruby was looking around frantically.

'Dark Magic,' said Jones. 'Whether we're breathing it in or it's coming up from the ground through our shoes, I don't

157

know, but it's getting inside our heads and speaking to us somehow. It wants us to know everything about this place, give us all the answers.'

'Why?'

'It's taunting us. It's telling us everything we want to know because we can't do anything about it, not if there's no way out.' Jones kicked at the ground. 'It wants us to lose hope and make us suffer.'

'Well, I won't let it,' shouted Ruby. 'It won't beat us!'

'Keep your voice down. We don't want to attract anything,' said Jones as he looked about nervously. 'Let's keep moving, and just do your best to ignore the voice for now.'

But all Jones heard was the gentle sound of laughter from time to time as they walked on and he knew Ruby could hear it too. As he thought more about their situation, he started to wonder about Maitland and the man's special connection to him. He whispered his old Master's name, calling on him to appear and help them out. But the man didn't appear. Jones didn't feel a flicker of anything or sense his presence at all. And he knew that even the bond between them had been broken by this world they were in and tried not to think any more about it.

When they reached a stream, the *Scucca* paused to lap greedily at the cold, clear water. Jones and Ruby cupped their hands and drank from it too after observing no ill effects to the hound. They were tired and hungry and didn't have much to say to one another. Ruby kicked a stone into the water with a *plop* and watched it disappear and couldn't help but think about how they had disappeared too from Great Walsingham like every other Badlander before them.

When the *Scucca* gave a short whine, they looked up, expecting to see a creature of some sort coming through the trees. But the hound had its head in the air and its tail was swishing gently. It whined once more and then set off again.

'Not a creature?' asked Jones.

'I don't think so. Should we follow it?'

Jones shrugged. 'We've got nowhere else to go.'

They walked behind the *Scucca*, as it slipped between the trees, following a scent. From time to time, both Ruby and Jones thought they heard something following them, but there was nothing there when they looked. The spaces between the trees and the high-growing ferns and brambles looked so deep and dark that it was difficult to shake off the feeling they were being watched.

As they became more tired and hungry, the heat made their brains spin. When Jones took a breath and tried to clear his head, he realized he must be imagining many of the sounds he was hearing. He began to wonder if this world was turning his mind to mush. He heard the voice of Dark Magic speaking to him from time to time but he did his best to ignore it. He started to hum to himself instead to try and keep his spirits up. He heard Ruby grumbling under her breath and figured she was handling the voice her own way. When it occurred to him to look at his smartwatch, because the sun hadn't seemed to move in the sky at all, he saw that it had stopped at 12.50 a.m. He stared at the screen. It must have been the exact time he'd passed through the doorway and left Great Walsingham.

Eventually, the *Scucca* paused at the treeline and stood looking out at a large clearing ahead of them, tail wagging, nose still twitching.

Trees had been pulled up and dumped to one side, stacked in great piles. Vegetables were growing in rows. Jones thought they might be carrots or perhaps parsnips. There were other taller plants bound on cane frames and he spotted long green runner beans hanging on their stalks. Fruit was growing on rows of bushes too and he could see blobs of redcurrants and blackberries. A block of green and yellow vegetation in the centre of the clearing was made up of sweetcorn plants. On the far side of the clearing was a fenced-off square of land containing sheep and horses.

A long shed stood to one side. It had a triangular roof covered in wooden shingle and a silver chimney pipe sat on top, a plume of smoke drifting out of it.

'What do you think?' asked Ruby. Jones wasn't sure what she meant. 'Aren't you hungry?'

'We don't know what this place is. Or who it belongs to. It's probably dangerous to stop.'

'It won't matter, not if we're quick.'

Jones's tummy gurgled as though replying for him.

'Who knows when we'll get another chance to get something to eat? All we've seen up to now is trees. The *Scucca* needs food too.' She pointed to the shed. 'Know what

160

that is?' Jones shook his head. 'It's a smokehouse. There are no windows. Can't you smell what's smoking?'

Jones had already caught the woodsmoke scent earlier and now it was impossible to erase it from his nostrils. His stomach rumbled again.

'The *Scucca*'s hungry. That's why it brought us here. If we can feed it then it'll grow again and I think that's probably a good thing under the circumstances, don't you?'

Jones looked out across the clearing once more and watched for anything moving. The sheep and horses seemed to be the only living things, munching happily on grass. An old wooden house had been built some distance away but it looked lifeless.

'Okay.'

Ruby took a step and paused as a figure emerged from the smokehouse. It was a woman. Stooped and curled over like a question mark, she was using a cane to totter over the grass. Even from a distance, Ruby could tell the woman was old. She made her way slowly across the grass towards the wooden house. Halfway there she paused and sniffed the air, looking in the direction of where Jones and Ruby stood. They crouched down, pulling the *Scucca* back.

'I think it's a Wrinkle-Toed Witch,' whispered Jones. 'You can tell cos they almost always have canes, on account of their deformed feet.' Ruby shrank lower as she remembered the first Witch she had ever met, Mrs Easton. It had taken a lot to defeat her.

'Can she smell us?'

161

'None of their senses are that strong. They like to eat, though. Appetites like *Ents*.'

The old woman carried on and eventually went in through the front door of the house, shutting it behind her.

'So what do we do?' asked Ruby.

The *Scucca* whined and licked its lips, huge raindrops of saliva dripping from its mouth and frosting the grass.

'It's too dangerous. If we get caught by that Witch, I'm not sure my catapult will be enough and I know the gun won't be.'

'But, Jones, we don't know when we'll next get the chance to eat.'

Jones sighed and then his tummy groaned so loudly that the *Scucca* stared and cocked its ears at him. Ruby stood up and brushed the dirt off her knees.

'We can move through the trees and come out on the far side of the smokehouse so we won't be seen.'

Jones tutted. And then he nodded. 'We move quickly,' he said. 'In and out as fast as we can.'

They used the trees as cover. Jones could barely hear anything above the beating of his heart. He knew that Ruby was right, that they needed to eat something, but he didn't want to get caught. He didn't want to risk ending up like the other Badlanders who'd come here. He thought again of the remains of the jacket they'd seen after they'd arrived in this strange world.

When they finally broke out of the treeline they kept low

and moved fast up to the smokehouse, and Jones clicked up the latch to open the door. Through the wafting smoke he could see rows of sausages as long as an arm gently curing, as well as large chops and shoulders of what he presumed was lamb. He moved deeper into the dark room, Ruby following with the *Scucca*.

When he noticed fish hanging up too, their tiny teeth bared over wrinkled lips, he took down a couple and began to nibble them. The meat was flaky and juicy and he realized just how ravenous he was. He looked back to see Ruby feeding the *Scucca* a large hunk of meat, turning it round as the creature bit off great chunks from it. Tossing the fish bones to the floor, Jones explored deeper into the building and saw a wooden table fixed to the wall at the back. He crept closer and saw an array of knives and other sharp instruments, including skewers and even a small axe and a saw.

Hanging on a large hook above was a leg.

A *human leg*, he thought, and took a few stuttering steps back, knocking into a row of hams on a stand, sending a couple thumping to the floor, while at the same time tangling with a line of sausages hanging from the roof. But then he saw it must be a leg from some creature since there were only three toes. Even so, as he stared at the hanging meat around him, he was glad he had only eaten the fish.

'We're leaving, Ruby,' he hissed as he turned to see her feeding the last of the meat to the *Scucca*, allowing it to lick her fingers. 'Take what you want and let's go.'

He marched past her. As he walked he thought he saw

other legs and arms hanging in the dark corners. He told himself it was just his imagination. But he didn't want to look to be sure.

When he reached the door, he opened it a crack and breathed the clean, fresh air and wiped the sweat from his brow with the sleeve of his overcoat, making dark streaks on the material. He heard his heart beating in his ears and wished it would be quiet so he could think more clearly.

But it wasn't his heart. The booming sound was somewhere outside of him. Distant but growing louder.

He peeked out of the door through the crack but saw nothing suspicious. And then he felt a tremor in the ground beneath him that rocked him ever so slightly, the structure of the smokehouse squeaking as it shifted on its foundations. The sheep started bleating and the horses stood with their ears pricked, looking into the forest.

The tops of the trees shook and Jones wiped his eyes to look again. The trees were definitely moving. Something was coming.

'Ruby!' he growled, looking back. 'We've got to go. Now.'

But she was having a tug of war with the *Scucca* over a ham.

'Ruby!'

'All right!' She let go of the ham and the *Scucca* backed towards Jones in the doorway, looking to try and get past him. Jones stood his ground and the *Scucca* started to gobble down the meat anyway.

Ruby stood beside Jones, looking through the gap with

him as a large ugly head emerged above the trees, their triangular tops barely touching its chin.

'It's a Grobbler *Ent*, biggest of the lot.' Jones reached a shaking hand into his pockets and searched for something as the ground trembled so much his ankles shivered. He took out the tub of ointment and showed Ruby the handwritten label on the lid: *Smellies*.

'It en't magic, just a mix of different plants, so it should work fine. Grobblers can smell humans a mile off.' He unscrewed the lid, then took a fingertip of the brown muddy substance and wiped it on his neck. He offered the pot to Ruby. 'Quickly, this stuff'll cover our smell.'

Ruby applied some of the mixture to her neck too and almost gagged. Even the *Scucca* seemed to turn its nose up at them, before it stared across the clearing at the trees as they parted, thumping its tail on the smokehouse floor as the Grobbler appeared. Jones reckoned it was almost sixteen metres tall. A great ugly brute with a fuzz of close-cropped black hair, each ear weighed down by a golden ring as big as a car tyre. It wore a brown butcher's apron of different pieces of material stitched together and Ruby realized with disgust it was made from the flayed skins of animals, their heads still attached. The creature had a bulging brown sack slung over its shoulder.

Jones pulled the door shut until they could see through just the smallest crack.

The Grobbler dumped the sack down on the ground. It sighed, clearly happy at getting rid of the weight from its shoulder, making the corn in the centre of the clearing rustle.

The horses in the pen whinnied and the Grobbler laughed, making a sound as deep as thunder, and blew through its lips, making the sheep totter backwards. When it saw them gamely trying to stay upright, it blew even harder and toppled the nearest sheep, much to its amusement.

'What's it doing here, Jones?' asked Ruby, shushing the *Scucca* as it whined, clearly wanting to leave the smokehouse and meet this creature.

Jones shook his head. The front door of the house opened and the Witch came tottering out, leaning on her cane.

The Grobbler beamed a big smile and knelt down beside the Witch, although it still towered over her. From the pocket of its apron it plucked a tiny, wriggling body. A girl in a nightdress, the material covered in blood.

Jones felt Ruby leaning forwards and had to hold her back. All they could do was watch as the Witch circled Olive, who lay shivering on the ground, poking at her with her cane and sniffing the air. She tapped her cane on the ground three times and conjured a spell from the end of it and the little girl floated up like a balloon. Olive drifted, kicking and screaming, through the open front door of the Witch's house, and disappeared.

The Witch pointed at the smokehouse with her cane and said something that Jones couldn't hear. The Grobbler seemed to understand though, nodding as it emptied out the sack it had been carrying. A group of grey-skinned Goblins came tumbling out, rickety-legged and sharp-faced. They cowered beneath the Grobbler as they picked themselves up, shivering in the shade its body cast. The Grobbler roared, waving its hands at the crops and the fruit bushes. And one big finger unfurled and pointed at the smokehouse as the Witch tottered back towards her house and shut the door behind her.

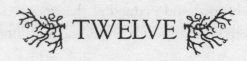

TWELVE

There was no way to escape from the front of the building without being seen so Jones and Ruby dragged the *Scucca* to the rear. They were breathing hard. The smoky air crept deeper into their lungs, and they tried their best not to cough. But when Ruby saw the leg dangling from the ceiling above the workbench at the back she let out a gasp that sent her into a coughing fit.

Jones was down on his hands and knees, looking for a way out, pressing the wooden planks to see if any of them were loose. But they were nailed in tight and there were no gaps for prying fingers. He paused when he heard the door at the front of the smokehouse open and motioned to Ruby to crouch down. They crept as quietly as spiders into the darkest corner they could find and made the *Scucca* lie down beside them. Its black fur seemed to melt into the dark, though its red eyes blipped as it blinked.

Jones could see two Goblins in the doorway, their silhouettes bickering with each other until they seemed to reach a decision and one of them set about removing great

168

loops of sausages, placing them into a basket near the door like coils of rope. The other Goblin climbed onto a stool and reached for a ham, unhooking it from a wooden rail and laying it on the floor, before repeating the process.

Ruby found the more she tried not to move the hotter she became. The *Scucca* was hot too and she could feel its heart thumping. It started to pant, the big pink tongue flopping out of the corner of its mouth. Jones glared at her and she tried to close the creature's mouth but it growled and shook her off. She edged back, wary of being nipped.

When she looked round, she saw one of the Goblins peering towards the dark corner where they were hiding. Ruby had the sensation that the creature was looking right at her. Her hand moved towards the gun in her holster but she was wary of the noise a shot would make and knew it was a last resort. The Goblin licked its lips, its ears flicking higher, then Ruby heard a tiny thud and a smoking hole appeared in the Goblin's grey forehead. The creature fell to the floor and twitched, before lying still. Jones was already reloading his catapult with a second silver ball bearing as the other Goblin came running at them. But when he fired again the creature dodged and the ball bearing thudded into a large piece of ham.

The Goblin leapt onto the rail above and swung around it like a gymnast then let go, landing on the workbench. It picked up a small axe and hurled it at them, sending it spinning end over end, the sharp blade winking as it passed through the bars of sunlight poking through the cracks of the building's wooden walls. The axe struck the wall just above Ruby's shoulder.

'Ruby!' shouted Jones, and she looked up to see that the Goblin had decided to retreat, heading for the open door, racing between the various sausages and meats.

A *thud* made her flinch and she saw Jones pulling a bigger axe out of the wooden wall. 'We need to get out,' he hissed as a commotion started up outside. 'We can make a run for it into the trees.'

Ruby nodded and picked up another axe in her shaking hands and smashed it into the wall.

Jones had already made a big enough hole for the daylight to come flooding in, catching the smoke and making it seem to churn faster and faster. He kicked to make it bigger, snapping a couple of planks, the broken ends falling to the ground outside. Ruby hooked the head of her axe into one side of it and pulled hard, ripping it even bigger. The *Scucca* seemed to get the idea too and bit down, tearing out a section of plank with its jaws.

The hole was large enough to crawl through now and Jones stuck his head out. He judged the trees to be around fifty metres away and he was about to turn and tell Ruby to get ready to run when there was a terrible wrenching sound and the walls of the smokehouse juddered.

The various meats hanging from the ceiling swayed and knocked together as the whole roof came away in the Grobbler's hand. It peered down, wafting away the smoke with its free hand. Jones darted quickly through the hole, catching his neck on a jagged splinter of wood, the pain making him gasp. He scrambled to his feet and sprinted for the trees, hot blood running down past the neckline of his overcoat.

Reaching the treeline he glanced back, expecting to see Ruby close behind, but her jacket had snagged on the edges around the hole and she was trying to free herself. He could hear the *Scucca* barking from inside the building as the Grobbler reached down.

And then Ruby was yanked back through the hole.

Jones saw her being lifted high in the air, one foot held between the Grobbler's thumb and forefinger. She was kicking her other leg and screaming. Jones stood by the trees, caught between wanting to help and knowing it would be useless, his catapult too small to make any difference.

Then the *Scucca* was bursting out through the hole in the back wall of the smokehouse in a spray of splinters, a Goblin riding on its back, knife glinting in its hand. It plunged the knife into the hound's side, making it howl, before the *Scucca* managed to crane its head round and grab the Goblin's leg in its jaws, dragging it to the ground. Other Goblins were clambering through the hole in the smokehouse wall and more were streaming round the sides of the building.

Ruby's screams disappeared as she was dropped into the pocket of the Grobbler's apron. Jones knew he had to save himself if he was to have any chance of saving her too. So he turned and ran into the trees.

He ran as fast as he could and for as long as he could. But it felt like there was a piece of elastic connecting him to Ruby that was trying to ping him back to her. He shouted that he'd go back eventually, that he wouldn't give up on her, and finally collapsed to the ground exhausted and wept, his heart heaving. When he heard a snapping of twigs and heavy breathing behind him, he turned, his catapult raised.

But it was the *Scucca*. It limped up to him, its bloody side sticky and glistening, and then it looked back at the trees and howled, the long note rising into the canopy.

Ruby sat in the dark smelly pocket of the Grobbler's apron. Despite the greasiness underfoot she managed to stand up in a corner, before toppling over and sliding in the dark as the creature moved. Its lumbering walk made it difficult to get off her hands and knees, and she collided with something else in the pocket's corner, though it was too dark to see what.

Suddenly, the mouth of the pocket opened and a large finger and thumb plucked her upwards. As the daylight flooded in she saw what she had been sharing the pocket with: a Spring-Heeled *Ent*. It lay dead in a heap, and she knew it must have been the one that had snatched Olive.

The big arm holding her brought her up and then down like she was attached to a crane as she was lowered closer to the ground.

Ruby shielded her eyes as the bright sunlight scratched

them. Still dangling from the Grobbler's fingers, she came face to face with the Witch. The woman leant on her cane, hooded eyes studying Ruby. She sniffed, then turned up her nose.

'Hmm. You're a long way from home, little girl. I wonder what stole you away from the life you knew and brought you to our sunny world?' Ruby didn't say a word. She kept her arms tight to her sides to keep the gun in its holster covered, not wanting the Witch to suspect that she was anything other than an ordinary girl. 'You must have escaped from something. Some terrible creature that gave you a fright!' Still, Ruby said nothing and the Witch smiled. 'Maybe it ate your tongue. Or maybe I might?' The old woman sniffed the air again and wrinkled her face once more, and Ruby remembered the ointment Jones had made her put on.

'Well, whatever your story, you're not for me. Too much pong. I think you've gone off. I like my meat fresh.' The Witch took a few steps back and looked up at the Grobbler. 'I'm happy with what I've got, dear, thank you,' shouted the Witch. 'She's past her sell-by-date and you know my appetite's not what it used to be, so I only treat myself to the best.' The Witch took another sniff and then waved her arms to make it quite clear she wasn't interested. 'Thank you but she's yours. I'm not trading anything more today.'

Ruby was lifted high into the air again and then plopped back into the pocket of the apron.

*

Once the Grobbler started moving, it was difficult to stand up and Ruby slid around in the bloody inside of the pocket, trying her best not to think too hard about the dead *Ent*. When she heard a swishing sound she realized the Grobbler had to be among the trees and wading through the forest, having left the clearing.

She tried to stay hopeful and trust that Jones would be working on a plan. But, in the dark, her mind began to play tricks on her. She couldn't be sure he had escaped the Goblins. And the last thing she'd seen as she'd been lifted clear of the smokehouse was the *Scucca* being stabbed with a knife. Its terrible howl echoed in her ears.

It wasn't just her own worries that drifted like bad dreams in her head. The Dark Magic in this world was taunting her too, as if it was feeding off her fears. *'This place is a secret world for creatures to hide in and prey on people in the ordinary world,'* it hissed. *'And because it's been made with Dark Magic it can never be undone without using Dark Magic. And guess what else? No Badlander who's come here has ever escaped.'*

Ruby tried not to listen, doing her best not to let the tiny flickers of hope inside her die. But it was hard when all she could hear was the voice telling her she'd *never* save Olive and that she'd *never* convince the Order to accept girls because she was *never* going to return to the Badlands. She wished the charm on the gun in its holster was still working. A friendly voice right now would give her some confidence.

In the dark, everything she'd achieved in the Badlands

seemed meaningless now. She was cold and empty without her magic, the same old Ruby, an unwanted foster child.

She imagined Sloop standing on the hill, announcing to everyone in the Order how he'd been proved right about girls not being suitable as Badlanders.

But as she saw Sloop's beaming face in her mind's eye, a spark of defiance grew in her belly. However much she didn't like the man, she decided she was grateful to him for giving her a steely determination to prove him wrong.

Thinking more clearly now, she reached into her pockets and searched for anything useful. There was nothing except the shrinking powders Jones had given her, the silver whistle, her scrying polish and some biscuits for the *Scucca*; somehow she had lost the Pocket Book Bestiary along the way.

'Come on,' she shouted into the dark. 'Give me a break!' All she heard in reply was a little peal of laughter and she knew it was the Dark Magic.

The next thing she knew, the Grobbler seemed to stumble and she slid across the bottom of the pocket, crashing into the body of the dead *Ent*. When she tried to scrabble away, her foot caught in some item of clothing and she had to contort herself round and reach forward to release herself. As she sat back, something occurred to her and she reached forward again, hands scrabbling in the *Ent*'s pockets. She found something sharp and tapered and guessed it was a knife. In the other pocket she found another one, although not as big.

She stood, wobbling for a moment, with a knife in each hand as the Grobbler suddenly turned very sharply. Ruby flung out her arms to keep her balance and one of the knives she was holding penetrated the leather of the apron far enough to give her something to cling onto and keep her upright. An idea fizzed into her head and Ruby stuck the other knife into the leathery wall too, higher than the other one, and hauled herself up off the bottom of the pocket. As soon as she'd pulled herself level with the second knife, she pulled out the lower one and jammed it in again above her head, then pulled on that.

She kept going, climbing like a mountaineer up a wall of ice, stabbing in one knife and pulling out the other. She was as slow as a snail, her hands slippery, her arms burning. The inside of the apron began to bulge as she reached the Grobbler's belly. The change of angle made it harder to climb and it squeezed her against the lining of the outer part of the pocket. Her feet kept slipping beneath her but she managed to hold on, pausing for breath as she hung from the two knives embedded in the leather. She could see the opening of the pocket above her, a thin horizontal line of daylight, gently opening and closing as the Grobbler walked.

She began to believe that she was going to make it out. But as the daylight hit her blood-covered hands and arms and she inched her head out, a tree branch came crashing past and she ducked back down just in time. The Grobbler seemed to be picking up his pace. There was no way out without risking being knocked unconscious or pinged to the ground many metres below. She waited for as long as she was able, hanging until her arms ached . . . and ached.

When the swishing stopped, she peeked up out of the pocket and saw they had emerged from the forest into a rocky landscape. The Grobbler's body see-sawed even more as it picked its way over huge boulders. She could see the sack over its shoulder, bulging with Goblins, and she tried not to think of Jones or the *Scucca*, focusing only on her determination to get away from the Grobbler.

Hauling herself up out of the pocket she came face to face with the head of a sheep, its skinned body part of the patchwork on the front of the apron which was dotted with the heads of other creatures. The sheep's eyes were missing but the sockets still had their large eyelashes. A set of worn yellow teeth was showing in a grin. Ruby started to try and work her way down the apron, finding other heads to rest her feet on. She tried not to look at the rocks on the ground, knowing that she would have to time her jump perfectly.

Suddenly the *Ent* slowed and Ruby realized they were nearing the mouth of a huge cave. The drop was still too far to be safe and she worked her way down the apron until she was rising up and down on a knee, scared the Grobbler might see her. The boulders were fewer now, and the ground smoother as they entered the cave. As the knee came down, Ruby pulled out both knives and slithered down the apron, using the sharp points to keep in contact like brakes so she didn't go flying, before digging them in again to stop.

She was near the bottom of the apron now, roughly in the centre, between two large boots. The next time a leg came down she let go of the knives and dropped to the cave floor.

177

She lay face down with her hands cupped on the back of her head as the Grobbler walked further into the cave. Then she darted over to the nearest hole in the rock wall and hid, glad to be in a different, safer dark.

When Jones had got far enough from the smokehouse to know the Goblins were definitely not coming after him, he stopped. He was tired. The cut on his neck was sore. Feeling sick from the food he'd eaten, he leant over and threw up.

The *Scucca* gave a little whine. It was keeping its distance and kept glancing back in the direction they had come. When it gave another louder whine, Jones knew what it was thinking.

'We'll go and find her,' he said. 'But I need to fix you up first.' The bloody stab wound in the creature's side had clotted, making the black fur hard and spiky, but the cut looked deep. Jones glimpsed something pink and raw. When he noticed spots of blood glistening on the ground he started to worry that some other creature in the forest might be interested in the trail.

He knelt and beckoned the *Scucca* closer. It stared at him, its red eyes giving nothing away despite standing awkwardly. Jones edged a little closer, speaking softly.

'I know I en't your Master, cos Ruby hatched you and fed you and trained you up, but I would have been in another life. Wanna know why? Cos I was the one what found you. Me and Maitland were in a graveyard in Yorkshire. That's where you're from.' He was so close to the *Scucca* he could touch its head now. 'We spent months looking for a hound like you. Maitland said training a *Scucca* would help us and I'd get to look after it. We looked for you on the night of a blood moon. And I was the one what found you and dug you up.' When Jones put out a hand to try and pull back the fur to look more closely at the wound, the *Scucca* growled and bared its teeth.

'I en't gonna hurt you.' The *Scucca* watched his outstretched hand. And then he moved it closer. 'All I want to do is help make you better.' The *Scucca* growled again, louder this time, and Jones pulled his hand back as he saw more teeth.

He dug around in a pocket and pulled out a small tub of brown ointment with a black lid. The paste inside was treacle-coloured and Jones heaped a mound of it on his finger and held it out for the *Scucca* to smell and then he rubbed it into the cut on his neck. He felt the fizz of the paste and a twitching in his neck as the skin on either side of the cut pinched together. The numbing sensation of the ointment grew stronger until nothing hurt and he inspected the wound in the little mirror he carried in his pocket and saw that it had healed, although the skin was still puffy and red.

'See?' he said, pointing at his neck. 'It's a Healing Ointment, and I'm gonna help you too.' He took a lump of paste out of the pot for the *Scucca*. 'It's only special herbs mixed together with honey. You can eat it if you want, it'll help your insides.' He held it under the *Scucca*'s nose but that only made it sneeze. 'It's gonna heal you like it did me.

179

It'll make you feel better.' He pointed to his neck again and thought he saw some understanding in the hound's eyes. He leant forward and put his hand on the creature's wound so the paste was touching it. The *Scucca* flinched but didn't move and Jones waited for the numbing effect of the paste to kick in. Slowly he moved his hand around in a circular motion, massaging it in. When the paste had disappeared, and the *Scucca* had started to relax, he rubbed in more. A couple of times he had to stop the creature from licking the wound and taking off the ointment.

'Let it do its job,' he said, holding the *Scucca*'s head, before sitting back. He knew it was done when the creature shook and rolled onto the ground. The ointment had an itchy after-effect and he had been scratching his neck too. When the *Scucca* had finished, it stood up and gave a great shake before trotting over to Jones. It planted a big lick on the boy's face.

'Geroff,' he said, wiping his face on his coat sleeve. 'Geroff,' he said as the hound came in for another lick. And then Jones grabbed hold of the creature's neck and buried his face in the fur for a moment, grateful not to be alone.

'We're going to find Ruby,' said Jones. 'We're going to save her. We'll follow the trail you made with your blood back to that smokehouse. If that Grobbler took her, that Witch'll know where, or if Ruby was given to her, like Olive was, then that'll do just fine too.' He started walking purposefully and the *Scucca* gave a little bark, before catching him up and trotting beside him. It felt good to have the hound as his companion. But the dark feeling about what he might find when they returned to the smokehouse clung to his insides like oil. Deep down he knew he was just a boy with his wits and a catapult, and he wondered if it was enough.

THIRTEEN

The Grobbler was not happy at all. From her hiding place, Ruby had watched the creature stop a bit further on inside the cave, which was clearly its home, and feel around inside its apron pocket. It had expected to find her after pulling out the dead body of the Spring-Heeled *Ent* and throwing it on the floor. Its smile of anticipation had turned to a frown, and the Grobbler had quickly become so enraged it had ripped open the pocket, rubbing at the bloody interior before roaring its displeasure.

After picking up a large rock the creature flung it against the cave wall like a petulant child and then stormed off deeper into the cave, pebbles in the walls shaking loose and trickling down to the floor.

Ruby could see that getting to the mouth of the cave was going to be a problem. The Grobbler had emptied out its sack prior to looking for her so now there were Goblins wandering around the cave floor, busy as ants. Some of them were putting away the meat from the smokehouse, along with the fruit and vegetables they'd gathered. Others were cooking, adding ingredients to big bubbling pots, and the rest were sweeping and cleaning.

The cave was lit with huge fires laid on the floor, each one surrounded by a ring of blackened stones. Large, flickering torches were lodged into fissures in the walls too, sending shadows rippling around the cave. Ruby watched the flames moving, feeling their warmth, and then it occurred to her she could feel a draught licking the back of her neck. The crevice she was hiding in wound like a corkscrew deeper into the cave wall, twisting and turning so she couldn't see much further than a few metres. She decided to investigate in the hope she might find another way out.

It grew darker and darker as she crept cautiously, peering round the corner every time the passageway turned, letting her eyes adjust to the gloom. The draught catching her face every now and then gave her hope she might find an exit of some sort and this grew as she saw a pale blue light ahead.

But it wasn't daylight.

When she came into the small cave she saw a mound of glassy stones, piled like giant marbles, each one lit inside with an icy light. By their bluish glow she could see the cave was a storeroom of sorts, with various crates and sacks, plump as pillows with whatever was inside them, laid in rows. In the far corner was a metal cage, with bones inside it on the floor. A skull lay on its side in the corner, the lower jaw missing. Ruby noticed a red jacket, the velvet material faded and scuffed, hanging on a peg beside the cage and when she looked at the black lining inside she saw the label she was expecting but hoping not to see: *Deschamps & Sons.*

Noises echoed down the tunnel behind her and her hand went to the gun in its holster but she knew it was time to leave. Any sound of a shot would only bring trouble.

There were two other passageways leading out of the room but she was unsure which one to take and it was too dark to see far down either of them. The approaching footsteps grew louder and when she felt a gentle draught fanning out of the dark mouth of the passageway to her left she decided to take it. She heard Goblin voices behind her in the storeroom and kept moving as fast as she could, stifling a cry as she bashed herself on jutting fangs of rock that jumped out at her.

She began to worry that she might be doubling back towards the main cave as the tunnel twisted and turned, a fact confirmed by the orange flicker from torches and fires that made the rock passageway start to glow. When she reached the end, all her courage felt as if it was dripping away, because she could see that she was much deeper into the cave now. The entrance was a long way off to her right, the blue sky in it no bigger than looking at it the wrong way through a telescope. She was about to go back when she saw another metal cage perched on an outcrop of rock above her, a set of uneven stairs cut into the cave wall leading up to it. Somebody was slumped against the bars, head resting on their chest, hair tumbled in greasy curls around their shoulders.

'Hey,' hissed Ruby. The person didn't seem to hear. So she

crept up the stairs, keeping close to the wall, slipping through the shadows.

She could see the figure more clearly now. He was wearing a dirty blue shirt, ripped in places, and black trousers down to the knees, the ends frayed where the lower sections had been torn off. He had no shoes and his feet were filthy, his toenails long and black.

'Hey,' hissed Ruby again.

The person raised their head and Ruby stepped a little more into the light. Before their eyes met, she already knew who it was.

Ruby had imagined meeting Thomas Gabriel many times in her head and each time it had ended with her firing the most powerful spell she knew at the boy and smashing him into tiny pieces. Now, here she was, without any magic at all, looking at this pitiful person slumped in a cage, thin and raggedy and covered in grime. When her eyes darted to his bony wrists and she saw the Black Amulet peeking out from under one of his ragged shirtsleeves, she stepped back, reaching for the gun in its holster. She pulled back the hammer as Jones had taught her and aimed the gun, her hand shaking as she looked down the barrel at Thomas Gabriel.

Thomas Gabriel blinked at her, waiting for her to shoot, not a flicker of panic on his face. And then he closed his eyes and nodded, as if ready to accept his fate. When she heard noises below them on the cave floor and saw the dark shapes of Goblins moving around she crept back against the wall, the gun dropping to her side.

As she waited for the Goblins to pass, thoughts poked little chinks of light in her anger and she started thinking more clearly.

Shooting the boy wouldn't do her any good if anything else heard the shot.

Leaving the cave was the most important thing.

She didn't care about Thomas Gabriel. Not one bit.

Let him rot in that cage!

But, before she could turn around and leave, Thomas Gabriel began shuffling forward on his hands and knees across the floor of the cage.

The poor, wretched boy gripped the bars and tried to speak. But his mouth was hoarse and his lips were dry and he could only manage a shuddering groan. He started to shake and a tear dribbled from his eye and cut a bright, clean path through the grime on his face. Beside the cage there was a metal cup on a long wooden stick next to a bowl of water and when he pointed a shaky arm, Ruby understood. She shook her head.

'Ruby, help me, please,' whispered the boy. 'Please.'

But all Ruby wanted to do was run. She had to think of herself if she was going to escape this cave, not Thomas Gabriel. Not this boy who'd wanted to hurt her the last time they'd set eyes on each other. She started feeling her way back along the wall, away from the cage.

'Ruby, I know how to get out of this place and back to Great Walsingham.'

Ruby stopped.

*

Jones was hot and he was tired. He figured he'd been awake for hours although there was no way of knowing how long it had been since they had come through the doorway into this world, given that his smartwatch had stopped working as soon as they'd arrived. Time seemed to have no place here where it was constantly sunny.

The trail of blood from the *Scucca*'s wound had proved more difficult to follow than he'd thought and he was worried they were lost. When he stopped to wipe his brow, the trees seemed to shift closer. The *Scucca* paused to look back at him before trotting on ahead, sniffing the ground and looking up from time to time. Jones hurried on behind it. He had to trust it would find its way back to the smokehouse. Something wobbled inside him again as he thought once more about what he might face when they arrived there. There was the Witch, of course, and he couldn't be sure if the Goblins or the Grobbler might still be there. But he was determined to find Ruby and rescue her. It was all he had to hope for in this world. It was the hope that kept him going rather than sitting down on the ground and giving up. He heard the Dark Magic chuckling and he sped up to show just how determined he was to save his friend.

When the *Scucca* suddenly stopped and started looking around, Jones's heart dropped into his knees.

'Come on,' he said. 'We've got to find her. You can't give up.'

The *Scucca* whined and wagged its tail and sat down on its haunches, panting hard. Jones knew it was hungry and thirsty. Just like he was. He looked up through the branches at the spots of blue sky above as if looking for inspiration but there was nothing there to help him.

'Come on,' he said again, clapping his hands. 'We can't be that far away, now. We've been walking for ages.' He strode off in the direction they had been going and the *Scucca* joined him, wagging its tail and sniffing the air again, zigzagging through the trees.

After a few hundred yards, Jones stopped. In the distance to his left he'd spied through the trees a small clearing and what looked to be a tumbledown cottage. His stomach prickled because he was sure they hadn't passed it as they'd run from the Goblins, which meant they were definitely lost. *Perhaps we missed it the first time*, he thought, trying to reassure himself.

He watched the house for some time, leaning against a tree and thinking about things, the *Scucca* beside him. He took off his overcoat and tore out a piece of the red lining and tied it to a low branch, then made his way to the clearing, the *Scucca* following. He kept looking back at the piece of silk, to reassure himself he knew where to return to.

As Jones moved through the trees he could see the cottage more clearly. The roof was sagging and parts of the walls were missing. The building was not made of stone but from what looked like . . . food. The walls were made from large pieces of gingerbread, and the corners of the house were built from striped candy canes, one of them leaning alarmingly. The roof was made from sheets of yellow icing that had cracked and splintered. Half of the chimney had been sheared away and looked to be made from chocolate sponge.

Jones paused, watching the house again for signs of life, but it seemed deserted. Eventually, he crept up and peered through a window made of clear sugar and framed with long pieces of chocolate. The cottage was a mess inside, broken furniture and crockery littering the floor. He pulled off a piece of the window frame and nibbled it. The dark chocolate was the best he had ever tasted and he took another bite.

'It don't make any sense,' he said to the *Scucca* which was looking at him with its ears pricked and its head cocked to one side. 'If you knew about fairy tales, the stories what ordinary people read, then you'd know what I was talking about.' Jones walked around the house once and crossed his arms. He heard the *Scucca* whine, gazing back in the direction they had been going and Jones gave one final glance at the house before setting off back towards the piece of silk tied to the tree. But he stopped when he saw another clearing off to his left and veered towards it when he noticed an apple tree, loaded with shiny red apples, standing on its own in the sunshine.

The tree looked healthy and leafy and Jones sniffed one of the deep-red apples and licked his lips, before plucking it off the tree. It was so shiny he could see a blurred reflection of the tumbledown gingerbread house behind him as he held it up. His own reflection stared back at him too and he looked more tired than he thought. The *Scucca* gave a little bark to hurry him up and he shushed it.

'There's something special about these apples. You ever seen one so shiny?' he asked, holding it up. The *Scucca* just gave a little whine. 'Well, I have – in Deschamps & Sons, on a Death Apple Tree.' He stared at the fruit again and licked his lips.

He took a big bite and chewed the sweet white flesh inside. But what he was really interested in were the pips. He took another bite to get to the middle of the fruit. They were different, hexagonal and jet-black. He took one out and held it up to the sun.

'See?' announced Jones. 'I was right! We might have something here if we're lucky cos a tree like this en't charmed or made with magic like lots of other Badlander things, just grown from a seed.' He took out his Learning Book from his pocket. The *Scucca* sat down and sighed and then laid its head on its paws as if prepared to wait for whatever the boy was doing.

Jones leafed through his book until he found a page with a rudimentary picture of a tree surrounded by various notes and a few lines of what looked to be a rhyme. After giving it a quick read, he crouched at the base of the tree and read it out.

'Apple tree, apple tree, show me your heart
For I think you've been grown through the
    Badlander art
From seeds that have sprouted inside a good man
Who's left us this tree in order to plan

With knowledge he's known and wanted to share
Through one single fruit you've grown
   up to bear.'

The tree shook its branches, the red apples on it bobbing. Excited by what he'd seen but not sure what it meant, Jones consulted his Learning Book again. As his finger scrolled across his notes, he heard a great cracking sound as the trunk split down the middle, each side rolling back like paper curling up in the heat of a fire. Jones smelt soil and stones as he peered into the dark. Inside the tree was a hole about twenty metres deep with a golden light at the bottom. Tree roots jutted out through the soil wall at intervals to make for an easy climb down.

'Stay here,' Jones told the *Scucca*. 'Keep an eye out.' The hound wagged its tail and Jones wasn't sure it had understood. He made it sit in front of the tree and pointed a finger. 'Stay!' And then he climbed into the hole, finding a way down using the roots.

He remembered what Maitland had taught him about the various special seeds that Badlanders had cultivated over centuries, perfecting and developing hybrid ones to grow naturally in the manner required with a particular purpose in mind: to allow another Badlander to access the past of whoever had planted a seed. But the Death Apple Tree grew in a particularly grisly manner for that to happen.

As he reached the bottom, Jones stepped onto lumpy soil. A skeleton was embedded in the ground and the roots of the tree had grown out of it. Dangling from the centre of the ribcage, on a stalk, was a golden apple, filling the void with a dull glow. Jones took out the small collapsible books from his pocket and searched for the right one, allowing it to spring open and wiping the lint off the cover – *Rare, Rarer and Rarest Horticultural Wonders* by P. L. Tierney. He flicked through the pages until he found what he was looking for in the section titled: 'Death Apple Tree'.

Gegælen æppel
(Enchanted Apple)

A range of different varieties can be found in the root system of a Death Apple Tree. These various fruits are categorized by their appearance and the effects they produce (see list below). However, whatever type of fruit you find, its benefit is always the same: an enchanted apple gives knowledge to the one who eats it. This occurs by way of a conversation with the Badlander who gave life to the tree in the first place, having swallowed the seed prior to his death. Some scholars argue that such a conversation, between the living and the dead, is proof of life after death. But the most commonly held theory is the apple absorbs the memories of the person as it grows out of their dead body. The apple's hallucinogenic properties then enable these memories to be accessed by whoever eats it, in what feels like a real conversation with the person who planted the seed inside their body.

There was more information but Jones ran a finger down the page and found the entry relating to 'gegylden æppel' or 'Golden Apple':

A very old variety believed to have originated from the Kursk region in Russia. Characterized by a tart flavour and a tough skin. This fruit allows three questions to the person who eats it.

Jones didn't bother reading the rest because he knew the basics and was worried about the *Scucca* wandering off. He collapsed the book and put it back in his pocket.

He had to reach in between the ribs of the skeleton to pick the apple. The golden fruit hung like a Christmas bauble, tethered to the ribcage by a strong brown stalk, and it required a generous tug to free it. He pulled so hard some of the ribs broke.

Jones licked his lips and took a big bite.

The skin was tough and the white flesh inside was as tart as the book had said it would be. In fact it was so sour that he only managed a couple of bites. As he chewed and did his best to swallow he thought he heard a whine and looked up to see the *Scucca* peering down. Jones wondered whether it was bored before he started to worry if it might be trying to warn him. But it was too late to do anything anyway. The apple was taking effect.

The earth walls around him wobbled and he tried to stay upright. He heard whispers. The skeleton rattled and pulled itself from the ground, breaking free of the roots attached to it. As it stood, skin began to cover the bones, then came clothes, and Jones found himself face to face with a handsome, well-dressed Badlander with golden floppy hair that he swept back with his hand, before looking around and nodding.

'I see you found my tree, then,' he said.

FOURTEEN

Ruby didn't move as she stared at Thomas Gabriel crouched on the floor of the cage. Her eyes kept flicking to the Black Amulet on his wrist, concerned about its power in this world created by Dark Magic. But as she thought more about it, she realized that Thomas Gabriel must have lost his ability to use magic just as she had, which explained why he was trapped in the cage. Although the boy's shirtsleeve was pulled down, she could see that the skin around the amulet was black and puffy, as if infected.

'What do you mean, you know how to get back to Great Walsingham?' she asked. Thomas Gabriel licked his lips and pointed at the metal cup on the long wooden stick beside the bowl of water.

It was hot in this section of the cave. Ruby could feel the heat from a giant bed of embers set into the floor. It was the size of a large swimming pool and it prickled and glowered, the heat turning the air hazy above it.

She stole forward and dipped the cup into the water.

When she handed it to him through the bars, he drank it down in gulps and poured some over his face.

'What did you mean about getting out?' asked Ruby again. Thomas Gabriel licked his lips once more and smoothed back his tangled hair from his face. He pointed deeper into the cave. 'What's back there?'

'Someone who can do magic.'

'A Badlander?' Thomas Gabriel shook his head. Ruby frowned, trying to figure out what he meant. 'What's the point if it's a creature?' she hissed, and thought about turning round and leaving.

'It's not a creature. It's someone from the book.'

'What book?'

'The book that made this place.' Thomas Gabriel grabbed the bars of the cage and beckoned Ruby closer. 'This world tells you things. Taunts you. Tortures you,' he hissed, whistling through the gaps where his teeth were missing. 'I know things-s-s.'

He pointed at the metal cup. Ruby refilled it and handed it back to him through the bars of the cage and he gulped down some more water.

'This world was conjured up by a No-Thing, a Badlander gone bad with Dark Magic from a book of fairy tales. It's a place where creatures can hide from the Order. But it's not a place for Badlanders.' He laughed, spit jumping in frothy beads from his mouth. 'But you probably know that if the world's been talking to you too.' He wiped the sweat from his brow as the embers in the pit below glowered and burnt.

'Back there,' he said, pointing into the darker reaches of the cave, 'is someone from the book who can do magic. But she'll only do it for girls. Not for men and boys.' He chuckled. 'The Dark Magic in this world has taken great pleasure in telling me that deeper in the cave is someone who *can't* get me out of here.' He licked his lips and tried his best to smile. 'But she could do magic for you.'

'And why should I believe you, Thomas Gabriel? After everything you've done?' She nodded at the Black Amulet. 'I can't believe you're even still wearing that horrible thing,' she said, 'when it's impossible to do any magic here.'

Thomas Gabriel pulled back his sleeve and Ruby saw that the whole arm was wizened and black. 'The amulet won't come off,' he said. 'It's another form of torture, reminding me what I could do once but can't any more. The amulet's slowly rotting me away.' He prodded his blackened arm and a little section of flesh flaked off like a burnt piece of meat.

'How long have you been here?'

Thomas Gabriel shook his head. 'Long enough.' He giggled and shrugged his shoulders. He started playing with his hair, twisting it round and looking at it as if everything he wanted to say was lost among it. And then he looked at her again. 'Long enough for this world to tell me its secrets,' he said, gripping the bars so hard his knuckles bleached white. 'If you take me back to Great Walsingham with you, I can close this world.' He raised his wizened arm and the green eyes of the two serpents that formed the Black Amulet flashed in the fiery light from the warm embers below. 'This amulet's powerful enough to do it once I can do magic again. This place told me.' He laughed. 'It told me because it knows I'd never be able to get out of this cage, let alone back to Great Walsingham. At least I couldn't have till now.' He grinned at Ruby and shook his head. Then he scratched at his face and started muttering under his breath, eyes darting this way and that as if looking for things in the shadows that Ruby couldn't see. Suddenly, he seemed to remember that she was there again. 'I went to Great Walsingham to hide away, you know? No Badlander would ever come after me there, I thought.' He laughed. 'But you did, didn't you?' He cackled another little laugh and slapped the bars of the cage.

Somewhere inside Ruby a dial was turning as she watched the wretched boy muttering and shaking his head. All her anger was switching off. This was a different Thomas Gabriel to the one who'd tried to hurt her. He looked so fragile that she thought any more strong words might shatter him. But whether she could trust what he was telling her, she wasn't sure, given how broken his mind seemed to be.

She peered into the depths of the cave. Was there really someone there who could help her? She turned to ask Thomas Gabriel another question when a great noise started up, shrinking him back into the cage. Ruby crouched low too, like a crab against the wall, as the Grobbler came striding out of another part of the cave with a huge pair of bellows. The creature pointed the nozzle at the bed of embers and started to pump, making the hot orange rectangle burn an angry red.

Thomas Gabriel let out a little sob. He grabbed at the bars of the cage and peered over to where Ruby was hiding.

'I never meant to hurt you. It was the amulet. It made me think differently and now it's torturing me. I'd never hurt you again. Never!'

'Sssh,' she hissed. 'Thomas Gabriel, you need to keep quiet. I'm going to get you out of that cage and then you can show me what you're talking about.'

But he didn't seem to understand what she was saying and began to sob more. Ruby saw the Grobbler lift its head and glance over in her direction. It rumbled a laugh as it watched Thomas Gabriel crying and tugging at the cage bars, and then went back to its work, pumping harder on the bellows and raising the heat higher in the cave. Ruby wondered why the Grobbler hadn't eaten the boy and seemed to enjoy watching him suffering. Maybe the creature had been told to imprison him by the Dark Magic in this world? Whatever the answer was, it didn't matter now; there was no time to ponder it further. She had to focus on getting out.

When Ruby breathed in it felt like she was swallowing hot coals and she watched the Grobbler thrust a long piece of metal into the fire. It came out white-hot, and the Grobbler laid it on a giant anvil and started hammering away, great sparks flying into the air.

As the Grobbler worked, Ruby crept to the wall and reached up to Thomas Gabriel's old herringbone jacket hanging on the peg beside the cage. She felt around in the pockets.

199

'Did you have anything in here that might help me get you out?'

Thomas Gabriel just looked at her. Then he smiled and shook his head.

Ruby felt her fingers grip something and she drew out a silver pillbox. But when she opened the lid the Door Wurm inside was shrivelled and black, dried out like a fig. Cursing, she put the pillbox back and searched again. There was nothing else in either pocket. It was difficult to think about what to do next with the Grobbler banging so hard on the anvil, making the cave walls shake.

BANG ... BANG ... BANG.

BANG ... BANG ... BANG.

Ruby closed her eyes to try and block out the noise.

BANG ... BANG ... BANG.

She thought of something and her eyes flicked open.

'Stand back,' Ruby warned Thomas Gabriel as she drew out the gun from her holster and pulled back the hammer.

BANG ... BANG ...

She tightened her finger on the trigger and aimed for the padlock ...

BANG.

The bullet struck the padlock and broke the arm holding the door of the cage. She held her breath as the Grobbler paused and peered at the metal it was working on. It stuck a finger in its ear and wiggled it around, before plunging the metal back into the embers again.

Ruby opened the cage door just enough for Thomas

200

Gabriel to creep out. He was wary, like an animal not used to its new surroundings. She pulled him on, grabbing his coat on the way past and handing it to him.

'You're a Badlander, Thomas Gabriel, and Badlanders help each other. And you're going to help me. So show me this person who can do magic.'

Thomas Gabriel nodded and Ruby led him down the steps, where they hid in the shadows.

When the Grobbler stopped hammering, it picked up the metal which it had fashioned into a blade and started swinging it through the air, assessing the weight of what was going to be a sword. When it turned its back, Thomas Gabriel pulled Ruby deeper into the cave.

As soon as the skeleton started moving, Jones had been thinking about his three questions. Now the man was standing in front of him, he was finding it difficult to concentrate. His book had warned him the apple's natural effect was strong but Jones hadn't expected it to feel so powerful, given it didn't work with magic.

He was tingling all over, and his skin felt so tight he thought it might split open with the slightest touch. The walls of the earth chamber rippled if he looked too hard at them and the floor seemed to shift under his boots. There was a curious buzzing sound, like a fly trapped in his head, which kept fading in and out. He did his best to ignore it and focus on the man in front of him.

'Silas Weaving, at your service,' said the man, clicking

his heels together. 'What would you like to know?' he asked, adjusting his tie as if the collar of his white shirt was a little too tight.

'I . . . I . . .' Jones heard the buzzing again and it seemed to take away the words he wanted. He felt an itch at the back of his head that he was forgetting something important.

'Spit it out!' growled Weaving. 'This tree grew out of me because I had something to say. My last act as a Badlander before dying was to swallow a seed to make sure there was someone to hear me one day. And it seems to be you.' The man looked at Jones as if not entirely convinced by him.

When Jones swallowed his throat crinkled like tin foil. He was starting to feel sick.

'What . . . what is this world I'm in?'

Weaving nodded, as if it was an obvious question to ask. 'What I discovered is that this world was created by a No-Thing, for creatures to hide from Badlanders. And as I've lain in the earth, I've learnt more about it, absorbing its secrets as I've rotted and we've become one. This world was conceived with Dark Magic, *áglæccræft*. The No-Thing used its particular type of magic on a book called *The Classic Book of Fairy Tales*. The made-up world in those pages was made real. But it's changed from the one in the book, of course. It's very much a different place, turned rotten by the Dark Magic used to create it. Not a place for *ordinary* children. And not a place for Badlanders either.'

The man laughed and the vibration wobbled Jones as if he was on the deck of a ship in a storm. But he steadied himself.

'My next question is how do I get ou—'

'Why don't I ask you a question?' Weaving grinned and smoothed back his floppy golden hair once more. 'That's fair, isn't it?'

Jones thought about that because it didn't sound quite right and he wondered if he should consult his book again.

'One question for you, then one for me and so on,' continued Weaving. 'You can't just take and not give anything back.' The man stared at Jones as if what he was asking for was the most natural thing in the world.

'That en't how it works,' said Jones. 'I'm supposed to ask three questions.'

'All I want to know is your name?'

'Why do you want to know that?'

Weaving tutted, shaking his head. 'That's your second question!'

'No, I didn't mean—'

'That's all right. I'll tell you the answer, and then I get two questions. Clearly, I need to know your name if you're going to stay down here with me.' The man grinned and stepped forward. Jones retreated instinctively, and bumped up against the earth wall behind him.

'This en't right,' shouted Jones. He felt something tickling his hand and looked down to see a maggot crawling out of the apple where he'd bitten into it. More were wriggling out of the white flesh. He dropped it in disgust and kicked it away before wiping his mouth on his sleeve.

'Oh, dear, looks like you ate a rotten apple.' Weaving

203

started to laugh. Must be something to do with the earth it grew in. You can't trust this world at all.' He tutted and shrugged. 'That Dark Magic just gets everywhere, doesn't it?'

Jones balled his hands into fists and did his best not to appear afraid. 'Tell me how to get out of this world made from a book. You're supposed to answer me three questions.'

The man stifled a giggle with his fingers. 'Take it easy, you should be more concerned about getting out of this hole, to start with.'

'You en't real. I en't scared of you.'

Weaving touched his hand, making him flinch. 'How real is that for you?'

'I'm just imagining it,' shouted Jones. But the man reached out and grabbed Jones by his arm. 'You're going to stay down here with me. This tree can grow even more if you give your body up to it. Make the apples even more red and shiny.'

Jones lashed out with his other arm and sent Weaving reeling. He turned and started to climb the roots. When he felt a hand grab his leg, he tried to kick himself free but Weaving clung on.

'There's no getting out of here.'

'You en't real,' shouted Jones. He put his fingers down his throat and threw up a chunk of the apple in a foamy yellow puddle. The man's grip started to fade and Jones stuck his fingers down his throat again.

'I gave birth to this tree. And that's real. You didn't imagine climbing down here, did you? If you stay here, you'll be safe,' said Weaving desperately.

'No, I won't!'

'Stay down here. Help the tree grow,' pleaded Weaving.

As Jones brought up the rest of the apple, the man disappeared and all that was left was the skeleton again embedded in the earth, the ribs in pieces where Jones had broken them.

The buzzing in his head had gone, replaced by the *Scucca* barking above him. But there was another sound too. The tree roots were moving. A great clod of earth fell from the far side of the chamber and landed on the ground. More started to fall as Jones climbed higher, doing his best to negotiate the moving roots that batted back his hands and pushed at his feet, trying to trip him up and send him falling. Another clod of earth dropped past and he looked up to see the passage back to the top narrowing, the roots binding together and weaving a barrier above him. He aimed for a gap and just managed to squeeze through before it closed.

The *Scucca* was still barking and he could see its head in silhouette as it peered down. Jones tried to climb faster, but his foot slipped and was caught by a root that whipped around his ankle. Another larger one slithered round his waist. He dug out a sharp stone from the earth and sawed at the root around his waist until he could snap it and then pulled his foot free.

The light was fading all around him now and Jones could see that the door in the trunk above was closing. The *Scucca* was doing its best to stop it, grabbing one side in its mouth and pulling. But the other side just rolled further round, shutting out the light.

Earth poured in and Jones took a gritty mouthful, pebbles hitting him on the head and setting off sparks behind his eyes. More roots grabbed hold and then a great shower of earth fell on top of him and he tucked his chin into his chest. When he opened his eyes, he could just hear the muffled sound of the *Scucca* barking. And then more earth was falling on top of him, and the *Scucca*'s barks became distant.

Thomas Gabriel jabbed a finger upwards.

'There,' he said triumphantly. Ruby followed his outstretched arm and looked up at a middle-aged woman wearing a chiffon dress and a silver tiara. She was sitting in the bottom of a cage suspended from the ceiling of the cave, her legs dangling through the bars. A pair of red-and-white stripey stockings covered her legs and her blue high-heeled shoes winked when they caught the light.

'Who is she?' asked Ruby.

'I don't know. But I *know* she can do magic.'

'Because this world told you, to taunt you?'

Thomas Gabriel nodded. 'I've seen her do things too, to amuse the Grobbler. I think that's why it kept me in a cage, because I made it laugh.'

'What sort of things does she do?'

'Magical things.' Thomas Gabriel twisted his hair around his fingers and Ruby watched the Black Amulet glinting

206

as it caught the light from a fire set into the floor. It gave her the shivers even though Thomas Gabriel was unable to use it.

'If she can do magic, why's she still in a cage?'

Thomas Gabriel shrugged. Ruby began to wonder if the damage the amulet had wrought on Thomas Gabriel's mind was too much, if he was too confused to be of any real help. Her hope of them getting out of the cave, let alone out of this world, started to fade.

'That's what she needs, of course,' said Thomas Gabriel, perking up and pointing at the wall, his greasy hair sticking up in tufts. When Ruby squinted, trying to see what he was so excited by, he grabbed her hand and led her towards a ledge carved into the wall. Standing on it was an old tin cup with a stick inside. At least, Ruby thought it was a stick until she picked it up and found a five-pointed star carved at the other end.

'The Fairy Godmother,' said Thomas Gabriel, hopping from one foot to another, as if pleased with himself for remembering. 'That's what she calls herself. *You can't do this to me*,' he squawked in a high-pitched voice in some bad impression. '*I'm the Fairy Godmother*. That's what she shouts at the Grobbler.'

Ruby swished the wand from left to right and the air behind it sparkled with blue stars that faded. When she looked up, the woman in the cage was peering down at them and jabbing a finger at the rope that ran from the cage down through a pulley system of rusty old cogs and gears fixed to the wall. She wound her hand round and round as if trying to get them to hurry up.

If he really listened, Jones could just hear the *Scucca* barking, the sound muffled by the earth packed around him. He moved and breathed and coughed. Keeping his head down low on his chest he began to wriggle his way up through the soil, his hands pressed together like a swimmer underwater. Every now and then he paused to listen for the hound to make sure he was going in the right direction.

Stones trickled around him. He heard roots shifting, slithering past his legs and over his back as if some great tentacled beast was dreaming in its sleep. Jones tried not to panic. He imagined the *Scucca* hound above, and was thankful for its loyalty. A couple of times, the sound of its barking played tricks on him and he found himself having to focus very hard on where he was going. In those moments, a dark part of him whispered he would never find his way out.

The roots became more tangled the higher he went and he had to pick his way carefully between them. As his route became more and more blocked, he decided to veer off and tunnel sideways, aiming to come out above ground some distance away from the tree. He made sure to keep the barking on his left and wormed on through the loose soil. But his legs and arms were tired and his breathing was growing more laboured. The soil was sucking the energy out of him.

He cursed, panicking, when the hound stopped barking

because it felt as though it had given up on him. It scared him enough to try and kick on. But he barely had the strength to move and the dirt felt so heavy.

'Over here!' he shouted, realizing that if he could hear the *Scucca* then it might be able to hear him too. 'Over here!' He heard a noise and his heart pounded harder, hoping it was the hound, but it was the sound of roots moving, seeking him out. He felt something wrap around his ankle and he tried to kick it away.

'Help!' he croaked.

More roots moved and the ground shuddered. One root hooked round his waist. And then there was another sound above him. He knew it was the *Scucca* because he could hear it barking, and it was digging too.

'I'm here,' shouted Jones again.

When a ray of daylight came streaming in, it struck his eyes so hard it made them water. The hound was digging hard, panting, shovelling away the earth with its big black paws. Jones felt the root around his waist start to drag him back, away from the light. The *Scucca* growled and reached into the hole it had dug, grabbing the collar of his overcoat in its teeth and starting to pull. Jones cried out, thinking he might split in two, and then he was cutting at the root with the stone he was still holding.

There was a great cracking sound as the *Scucca* pulled him so hard the root snapped and he came up through the hole and landed on top of the hound. Other roots slithered up out of the earth, looking for him, and Jones got shakily to his feet and ran towards the treeline, the *Scucca* following.

As he ran, he felt the strength flooding back to him. The sun on his face refreshed him, burning off the chill from the dark earth. A movement in the trees made him glance to his left and he saw something flapping through the air. His mouth opened and he paused, because his first impression was that a huge butterfly was pulsing towards him and then he felt it land on him and he knew exactly what it was. His fingers clawed the fine wire mesh of the net as he tried to lift it off but it was weighted down at the edges and the harder he struggled, the more the net clung to him. He came crashing to the ground and saw a band of creatures running towards him. As one of them raised a cosh he realized it was a Grim Dwarf, its white beard tied in a knot, the grey skin on its cheeks, nose and forehead speckled with dark blotches. Jones glanced back, hoping the *Scucca* would help him, but it was thrashing around in its own net, and he knew its continued barking must have attracted the pack of Dwarves.

He turned to face the Dwarf, teeth clenched, but all he heard was the *thunk* of the cosh on the side of his head and the instant ring of it in his gums before the world fell away.

It took a long time to lower the cage. Ruby turned the handle as fast as possible, the rusty cogs grating and squealing, making Thomas Gabriel hop up and down, his hands flat against his ears. She worried the noise would bring unwelcome visitors but the vast cave was so alive with sounds and echoes that it just merged into the soundtrack of everything around them.

When the cage touched the ground, the woman opened the door and stepped out gracefully onto the dirt, her blue shoes leaving a slipstream of sparkles that glittered and faded away. Up close, Ruby could see she was more beautiful than she'd realized, though it was hidden beneath grime and straggly hair that tumbled either side of the tiara perched precariously on her head. But there was a sparkle in her blue eyes and when she smiled, Ruby felt a tingle in her belly that made her smile straight back.

'Right, the first thing I need is a pee,' said the woman, hitching up her dress and looking for a corner.

'Oh, right,' said Ruby. 'I mean '

'I've been stuck up there for hours,' said the woman as she squatted down, her tights around her ankles. Her dress, big enough to cover her modesty, looked like a giant upturned teacup. Ruby and Thomas Gabriel didn't know where to look as it became obvious what was happening and a look of contentment spread over the woman's face.

'Thank you, by the way.' She smiled. 'I'm not great with heights at the best of times, not least in this awful place.' She found a handkerchief from somewhere and used it, scrunching it up and tossing it away as she stood up and walked towards them. 'I'm Precious. Precious McGinty Flora Aurora Stella Glorinda Bunty Smith.' She held out a hand. It was slender and looked like it was made of bone china, but it was filthy and she hadn't washed her hands after spending a penny either. She seemed to realize this, because she spat on her dirty palm and wiped it over her dress before holding it out again.

'Pleased to meet you, Precious,' said Ruby, shaking the woman's hand.

'Pleased to meet you, Precious,' echoed Thomas Gabriel, as though trying his best to be polite.

'Well, then,' said Precious, folding her arms and looking them both up and down, not quite sure what to make of the long-haired boy in his herringbone jacket. 'What's the plan?'

'Thomas Gabriel says you can do magic,' replied Ruby, remembering the wand in her other hand and holding it out. 'I think we're all agreed we need to get out of here.'

Precious snatched the wand and swished it back and forth in the air, like a sparkler. As a smile played over her face, her skin glowed and her blue eyes brightened, as if a bulb inside her had been turned up. Ruby had the curious sensation the woman had grown ever so slightly too. Everything about her had been re-energized by some sort of power in the wand.

'I *can* do magic, but like I said, what's the plan?' Precious pointed the wand at them.

Ruby opened her mouth but Precious sighed and shook her head, muttering under her breath.

'People never seem to care about anything other than themselves. It's just me, me, me. Of course I can do magic. I can give you whatever you need. That Cinderella got what she wanted, and there have been plenty of others too. But there's nothing in it for me except the glow.'

Ruby frowned like she'd just swallowed a worm. 'I don't understand.'

'The glow you get from doing something good for someone else. And between you and me that wears rather thin after a while.' Precious gave a little sigh. 'I mean, it's lovely helping others, of course it is, but not being able to do magic for myself is *not* okay. In fact, it's a curse. Especially when I'm rotting in a cage being forced to do magic by some vile ogre just for kicks. I'm a Fairy Godmother, not a circus act.' Precious jabbed a finger upwards. 'Being stuck up there means you get time to think and I've had enough of giving to everyone. I'm a different woman now. A deal-maker.' Precious hawked something into her throat and spat into the dirt. 'So get me out of this cave and you can have whatever you want. That's how I'm rolling. Because I've got to think of myself, not just others, for a change. This is a new world and it's turned me into someone new too.' She pointed the wand at Ruby and a little stream of sparks flew out and struck Ruby on the nose, making her sneeze. 'And I'm only giving *you* what you want, by the way. I don't do magic for men.' She shrugged at Thomas Gabriel. 'Just girls down on their luck, I'm afraid. That's the deal. It's how I'm made to the marrow in my bones. Ask any Fairy Godmother and they'll say the same.' Precious folded her arms as if that was the end of the matter. Then she raised her wand. 'And another thing. I'm not being difficult for the sake of it. Girls need to figure out things for themselves, not rely on the generosity of someone like me all the time. They have to find their own way. They're not helpless things, are they? Aren't I helping them realize their potential by not instantly coming to their aid every time?'

Precious refolded her arms as if that really was the end of the matter.

'So if you can't do magic for yourself, how did you end up here?' asked Ruby.

'Haven't the foggiest. One minute I'm minding my own business and then the world turns upside down and all manner of creatures are appearing. People panicked. Tried their best to fight them off. I was cornered in the forest by some horrible little creatures – Goblins of some sort, I think. They brought me here to this giant of a thing, the king of this awful cave, for his amusement. At least I presume it's a *he*, you can't always be sure with creatures like that.'

'And this world is supposed to be what exactly? When it's normal, I mean.'

Precious made a sound like a bottle of lemonade being opened as she sucked the air in through her teeth and studied them. 'I figured you weren't from around here. Like all the others, the men, anyway.' She waggled her wand at Thomas Gabriel, who cowered and put up a hand. 'All of them asking for help, which was difficult, given I *couldn't* help them.' Precious nodded over at a cage in the far corner of the cave, bones strewn over the floor, and clicked her tongue on her teeth, shaking her head. 'But you're different,' she said, brightening and smiling at Ruby. 'And I'll take that.' She put out her hand. 'Do we have a deal? Show me what you can do and I'll help you.'

Ruby looked at the hand. There were so many questions she wanted to ask, but now was not the right time. A clanging sound started up from somewhere in the cave and when it died away, she heard voices coming closer. The walls flickered black and orange as torches came towards them, the voices growing louder. Precious glanced behind her.

'Time to go, don't you think?'

Ruby felt something being screwed deep into her guts. She didn't have a plan. But she needed this woman's magic.

'I'll take my chances then,' said Precious, dropping her hand and hitching up her skirts, ready to run.

'No, wait!' hissed Ruby. 'I've got an idea to get us out of this cave.' She didn't, of course. At least not yet. So she was just going to have to come up with one as fast as she could to convince Precious to help.

FIFTEEN

A s the sun beat down, Jones took another sip of the water from the leather flask he'd been given and wondered if it ever got dark in this world. He was sure hours and hours had passed, but the sun was no lower or higher in the sky than when he and Ruby had arrived. He took another sip of the water, which was lukewarm. He guessed it had been stewing inside the flask for a long time as he picked small brown fibres from his tongue.

When the Dwarves began standing up and brushing themselves down, Jones knew the break was over. He was hauled to his feet by the chain wrapped around his wrists, the metal pinching his skin. Although he stood taller than the creatures around him, they weren't afraid of him. When he'd been freed from the net, he'd jumped to his feet, ready to fight, but the creatures had just laughed. It had only taken one of them to grab hold of him and pin his arms to his sides as another had bound his wrists. The Grim Dwarves were strong, sturdy creatures, built like pit ponies, and looked like they had been hewn from granite. Jones knew all about them in the Badlands. They stole children and small adults to work for them, digging in mines and underground tunnels, driving them until they dropped and died from exhaustion. No doubt that was to be his fate too.

The *Scucca* had been tamed with a silver chain looped around its neck and seemed subdued, plodding on as it was led by a Dwarf, one of them either side of it too, prodding it with a stick whenever it dawdled. Jones knew that certain creatures didn't get on very well and he figured this was the case for the *Scucca* and the Grim Dwarves. As creatures that built cave systems and tunnels, he presumed the Dwarves had no use for graveyards and the stench of death it brought. No doubt it explained why they held the hound without much regard.

But they had kept it alive.

And he was still breathing too. As long as he had strength, his mind was alive and bright, looking for an opportunity to escape. It was the main reason he was thinking about the sun. Night would afford him a better opportunity to try and work himself free of the chains. But night seemed a long way off.

An argument broke out among some of the Dwarves, their gruff voices rising and echoing round the trees. The creatures were always muttering and shouting at each other and the small group seemed to nurture disagreement, as if that was what held them together. A scuffle turned into a fight and Jones decided it was his chance. As more Dwarves joined in the disagreement, tempers flaring and minds drifting away from him, he took a few steps back, trying not to stumble, disappearing between the trees. And then he was running as best he could with his hands chained in front of him, parting a patch of bracken as he raced through it. The voices behind him changed to cries and shouts and he knew his absence must have been spotted. Changing course, he zigzagged between the trees and crouched beside one, panting hard. As he listened out for his pursuers, he noticed an inscription etched into the smooth base of the tree where the bark had come away. It was a *mearcunge* made by a Badlander.

D. PETERSON 24/03/55
WARGUM
SEE ↓ FOR A TUSK
GOOD LUCK IN THIS PLACE!

Jones had seen a Wargum drawn in books. It had two downward pointing tusks with razor-sharp edges that were capable of cutting through anything. The chains round his wrists clinked as he clawed at the earth around the base of the tree. Wary of cutting his hands on any tusk that might still be there, he decided to dig with his boot, hoping that no other Badlander had found the message before him and taken up the kind offer of D. Peterson.

When he saw a leather handle poking up at him through the soil he realized the whole tusk had been buried, tip down, a leather strap wound around the root to allow it to be held. Jones pulled hard and the tusk came up cleanly out of the earth. It was about three feet long and slightly curved, like a scimitar. Gripping the leather-covered end between his knees he leant over the tusk, the curved end pointing up, and placed the chain holding his wrists onto the sharp edge. It cut through the metal so cleanly that he almost fell forward on the tusk.

A Dwarf growled behind him as he threw off the chains and turned to face it. As he did so, his right hand was already coming out of his pocket, holding his catapult by its handle, and pinched between the fingers of his left one was a silver ball bearing. He slotted, aimed and fired in one fluid movement and the Dwarf crumpled to the ground as soon as the ball bearing hit its mark.

There were more Dwarves crashing through the trees now and when a wire net came whistling towards him he side-stepped and hid behind the tree, the net crashing into the trunk and flopping to the ground. He rolled around the tree and fired another ball bearing, felling a second Dwarf, before running to the tusk and picking it up by its leather handle. It was lighter than expected but he felt buoyed by the sharpness of both edges as he flashed it through the air and caught the sunlight. Another net came flying towards him and the tusk sliced through the wire, the two halves of the net sailing past and falling behind him.

The remaining Dwarves watched him carefully, growling commands at each other, and the group arranged themselves to form a ring around him. As they began to advance, Jones slashed the tusk through the air in an effort to keep them back, the sharp edges humming. But they seemed less afraid than he was. He felt something strike his arm and a rock dropped to the ground. Jones whirled around as more stones came at him. He sliced up some of them as he flashed the tusk wildly but then he felt a thud on his forehead and the trees seemed to grow taller as he fell. He felt a trickle of something over his face and licked his lips, tasting blood and sweat.

'Get back,' he shouted in desperation, his voice cracking. 'Get back!' He flailed around in the dirt for the tusk, catching one of the edges with his hand and not realizing he'd been cut until he saw a dark red slash across the palm. As the cut began to sting the Dwarves fell upon him and dragged him to his feet. 'No!' shouted Jones, tears in his eyes. 'No!'

He sensed the Dwarves leaving him, their arms letting him go as they backed away, so he shouted even louder, as if *No* was a magic spell that worked in this place.

'NO!'

Then he realized they weren't paying any attention to him at all. Someone else was there. He wiped his tears away and saw a man dressed in shining armour, his blond locks flowing as he brandished his sword. And not just any man. One so handsome the air around him seemed to crackle. His chiselled features and bright blue eyes were focused on the job at hand as he glided effortlessly in a dance around the Dwarves, slicing them easily with his sword. Blood erupted like red forks of lightning in the sunlight as arms, heads and legs went flying off at ugly angles.

To Jones it seemed that time only started ticking again when all the Dwarves had been felled and chopped into pieces. The man surveyed the scene and nodded, pleased with himself. He was barely out of breath. When he held out his hand for Jones to shake it the boy looked up into the bright blue eyes and realized the skin around them was as white and soft as cotton.

'I'm Charming,' said the man in a rich, booming voice. 'Prince Hugh Richard Charming. Judging by your attire, I'm presuming you're a Badlander.' Jones nodded, wondering how the man knew that, and did his best not to gasp as his hand was squeezed so hard he thought the fingers might drop off.

'I'm Jones,' he managed to say as his fingertips slowly turned pink again.

Ruby led Thomas Gabriel and Precious back through the passageway towards the storeroom, her brain working hard on what to do next. Precious had been quiet up to now, but she was starting to grumble under her breath the further they went.

'Where are we going?' she hissed after a few more steps.

Ruby said nothing as they turned the corner into the storeroom with the strange blue balls and the first cage she'd found. She was hoping for some inspiration about what to do. What she found instead were two Goblins, inspecting a wooden crate full of what looked like green rocks, one of them scribbling strange characters on a pad of paper with a stub of pencil.

The Goblins snarled and one of them drew a ragged, dirty blade. Thomas Gabriel backed away, leaving Ruby and Precious wondering how to proceed.

'You don't have a plan, do you?' hissed Precious. Ruby didn't reply, and the woman tutted. 'Well, figure something out,' she said, 'or we're never getting out of here. We had a deal. Show me what girls are made of. That you really deserve my magic!'

Ruby already had the gun out of the holster and was pulling back the hammer. There was no time to worry about the noise it would make.

As she squeezed the trigger she remembered there were four bullets left so her aim had to be true. The gun went off and her arms jerked back. When she looked again, the Goblin with the knife was collapsing onto the stacked pyramid of blue balls. The structure broke apart and the balls bounced everywhere, one of them splitting open to release a bright silver substance that crept over the floor like mercury. It was so shiny Ruby could see her reflection moving in it and she stepped back as it crept towards the tips of her trainers.

She heard footsteps and she remembered the other Goblin, her arms swinging round to aim the gun again. But the creature had disappeared down the passageway towards the main cave, judging by the echoes coming back. The pad and pencil it had been holding were left behind on the floor.

Ruby knew they didn't have long before it returned with help.

'Well?' asked Precious. 'What do we do now?'

Thoughts were flitting inside Ruby like butterflies as she bent down over the silver puddle. As soon as she'd seen the reflective liquid there'd been a buzz inside her. It was the sensation she always had when she saw a mirror or a shiny surface, a ringing inside her that only a natural scryer could feel. It went right to the centre of her heart. She tested the puddle with a finger. The liquid was lukewarm but there seemed to be no ill effects from touching it as she inspected her hand and a big droplet fell back into the puddle.

Thomas Gabriel's reflection appeared beside hers as the ripples disappeared.

'Are you going to leave us here?' he asked. 'I know you can do it because of how good you are at scrying. We both know it, don't we? Because of what happened last time ...' He tailed off and grabbed at her as she stood up. He was shaking.

'I'm not leaving you, Thomas Gabriel,' she said. 'You've got a job to do in Great Walsingham with the amulet, remember?' She pointed at the Black Amulet on his withered arm.

'Oh, yes,' he said, his face brightening. 'Yes, I can do it. I can close this world using the amulet once I've got magic inside me again. I know because the Dark Magic here told me I could. And I know it wasn't lying because it wanted the truth to hurt me.'

'Good, but there's something you and Precious have to do before that if you're going to come with me.'

'And what would that be, exactly?' asked Precious.

Ruby brought out the vials of fungal shrinking powder that Jones had given her and popped off the lids. 'I can get you out of here but only if you're small enough.' She took a pinch of the red powder and flicked it onto Thomas Gabriel, making him sneeze. And then she took a pinch of the black powder. 'You're going to be okay, I promise.' Thomas Gabriel nodded and then he smiled as something dawned on him.

'It's Shrinking Pow—' His voice tailed off into a tiny squeak as he shrank down to something barely tall enough to reach Ruby's ankle. Ruby scooped him up in her hand as carefully as she could and dropped him into her jacket pocket.

Precious was staring, her mouth so wide that Ruby could see the back of her throat. 'How did you ... how did you do that?'

'Something to do with mushrooms ... I don't know exactly.' Ruby looked towards the passageway as she heard the sound of footsteps echoing round them. Whoever was coming was running.

'It's time to go,' she said. She flung a pinch of red dust at Precious, followed by the black dust. Precious's surprised cry became a squeak as she shrank to a tiny figure, no bigger than a Christmas cracker toy. Ruby popped the tiny figure into her pocket. She made sure the vials were closed and placed them back in her jacket too.

Quickly, she crouched by the mirror-like liquid again and asked to see Jones in the shiny surface.

He was with the *Scucca* hound and a handsome-looking man she didn't recognize. Her mind tingled as she smiled for the first time in ages, relieved they were both still alive. But she knew she couldn't go to a place that she'd never physically been to before so there was no way of reaching them.

The image faded as she stood up and fetched the Goblin's pad and tiny pencil and wrote quickly on the paper. Kneeling by the mirror-liquid again, she could just see the faint outline of Jones. It grew stronger again as she thought about him once more.

Having scrunched her note into a ball she pushed her hand through the liquid as far as it would go. It was grainy and stickier than a normal mirror. When she felt that her hand would go no further she released the piece of paper. It dropped at Jones's feet. He looked around and picked it up, shouting her name as soon as he'd read what she'd written. But Ruby let the image disappear when she heard something and looked up.

Rushing through the entrance to the passageway were a group of Goblins, teeth bared and knives out. Ruby had to leave now or never get the chance again.

She focused on the silver pool in front of her and the inside of the smokehouse appeared. It looked safe enough but it was difficult to be totally sure in the murky, smoky dark. All she could do was hope that it was as the Goblins advanced towards her, fanning out around the storeroom.

When she stepped into the liquid, it splashed and lapped against her trainer. She pushed harder and watched her foot sink through up to her knee, her other foot disappearing too as it landed in the shimmering pool.

She felt hands grabbing at her shoulders and hair and she

yelled as she heard the roots tearing and a clump come free. Claws ripped through her jacket and then there was nothing and she was landing on the floor of the smokehouse in a heap as she looked around, listening for anything else that might be in the building. But the only thing that moved around her was the smoke.

When she felt something tapping her hand, Ruby almost screamed until she realized that it was a tiny Thomas Gabriel peeking out of a pocket. And as her heart stopped fluttering she told herself that she had done it; she'd escaped the cave. As she helped Thomas Gabriel out and put him gently on the floor she imagined how impressed her other passenger would be with what a girl had done.

The *Scucca* had started licking Jones's face once the silver leash had been slipped over its head and removed.

'Geroff,' said Jones, trying to push it back. But it was too strong and as it reared up and the two front paws landed on his shoulders he collapsed onto his backside. Sitting up, he wiped the slobber off his face as the man called Charming watched on.

'What sort of beast is that exactly?' asked the man, eyeing it warily, the sword twitching in his hand, flicking spots of Dwarf blood to the ground.

'It's a *Scucca* hound. They en't normally friendly, only this one's been trained up to help Badlanders.'

'I see.' Charming nodded and seemed more at ease and began wiping his sword clean on the grass, leaving shiny red stripes. 'I suppose that's hardly surprising,' he said, inspecting his blade.

'What do you mean?'

'The Badlanders I've met certainly needed all the help they could get. But without exception they all died one way or another.' Charming pointed his sword at Jones. 'That doesn't bode well for you, boy.'

Jones patted the *Scucca* and tried not to think about that. He had a pretty good idea who this man was now that he'd thought about it, given what he'd learnt from eating the rotten apple. But Charming wasn't a Prince in a fairy tale any more, made of words and pictures in a book. This man was a living breathing person, because the book had come alive. Someone, Jones decided, who must have some answers. 'What did the other Badlanders tell you exactly?' he asked, wondering if he should be addressing the Prince as 'Your Highness'.

'That they'd come here to help. Once upon a time this land was a fair and just place. We had our problems, of course, which it was my duty to help sort out, from rescuing damsels in distress to battling foul creatures. Mostly the former, to be honest.' Charming smoothed back his golden hair and grinned a big, pearly smile. 'Everything ended happily whenever I had something to fix. But then something went bad here that changed everything, turned the whole kingdom on its head.' His smile faded. 'The whole place became overrun with creatures. No one knew where they'd come from. This is a magical place and anything is possible and, believe me, we've had our fair share of evil. But no one was prepared for what happened. The amount of creatures that descended on us made it feel like the land was suffering a curse. Giants, Goblins and all manner of other strange things. It was as if they'd crept out of the nightmares of simple folk. They made this place their own and however much the people of this fair land fought back, it was no good. There were too many of them. They were strange times. Wicked stepmothers and honest villagers fought together. Princesses battled alongside their Ugly Sisters, ageing Kings and clever Youngest Sons. But that was a long time ago. There aren't many of us left now.' Charming clicked his tongue against his teeth and grumbled something under his breath. For the first time, his hair lost a little of its shine and Jones thought he looked worn out and sad.

'And with the creatures came Badlanders, after a while. Men and their apprentices telling us they were from the same faraway world these creatures had come from, with the intention of helping us fight them. We thought we'd be saved at first. These men were so knowledgeable about the beasts that had ravaged this land and seemed to know their weaknesses. But they were doomed from the start. They could never leave once they'd got here. As if whatever had turned it bad in the first place knew they'd be coming and had prepared for it.'

Charming kicked at a piece of Dwarf.

'One man I rescued from a foul creature like this showed me how he'd got here. It was through a magical doorway that looked out into a town I'd never seen before. A strange-looking place. I've forgotten the name. Neither of us could get through. We tried following creatures coming and going through these doorways but it was impossible. The Badlander was trapped here. He was killed by an Ogre who smashed him to smithereens. Your lot must have got the message this place is so dangerous because fewer and fewer Badlanders came through until there were none. You're the first person I've rescued in a long time, so that's some small comfort. A man needs to have a purpose to feel worthy.'

'Thank you for saving me.'

Charming waggled a hand. 'Like I said, my pleasure.'

Jones heard something behind him and took a step back as a ball of paper landed by his feet. He stared at it for a moment and then picked it up and opened it.

Meet me back at the Witch's Smokehouse as soon as you can. I know how to get back to Great Walsingham and solve this mystery.

Ruby xx

As soon as he'd read the note, Jones shouted Ruby's name, whirling round to try and see where she was. But there was no sign of her anywhere.

Charming was looking at him and the *Scucca* was barking at hearing her name, jumping up in the air, its tail wagging.

'My partner, Ruby, she's alive!' Jones held out the note as proof, a smile blooming on his face.

'She's got a funny way of showing it,' said Charming, scratching his head. 'Your partner, she's a girl, eh?' He smiled as if a gentle electric current had been passed through his body, making his lips curl.

'Yes.'

'Then she'll need rescuing for sure. The fairer sex are always getting themselves into trouble, needing a man to sort it out. You'll understand what I mean, being a boy, of course, and seeing as all you Badlanders are male.'

'Ruby's different. She's the first girl Badlander there's ever been.'

'Really? That's a turn-up for the books. But if she's a girl I'd be happy to help her in any way I can. Coming to the aid of men and boys doesn't have the same . . .' He raised his hand, as if looking for the right word. 'Well, it's just not my job.'

Jones smiled at that.

'What's so funny?' Charming folded his arms and stood tall, his square chin jutting out. 'It's what I do.' Jones wasn't sure what to say to someone who was just supposed to be a character in a fairy story. Everyone was entitled to their own way of explaining themselves, he decided.

'I en't laughing at you, sir. I'm sure she'd appreciate your help, especially cos of where I'm supposed to meet her,' and he waggled the note she'd written. 'I'm just thinking that Ruby en't exactly the sort of person who thinks men are any better than women.'

'Nonsense.' Charming laughed and slapped Jones's

230

shoulder. 'Once she meets me, she'll change her tune, you can be sure of that. Now where are you supposed to meet her?'

'It's a smokehouse we found. Owned by a type of Witch.'

Charming clicked his fingers. 'I know the place. Tend to steer clear of it most of the time. Witches aren't really my scene. Damsels in distress are more my thing, as you'll no doubt see once we get to the Witch's dwelling. Because this Ruby of yours is bound to get into trouble there, mark my words. And when she does, and I save her, you'll get to hear my fanfare. It only plays when I rescue maidens in trouble. Just comes with the territory. A gift I was born with.'

Jones watched the man swing himself up onto his horse in one athletic movement and smooth back a wisp of hair that had fallen out of place. He decided that he wasn't the person to tell Charming anything different to what he believed. He'd let Ruby do that.

Patting the *Scucca* he hauled himself up and grabbed two fistfuls of black fur.

Charming looked mildly amused as he trotted over and looked down at the boy on the large black dog.

'You sure that thing's safe?' he asked.

'He's fine,' said Jones, rubbing the *Scucca's* neck.

'Well, let's get going,' said Charming, geeing up his horse. 'I'm keen to save a girl! It always works out when I need to. I've always been lucky that way. A bit like the fanfare. You sure you can keep up on that hound?' he shouted back as he turned his horse into a gallop.

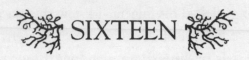

SIXTEEN

As soon as Ruby placed the tiny figure of Precious on the floor beside Thomas Gabriel, she reached into her pocket for the two vials of fungal powder. She paused the moment she heard something outside the smokehouse. Putting her finger to her lips to tell her tiny passengers to stay quiet, she peered through a window.

The only thing moving was the sunlight playing over the heads of corn and the wind working the leaves on the trees saying *Sssh* to the world. The front door of the Witch's house, on the far side of the clearing, was shut and Ruby suddenly heard an urgent voice in her head reminding her that Olive was somewhere inside. *Was she even still alive?* wondered Ruby. A fizz started up in her bones as she remembered the promise she'd made to the little girl. As Ruby reached for the vials of fungal powder once more, her hands were shaking and her heart was thumping.

And then there was another noise outside again.

Ruby could make out a voice, gently singing a song. She tried her best to listen over the sound of her beating heart and work out where it was coming from. Slowly, she swivelled on her haunches and looked between the various shapes of hanging meats towards the rear of the building.

The hole that she and Jones had made was still there, full of sunlight, and Ruby could just see a thin slice of green grass. And then a figure bent down on her hands and knees and peered through the hole from the other side.

Ruby almost bit off the tip of her tongue as the Witch, still singing to herself, surveyed the damage that not only Ruby and Jones had made but the *Scucca* too. As she made her assessment the old woman started mumbling and shaking her head. And then the Witch paused and licked a piece of the jagged wood and Ruby wondered why until she realized it was where Jones had caught his neck. She didn't dare look away and risk making a sound.

The Witch licked the sharp piece of wood again and again, as if cleaning it with her tongue, and then started to crawl through the hole to inspect the damage more carefully. As the old woman heaved her body through, Ruby quickly picked up Precious and Thomas Gabriel and snuck them into her pocket, popping the vials of fungal powder back into her jacket too. She went as slowly as she could and hid behind a large joint of meat.

The Witch sat with her back facing Ruby, inspecting the inside of the hole, as her legs stuck out into the sunshine. She rapped a knuckle on the damaged wood, moving any loose bits around and listening to the various noises she made.

Apparently satisfied, the Witch slid her cane in through

the hole and used it to stand up, knees popping and her body creaking. And then she started singing again. As soon as the first few notes had left her mouth, a selection of tools floated in through the hole and went to work, cutting and sawing away at the misshapen wood, removing the broken ends and tidying up the damage.

Ruby took her chance. Using the noise to cover any sound she made, she scuttled across the floor and stood by the front door of the smokehouse, her finger on the latch. Carefully, she raised it without making a *clink* and crept out of the tiniest gap she could make without letting in too much sunlight.

Once outside, she shut the door and took a deep breath to settle her heart which was beating so hard she could barely stand up. The sun helped, taking the chill off her skin and then, with the tools still working away, Ruby kept low as she ran towards the Witch's house.

She had no idea how long she had been in the Grobbler's pocket or in the cave. But she so wanted to believe that Olive was still alive. This was her chance to find out.

The dark windows either side of the front door were dirty and Ruby rubbed a bright little hole in each one. She couldn't see much. She tried the door and it opened into a sitting room with a rocking chair and two armchairs full of cushions. A fireplace was set with kindling and logs but there was no sign of Olive.

She walked on and saw a bedroom off to her left with a large iron bed covered in a colourful, patchwork eiderdown.

She moved further down the corridor and found a simple bathroom behind a door to her right with a copper bathtub on the floor and a white bowl set in a washstand. Ruby carried on towards the rear of the house, trying not to worry about the Witch coming back. When she felt a tug on her pocket she almost screamed, until she looked down to see Precious and Thomas Gabriel peering up at her. Precious didn't seem very happy but Ruby just shushed them again and shoved them back into her jacket.

Reaching the end of the corridor, she peered into a large kitchen with cabinets arranged around the walls and a white enamel sink. Bunches of herbs hung from a wooden rack suspended from the ceiling. A large black cauldron was hanging on a tripod in the centre of the room, a single blue flame dancing magically below it without burning the floor. Whatever was inside the pot was bubbling as steam rose in wispy fingers before drooping down over the sides and drifting like mist across the floor.

When Ruby noticed that the kitchen bent round a corner to the right, she stepped through the doorway, and passed the cauldron to be able to see what was round the corner.

She saw the edge of a black wire cage, and her heart dared to hope a little. There was little Olive, locked inside, her hands wrapped around her knees and her head buried in them.

Ruby felt such a sense of relief that she didn't notice something else in the kitchen. Only when the black shape dropped down from a shelf like a large blob of ink did it catch her eye. It was a cat. The animal stared at her, tail swishing, the vertical black slits in its green eyes narrowing.

Ruby's brain fizzed. She knew Witches often had familiars to help them and keep them company, creatures that were loyal and protective.

Or perhaps this cat was just a regular one?

The answer to the question came within a couple of seconds as the cat padded towards her, mewling, and started to rub against her leg. When it purred, arching its body as it rubbed against her, the tail curling into a question mark, she decided it had to be an ordinary cat.

'Olive?' she whispered and the little girl raised her head. Olive gave such a big smile that Ruby couldn't help smiling too. 'We're getting out of here,' she whispered. But when she tried to take a step towards the cage, she realized she couldn't move.

Olive's smile faded.

Looking down, Ruby saw the cat's tail snaking longer and longer, wrapping round her legs like a vine. Suddenly the tail pulled so tight her feet were whisked into the air and she toppled over onto the floor.

She tried to reach for the gun in her holster but the tail kept lengthening, wrapping around her arms. She could feel Precious and Thomas Gabriel moving in her pocket and when they peered over the edge and saw what was happening, they ducked back down as the cat hissed, wafting a paw in their direction, the claws flicking out.

Ruby was tied up tight in the long black tail, the soft fur

236

tickling her face. She could barely breathe. She became aware of Olive crying out and saw her looking through the cage, fingers poked through the bars and rattling the chain around the door. She lost sight of the little girl as the cat proceeded to walk out of the kitchen, dragging Ruby behind it.

As she slid along the wooden floor towards the front door, she heard a little peal of laughter and knew it was the voice of the Dark Magic that had created this world she was in. It had been quiet for a while but now, in a moment of extreme danger, it was taunting her again.

'If only Precious had been able to grant you a wish,' it hissed, 'and return you to Great Walsingham, then I have no doubt such a resourceful girl as you would have found The Classic Book Of Fairy Tales with Thomas Gabriel's help. You'd have shut all the doorways to this world, then. But you've blown it now. All because Olive is so important to you. You'll never make it out of this world now.'

The cat pushed open the front door of the house. Ruby was dragged outside, her head bumping over the sill as she struggled to try and free herself. The bright sunshine made her eyes sting.

'Yes, that's right, Ruby,' whispered the voice. 'Give up on your hopes. Escaping from this world is just a dream now.'

The cat's tail squeezed tighter around her. Sparks danced in front of Ruby's eyes and her ribs started to creak. She knew they were going to crack and there was nothing she could do about it. Precious and Thomas Gabriel were trying their best to release the tail but they were too small to shift it, their little cries rising helplessly into the air.

Ruby smiled. *I've tried my best*, she thought. *I almost did it. I almost beat this place. Not bad for a girl.*

As the world started to fade, she heard music and knew this was the end. Perhaps this was the way life ended in this world, with a fanfare to play you out, taunting you even more?

As the music grew louder, she closed her eyes.

Charming galloped faster when he saw what was happening. The girl lay on the grass in front of the Witch's house and was slowly being squeezed to death. Her face was the colour of bone against the black fur of the tail around her.

He smiled at the prospect of saving this girl as he unsheathed his sword and twirled it in his wrist, the sun glancing off the sharp bevelled edges. The cat saw him before he could get close enough to strike and sprinted away, its long tail releasing from Ruby and slipping behind it like a long snake over the grass, retracting as Charming took a swipe at it and drew a furrow in the ground instead.

He pulled the horse to a halt in a spray of turf and turned it round to face the cat.

But it wasn't a cat any more. It was changing into something large and cumbersome. A Troll or Ogre, the like of which Charming had never seen before. The horse snorted and pawed the ground as the creature lumbered forward, gathering pace like a boulder rolling down a hill.

Charming heard his fanfare, trumpets rising and falling in

regal fashion, blasting a tune into the air. It filled him with absolute clarity about what he should do and he drew back his sword arm. He threw his weapon with such precision it struck the oncoming creature in the centre of its forehead. The beast plunged onto the grass, sliding on its chin to land only a metre away from the horse's hooves. Charming reached down and plucked the sword from the creature's head, splashing a fountain of red onto the grass.

He trotted over to the girl, hopped down from the horse and offered her his hand, the fanfare reaching its climax, before it cut out to allow him to speak.

'The name's Charming,' he said in a deep, golden voice. 'And you must be Ruby.' He waggled his fingers to tell her to grab hold as the girl looked up at him. The next thing he knew, Charming was lifted into the air by some unseen force and thrown across the grass, landing in a heap. He scrabbled round to see who else was there and saw an old crone beetling her way towards him with her cane. She didn't look happy. Even less so when she passed the dead creature lying on the grass and had to circle round the large puddle of blood.

The woman raised her cane and pointed it at Charming, lifting him into the air, his hands and feet flapping. Then she did the same to Ruby and moved her through the air until she was floating in front of Charming, both their faces staring at her. Charming's sword rose into the air too, the sharp point slowly turning and aiming itself at both Ruby and the man behind her.

With another flick of the cane the sword sped towards the suspended pair. For the first time in his life, Charming cried out in fear.

The *Scucca* had tried its best to keep up with Charming's horse, but fell behind, its great loping strides no match for the stallion's speed. It galloped between the trees as best it could and as they started to thin, it came to the edge of the treeline and looked out across the clearing as the sound of a fanfare died away and Charming leant over to pull up Ruby.

Jones gasped as the man went flying into the air and the Witch scuttled forward. He reached for his catapult, but the *Scucca* took off and he fumbled his weapon. With his hands full, his legs weren't strong enough to keep him on and he tumbled to the ground.

'Stop!' he shouted. 'Stop!' But the *Scucca* had its head down as it sprinted across the grass.

The hound had one thought on its mind. Happiness. It was happy to see Ruby, the person who had fed and loved it with strokes and soothing words. It hurtled towards her as a shiny-looking thing flashed in the air and turned its tip towards its Mistress and the strange gold-haired man it had already met.

With a joyful bark the *Scucca* leapt into the air. It sailed towards its Mistress, clattering into her and the man, knocking them flying. But as it landed, it felt a terrible pain in its haunch and yowled, landing in a heap. The strange shiny thing was stuck in its leg, sending sharp, burning ripples of pain in waves. Its Mistress and the man were still bobbing in the air planting shadows on the grass.

There was someone else there too. It could smell her now. A small, wrinkled person dressed in black. The woman waggled the long stick in her hand and the sharp thing in its leg moved and slowly began to come out. The *Scucca* howled in pain. It heard little scutterings in its brain and it started to realize that this woman was the cause of all the hurt it could feel in its leg. She was cackling and laughing now as the shiny spike came out dripping red. And the *Scucca* saw red too.

It lurched to its feet and ran towards the woman who stretched out her cane, the brown end dirty with mud. The *Scucca's* leg burnt as it ran and then the hound slowed right down as if someone was pulling it back. It bared its teeth, grinding to a stop and growling in anguish because the old woman was so close. She cackled again as the hound snapped its jaws, desperate to grab hold of her.

Suddenly, something fizzed through the air and struck the long stick the woman was holding, sending it flying from her hand. Whatever was holding the *Scucca* back disappeared immediately and the creature leapt onto the Witch, its jaws closing on her scrawny neck.

Jones advanced with his catapult ready to fire again. But there was no need as the old woman's screams died away until all that could be heard was the growling of the *Scucca* as it shook her like a ragdoll, bones breaking and limbs flopping.

When the hound was finished, it stood over the dead Witch and remembered the deep wound in its leg. It howled and started licking the blood on its thigh, its tail tucked between its legs. The hound looked up at Jones as he came forward, fumbling the pot of ointment out of his pocket. He undid the lid, holding out his hand so the *Scucca* could smell what he had. It licked its lips and Jones carefully dabbed a pea-sized ball of ointment on the wound. The *Scucca* growled, before wagging its tail as the ointment started to take effect, and Jones rubbed in some more, as gently as he could, the dead Witch lying at his feet.

SEVENTEEN

As soon as Ruby emerged from the Witch's house holding Olive's hand, she smelt fish and biscuits and the pongy insides of gym shoes as the *Scucca*'s big tongue licked her face. She grabbed the dog's fur and buried her face in it. The smell reminded her of home and she breathed a deep sigh. She turned and hugged Jones too.

'We're going back to Great Walsingham, Jones,' she whispered. 'We can close this world down and finally solve the mystery.'

'How do we get back?' asked the boy.

Ruby held up a finger and then dipped it into her pocket. Out came Precious and Thomas Gabriel, hanging like acrobats, and she placed them gently on the ground. Her vials of fungal shrinking powder were broken, crushed by the cat's powerful tail, but Jones still had his share and popped out the corks before handing the vials to her. She sprinkled the red and black powders over the two tiny people in the correct order, making them cough and sneeze, and stepped

243

back as Precious and Thomas Gabriel grew back to their normal size.

Ruby felt as though her heart had been sprinkled with powder too as she watched them smile and clap their hands as they checked themselves over and realized they were back to normal. For the first time since Ruby had come to this wretched world it seemed that something had worked out as it should. There was no voice in her head taunting her now, which made her smile just that little bit more.

Jones was staring at Thomas Gabriel, his brow furrowed as the other boy grinned at him and held out his arms. The sun glanced off his dirty skin, making his rotten teeth look darker and his long locks even greasier.

'Jones!' shouted the boy. 'It's Jones, the Badlander. Not Ed. Not Ed when you're hunting creatures and not being an ordinary boy.' The dishevelled Thomas Gabriel laughed and waggled a finger. Jones took a step back.

Thomas Gabriel raised his hands like he was surrendering, because he already knew what Jones was thinking, that he might hurt him. He waggled his black wizened arm. 'I'm not going to hurt you. The Black Amulet can help us, Jones. I already told Ruby about Great Walsingham. She knows.'

Jones looked over at her and Ruby nodded.

'The world's been taunting him like it's been taunting us. It's told him things like it has with us. It said he could use the amulet in the town.' Jones looked at the ragged boy.

'And you trust him?'

'Do you have any other suggestions about what to do?'

Thomas Gabriel wiped his face. He held out a shaky hand to Jones.

'You can trust me, Jones.'

Jones looked at the hand and muttered something under his breath, then he coughed and looked Thomas Gabriel in the eye.

'Let's see, shall we?' He rubbed his face as if there was too much to take in and then looked at Ruby. 'You still en't said how we're supposed to get back to Great Walsingham.'

Ruby pointed at the middle-aged woman crouched down in front of Olive. Streams of sparkles trailed in the air as she flashed her wand back and forth, making the little girl laugh. A tiara on her head flashed in the sun.

'Who is she?'

'The Fairy Godmother. Precious McGinty Flora Aurora ' Ruby paused as she went through the names in her head – 'Stella Glorinda Bunty Smith. And she owes me, now I've shown her what girls can do.'

Jones watched the woman make Olive laugh again as Charming led his horse over to them and hoisted the little girl onto the saddle. Both the man and the woman beamed at her as she patted the animal and each gave her a hug.

'Mr Charming told me this is a world made from fairy tales that's gone wrong cos of Dark Magic. But I guess you know that.'

'Yes, I do. And I also know that all we have to do is find *The Classic Book of Fairy Tales*.' Ruby pointed at Thomas

Gabriel. 'And that's up to him. It's his chance to help us and make up for what he did.'

Jones stared at the smiling, gap-toothed boy who was rubbing the *Scucca* hound and shaking his head as though he could not believe he was so close to such a creature.

'Well, let's get on with it, shall we? Before this place tries to stop us.'

When they were ready to go, Ruby stood with Olive and the two boys beside the *Scucca* and Precious raised her wand.

'Ruby dear, this spell's for you
You've shown me that your heart is true
And not just that but honest too
As well as brave, like very few.
So by this wand, I honour you
And grant your wish to send you through.'

Precious swirled her wand round and round, generating a flurry of blue sparks that boiled the air, churning faster and faster as a tiny hole appeared at its centre.

'Safe journey home, dear!' shouted Precious. 'Do what needs to be done! We're relying on you!'

The hole opened wider and wider, revealing a kaleidoscope of colours and strange runes that flashed. Ruby and the others began to float off the ground. Olive clutched her hand and cried out with delight.

Jones couldn't help smiling too. He knew it was a different

magic to the type that Badlanders used, something purer and brighter, only meant for the good of people. Even the words that Precious had spoken sounded kind, not like the rough-sounding Anglo-Saxon taught by *The Black Book of Magical Instruction*. It was a way of using magic that felt better to him than the method Badlanders used, severe and disciplined in their learning of spells. Badlanders forced magic to do as they asked but Precious just seemed to be at one with it. Jones wondered if casting the spell felt as good for her as it did to him receiving it. As he was lifted higher into the air, he decided it was the type of magic he would have wanted if he'd Commenced as Maitland had wanted him to.

The magic from Precious's wand felt good to Thomas Gabriel as well, tickling him like someone was gently stroking him with a feather. He clapped a hand around his mouth to stifle a laugh as the sensation grew and he rose up into the air.

It was a long time since he'd laughed with joy. After all the pain and suffering he'd experienced since arriving in this strange world, everything was feeling better inside.

At least, almost everything.

Even as he smiled and nodded at the others a dark question lurked inside him that was too heavy to throw out of his head: *What would happen with the Black Amulet?*

Before coming to this world, it had turned him into someone else when he'd been in the Badlands, urging him to hurt his friends. He'd listened to it and left them to die.

The memory of locking them in that secret stone chamber still burnt bright, even though it seemed like a lifetime ago. He'd had a lot of time to think about what he'd done.

Thomas Gabriel had noticed Jones and Ruby shooting him sideways glances as if still wary of him. He didn't blame them, although the amulet was lifeless on his black withered arm and his connection to it severed as soon as he'd arrived in this world. He knew it would come alive to him again once he was away from this place where Badlanders could do no magic.

As he floated higher with the others he told himself he'd be ready for it this time. That he wouldn't listen to its whispers. He'd fight the power it had to warp his mind and turn him into someone he didn't want to be.

A sudden pulse of light enfolded him and the others. A giddy sensation lifted his stomach into his head and took his breath away as they were all whisked through the hole Precious had created.

They appeared beside the VW van as Ruby had asked, the ground gently settling under their feet.

It was dark and Jones checked his smartwatch. The seconds ticked merrily on. It was 12.52 a.m. Only two minutes after the time his watch had stopped when they'd passed through the doorway. This emboldened him. Not only were they the first Badlanders ever to have returned to Great Walsingham, but barely any time had been lost on their trip at all. He closed his eyes and breathed in the fresh air, glad to feel it cooling his lungs and his sun-blasted face.

'It's good to be back, en't it?' he said, suddenly feeling just how grubby he was. The stench of the smokehouse was wound tight into his clothes.

'It's better than good, Jones,' said Ruby. 'I don't think I'll ever feel quite as relieved ever again.' She crouched down and placed her hand on the ground to check it was real.

'Are we really back from that world and in Great Walsingham?' whispered Olive as she clung tight to Ruby.

'Yes, we are,' said Ruby. She pointed to the van. 'You wanna see inside?'

Olive nodded. As Ruby went towards the vehicle in the moonlight, she saw through the window that the interior had been ransacked. It wasn't something she was expecting to see and it sent a shiver through her blood as she looked about, listening for anyone or anything close by.

Jones had noticed too. He pushed his nose to the window. All the cupboards had been opened, their contents strewn over the floor. There was broken glass everywhere. Different coloured powders coated every surface and liquids lay in puddles. To his dismay he saw that the vials of expensive potions they'd bought from Deschamps & Sons had all been smashed. Preserved beetles and various herbs had been decanted from their various jars and poured out. Even the *Scucca*'s silver cage had holes torn in it.

'That's how they got in,' said Jones, pointing at the door, which was hanging down at an ugly angle. Large gouges shone silver through the paintwork. The metal panels had been battered by something powerful.

'Was it a creature that did this?' asked Ruby.

'Most likely.' Jones scanned around, looking for anything that might be hiding in the dark. 'Just cos we're back in Great Walsingham don't mean we're safe, not when we're in the Badlands.' He turned to Thomas Gabriel. 'We'll get what we need and then we'll find that book of yours and solve the mystery of Great Walsingham once and for all.' His eyes darted down to the amulet on the other boy's blackened wrist. 'How are you feeling?'

'Fine,' whispered Thomas Gabriel. He flinched as the snake heads at either end of the amulet suddenly moved, yawning as if they were waking up after a long sleep, their little forked tongues flicking out to test the air around them. Their eyes blinked and then the amulet started to shine a little brighter.

'It's happening,' said Thomas Gabriel. 'I can feel the amulet reaching out to me, wanting to know me again so it can help me use magic. It's still drowsy after not being used for so long.'

'Well, you keep it that way till you need to use it,' said Jones, 'or else I'll have something to say about it. One of us keeps an eye on him all the time,' he said to Ruby.

'You don't have to worry,' said Thomas Gabriel. 'Not after last time. I know what I did was wrong. I'll start taking a Bitter Potion now, if you've got one, to prove it.'

'If they're not all broken, we have. And if we do, you'll

take all of it in one go,' growled Jones. 'Let's get moving and see what we can find.'

They left the *Scucca* outside with Olive, guarding the van, and they picked their way through the mess inside, looking for anything that might be useful. As Ruby picked up a few things and popped them in her pockets, she realized they were starting to recover their limitless quality again. The unlimited space inside them felt lumpy and any items she put in a pocket took a while to sink down, as if they were dropping through a layer of mud. Just as the Black Amulet was taking time to recover its power, so the charm on her pockets seemed to be too.

Ruby still had that hollow feeling that came with losing her ability to do magic, and she'd been waiting patiently for something to happen as soon as she'd seen the amulet move around Thomas Gabriel's wrist. As she bent to retrieve an unbroken vial of salt and rosemary, she felt a tickle in her guts and little warm spots dappled the insides of her tummy. She knew at once it was the magic, though just a notion of it. The warmth felt fleeting, like a match being moved around. She raised her hand and drew on what little there was inside her. The sparks at the ends of her fingers stood proud for a while but faded away quickly, leaving her fingers red at the ends.

As she picked up more things in the van, the warmth inside her grew a little more. She tried not to think about it in an effort to make it hurry up.

When something else occurred to her she took the gun

out of its holster. But it didn't say a word and there were still only three bullets left in the chamber. She tapped it thoughtfully as Jones looked at her.

'You think it'll work again like before?'

'I en't sure. Will you?'

'The magic's coming back slowly.'

'Well, you'll always be able to redo the charm on it then, if you want to.' Jones managed a smile. 'It's a bit quiet without it, but I en't saying that's a bad thing.'

'You should try working with it all the time,' said Ruby as she put the gun back in its holster. But, secretly, she missed its voice.

Jones nodded, he understood what she meant. Talking about the gun had prompted him to think about Maitland, who'd placed the charm on the weapon in the first place. He whispered into the air around them, asking if the man was anywhere nearby. But Maitland did not appear to him. He wondered if the magic Maitland had used to remain attached to him had been broken like it had been on the gun, perhaps for ever. If so, then he would never see his old Master again. Something sharp prodded his guts as he thought about that, at not being able to call on Maitland for help when they still had so much to do to close this mystery once and for all.

But he was sure he could feel someone near. A presence. Even if he couldn't see anyone. Or maybe he was just imagining it? As he looked around again, he decided that perhaps he was just feeling on edge about the van.

*

It took them an hour or so to sort through things and find what little they could. When Jones discovered a bottle of Bitter Potion in the back of a cupboard he made Thomas Gabriel drink all of it in one go, just as he'd threatened to do. Thomas Gabriel screwed up his face as he glugged the potion, stopping whenever he thought he was going to be sick. But he kept nodding and putting the bottle back to his lips.

From time to time the Black Amulet would move, stretching itself, the two serpents showing their fangs and tasting the air. At one point the whole thing spun round and round and picked up speed into a blur. When it slowed and eventually came to a stop the amulet shone brighter on Thomas Gabriel's blackened wrist. Jones watched Thomas Gabriel carefully for any sign of change after that.

'Right,' said Jones finally when he thought they were ready. 'Let's see what you've got.' Ruby couldn't be sure if he was talking to the amulet or Thomas Gabriel or both. She wasn't surprised at his gruffness. She felt tiny pricks of doubt inside her as Thomas Gabriel stepped outside and rolled up his sleeve all the way to his elbow, his arm still black and wizened. She had never imagined she'd be working with Thomas Gabriel ever again, after all that had happened. She felt her hand twitch and little white sparks fluttered out, stronger than before. Thomas Gabriel gasped when he saw them and then nodded, as if remembering what he'd already been told, that Ruby had magic now and Jones had none, and she'd use it if he gave her any cause to do so. Jones was holding his catapult, arms folded as he glared.

Thomas Gabriel licked his lips and conjured up the magic inside him, commanding what there was of it to come forth from the very marrow of his bones. His mind felt rusty and heavy and it was a struggle at first to make anything happen. But as he focused on what he wanted, he became aware of a little flicker of warmth somewhere in his stomach. It made him laugh out loud, such was the relief of feeling the magic in him after all this time. He had thought he'd never have the privilege again of wielding such power. As little sparks rose off his fingers, he shivered at the thought of the cage in the Grobbler's cave. His mind struggled to hold the magic and he began to weep.

Ruby stepped forward and held Thomas Gabriel as he sobbed on her shoulder. She understood, not only about the relief he felt with the magic returning, but also that it was bringing back everything that had happened to him after arriving in Great Walsingham.

'It was so horrible in that place, Ruby,' whispered Thomas Gabriel as he wiped his nose. 'I never thought I'd leave that cage. Never.' A great rasping sound chugged up and down in his throat as he tried not to cry so he could say something else. 'And coming back here has made me realize even more how terrible I was to both of you after putting on the amulet.' The boy tucked his long straggly hair behind his ears to make sure he could see them both. 'I would never do anything to hurt you again. Not after what you've done for me.'

'We believe you, Thomas Gabriel, don't we, Jones?'

Jones looked at the boy. His face didn't move. 'You saved him more than I did.' But then he dug a heel in the ground and ground it into the grass. 'I en't saying it'll be easy to forgive you, Thomas Gabriel, but I'll try. And if we get done what needs to be done then that'll make it a lot easier.' He took a deep breath. 'It's good being together again in the Badlands, doing what our job's supposed to be and keeping people safe.' He smiled at Olive and the little girl grinned. 'And now we're gonna keep Badlanders safe too by getting rid of what we've found in Great Walsingham. And we're gonna honour the memory of every Badlander who ever tried to do the same thing. So go ahead and do what you need to do, Thomas Gabriel, and we'll do our best to help.'

Thomas Gabriel wiped his eyes once more and refocused. He thought hard, drawing out the sparks from his fingers as he conjured up the magic inside him. They drooped and paled as he shuddered, his mind darting to darker thoughts again. But he focused on the amulet which was starting to move, the two serpents' heads peering up at the sparks of magic, excited by them.

'Help me,' said Thomas Gabriel softly. 'Help me with this spell I want to use, and find that book wherever it is.'

Ruby held open a copy of *The Black Book of Magical Instruction* they'd found in the van to help Thomas Gabriel with the spell she'd chosen for him, given how shaky his mind was. He thought the magic into the words as he spoke them.

'*Gefind þá bóc.*' The heads on the amulet swayed, as if

transfixed by the Anglo-Saxon words. '*Gefind þá bóc!*' he shouted. The amulet moved, coming alive on his wrist. '*Gefind þá—*' He didn't finish as the two tiny mouths bit down into his wizened arm, making it twitch. Strange patterns swirled bright on his blackened skin. He felt the magic in him surge. The white sparks streamed out of his fingers and joined into one point in the air in front of him. When the sparks flashed and disappeared, all that was left behind was a small blue light, bobbing in front of them. It faded from the view of everyone except Thomas Gabriel, who nodded when Ruby asked if he could still see it.

'It's a spell that only works for the Badlander who cast it, Thomas Gabriel. Because we don't want to arouse any more suspicion than we have to.'

'It's moving,' said Thomas Gabriel, looking back at them. 'I think it wants me to follow it.'

'Follow it, then,' hissed Jones, 'and we'll follow you.' Thomas Gabriel turned and followed the blue light, shuffling forwards in his bare feet, Ruby and Jones beside him, and Olive sitting on the *Scucca* as it came behind them, sniffing the air.

The blue light moved at a gentle pace through the streets of the town, occasionally pausing if it floated too far ahead of Thomas Gabriel. His arm was still thrumming where the Black Amulet's tiny serpent heads had bitten him. Every now and then the strength of the blue light faded before growing brighter again. It troubled him slightly because he worried it meant he hadn't cast the spell as correctly as he should have done. He whispered to the light to keep going and for the spell to work because he didn't want to let Ruby and Jones down.

Jones stayed alert in the dark, his catapult clutched in his hand. Any figure that came towards them meant he coiled his arm like a spring ready to aim the weapon. But the odd person they saw only proved to be someone interested in their phone screens or talking to a friend. Nobody seemed to notice Jones and the others as they walked past, not even Olive riding on the back of the *Scucca*. Such a thing wasn't strange. Jones had often thought that ordinary people were far too wrapped up in their own thoughts and lives to notice much, most of the time. He'd noted the same thing about himself when he was with his parents, barely thinking about much beyond who he was talking to or what he was looking at. It made the work of Badlanders even more important. Thinking of his mum and dad, he looked again at his watch to reassure himself that no time had been lost while they'd been away. The screen read 2.10 a.m. which was about right, given the time they'd spent looking through the van. He walked on, eager to get the book found and the Mystery of Great Walsingham solved. But he couldn't shake the feeling that it was not going to be easy.

'Don't you think it's strange that nothing's stopped us, given what we're aiming to do?' he asked Ruby.

'I do, yes.'

'You'd think there'd be creatures coming after us or some

sort of Dark Magic working against us.' He watched the amulet on Thomas Gabriel's wrist. 'We need to keep an eye on that amulet. I don't trust it,' he said.

As they walked on, none of them saw a figure lurking in the shadows, following them as they moved, another one by its side.

EIGHTEEN

Thomas Gabriel watched the blue light ahead of him fade and he scuffed his steps, slowing a little, as he waited for the light to reappear. But this time it didn't.

'What's wrong?' asked Jones, watching Thomas Gabriel as he peered into the dark ahead of them.

'Nothing. I think it's just deciding where to go.' Thomas Gabriel pointed at where he wanted the light to be.

'If it's stopped, maybe the book's here,' said Jones, looking around. 'Could that be it?'

They had paused at the top of a residential street, the houses on either side, tucked up asleep in the dark like their occupants. Street lamps stood on their little islands of orange light as Jones watched for anything unusual ahead of them.

'No, I don't think it is,' said Thomas Gabriel and started moving again. There was still no blue light in front of him, but as he walked he urged the amulet to bite him again to power up the spell. 'Come on,' he whispered. 'Give me what I want.' The two little serpent heads didn't move. Thomas

Gabriel scuffed another few steps, stubbing his toes on the tarmac path and cursing loud enough for his voice to rise in an echo down the street. The pain burnt a clean hole through all his worries and his frustration with the amulet. And through it he saw deeper into himself, into a private place where he was hiding a secret. The magic in him was rotten. It was almost gone.

He had known about it rotting away, ever since he'd stolen the key from his Master Simeon Rowell and Commenced without his Master's blessing. The punishment for such a deed he'd found out was that the gift of magic granted to him by his Commencement would inevitably decay and fade away. The process had paused in the fairy-tale world where no magic was possible but now he was back in the Badlands it seemed to have restarted with renewed vigour. He could feel it dying inside him. The Black Amulet could feel it too. There was barely any magic left inside Thomas Gabriel for it to work with. And what remained was too weak.

'Come on,' he hissed. One of the serpent's heads perked up and looked at him, as if asking a question. 'Please,' whispered Thomas Gabriel. 'Please let me find that book.' The tiny head bit into his arm again. This time the world wobbled because the pain was far worse than before, so strong it left him breathless. The amulet seemed to be taking something from *him* rather than working with what was left of the rotten magic inside him. His heart fluttered and a terrible coughing took root in his chest. He coughed so hard he could taste blood in the back of his throat before he swallowed it down.

His legs and arms became translucent for a moment and it was like looking through pieces of glass at the pavement. It scared him.

'Thomas Gabriel?' Ruby was at his side, holding him up as he stumbled forward. She could see dark spots of blood on the lapels of his coat.

'I'm all right,' he said. But he wasn't. He knew what the Black Amulet had done. It was taking all that was left of him, his spirit and his body, to be able to give him what he wanted. The spell he had cast strengthened again and the blue light reappeared in the air above him.

'I'm okay, Ruby,' he said, stumbling a little and then striding after the light as it floated down the street.

It took another ten minutes for them to reach the edge of Great Walsingham and Jones grew wary as the lights of the town died away and the dark folded in around them. As they passed a small copse of trees, the leaves rustled and he raised his catapult. But no creatures appeared. There seemed to be no trap laid for them. At least not yet, anyway.

'It just en't right,' he said again. 'You'd think that cos we're about to close off the world, it would be trying to stop us. Or the creatures living in it would be.' He clicked his teeth as he looked around. 'It don't make sense.'

Ruby fired little sparks into the air to light the way and they followed their shadows slip-sliding in front of them in the dirt.

'There!' shouted Thomas Gabriel, as the blue light that

only he could see landed on the ground in front of him and blinked three times before disappearing.

All Ruby and Jones could see was a crossroads ahead where the path they were on was bisected by another. Thomas Gabriel crouched down in the spot where the two paths crossed, dead in the centre. He laid a hand on the dirt. 'The book's here. The amulet knows it too. It can sense the Dark Magic.' Thomas Gabriel raised his arm and Jones watched the tiny serpent heads wriggle and flicker their tongues and his hand tightened round his catapult. 'All we have to do to close the fairy-tale world is shut the book that it came from.' As Thomas Gabriel beamed, Jones looked about, straining to see anything hiding in the trees.

'Well,' asked Ruby, 'what do you want to do?'

Jones chewed his lips and watched the *Scucca* for any signs it might be sensing a creature close by. But it was standing quite still with Olive on its back.

'I guess we go ahead and do what needs to be done. There en't nothing here, as far as I can tell, or your *Scucca*, for that matter.' He jabbed a finger at the ground. 'A crossroads makes sense. It's a special mark of a place. Somewhere betwixt and between where anything might be possible. Even a fairy-tale world.' He looked about again as he heard a rustle in the undergrowth. But still nothing appeared. 'So where's this book, then, Thomas Gabriel?'

'It's hidden deep in the earth, I think. Put there with Dark Magic. The amulet can find it.'

'Well, let's get on with it,' said Jones. 'And if you feel

anything strange – and I mean anything – you let me know, and I'll decide what needs doing, and Ruby will too.' He waggled the catapult and looked over at Ruby, who nodded.

Thomas Gabriel stood up and took a breath as he watched the tiny serpents that formed the amulet hissing and biting at the air.

'Do you need the right spell?' asked Ruby, holding out *The Black Book of Magical Instruction*. When she opened it, the words and letters were jumbled round, and he could barely read anything that made sense. There was very little magic left in him now.

He shook his head at Ruby. 'I know it. I know the spell.' He raised his hand and conjured the magic in him. But the sparks flickered and spluttered.

'*Gebíed mé þá bóc.*' His hand shook. Sparks licked the air. Then died again. '*Gebíed mé þá bóc.*' Nothing happened.

'Thomas Gabriel?' Ruby was looking at him. 'Thomas Gabriel, what's wrong?' she asked.

'It's the magic in 'im,' said Jones. 'It's gone. He stole his Commencement key from his Master, remember? He told us his magic was going rotten cos he'd cursed it.' Jones raised his catapult. 'He weren't following no light. He's been tricking us all along.'

'No, I haven't. I want to make up for what I did to you. You saw me drink the Bitter Potion.'

But Jones was looking all around, searching the trees. 'What have you brought us here for? What's going to happen?'

263

'Jones, I'm not a bad person,' cried Thomas Gabriel. 'I'm not!'

But as he spoke the words, he heard a whisper in his head telling him that it might be better if he was. The amulet was speaking to him. *You could have your magic back if you make a pact with us,* whispered the tiny serpents. *All you need is blood to use Dark Magic. You'll have as much magic as you want then. Becoming a No-Thing will give you great power.*

Thomas Gabriel licked his lips. And then he shook his head. 'No ... no ... I don't want to hurt them. I don't want their blood to do magic!' He looked at Ruby and Jones. 'The amulet's saying if I become a No-Thing I'll have magic again.' He started to weep. 'It says I can only use magic again that way.'

'You find that book, Thomas Gabriel,' said Jones. 'And then I'll put you out of your misery.'

'I can't,' he screamed. 'I can't use my magic. It's not there any more.'

'There must be another way, Thomas Gabriel,' said Ruby. 'There must be a way I can use my magic.'

'The Black Amulet is the only thing that's powerful enough,' said Thomas Gabriel. 'It's made from Dark Magic, just like the book is. Like that fairy-tale world is. I won't let it turn me against you. I won't. Not after last time. I ... I ... you're my friends. We're Badlanders-s-s.'

His voice mingled with the serpents' as they hissed and bit into his arm. The boy threw back his head and juddered and then licked his lips and took a step forward, arms

264

outstretched, his face hardened. He growled at Jones, baring his teeth, and Jones pulled back the sling on his catapult, ready to fire.

Ruby stepped between them.

'Thomas Gabriel, don't listen to the amulet. Don't let it turn you against us. You're right. We're your friends. We're Badlanders. All of us. I forgive you for what you did. I forgive you and if we can't solve the mystery of Great Walsingham by finding the book and closing it, then so be it. But at least we'll be together. All three of us.'

'Ruby, what about the Order?' asked Jones. 'The vote? Everything we've come here for.'

'I don't care. My legacy isn't more important than a life. If it was then I'd just be like all the other Badlanders there have been, and what good am I then?' She looked into Thomas Gabriel's eyes. 'Closing the world doesn't matter, Thomas Gabriel. Not now. But saving you does. You're our friend.'

Something clicked inside Thomas Gabriel as he stared into Ruby's eyes and knew she was telling the truth, that she'd forgiven him. And it filled him with such relief because he no longer felt alone. In fact, for the first time in his life he felt loved and knew instantly that he wanted Ruby to feel such a joyous thing too. He let the amulet's words about taking his friends' blood and becoming a No-Thing wash over him.

'I won't ever be a Badlander again,' he whispered. 'I won't ever be in the Order. Not after what I've done. But there's another way to help you.'

He pointed a hand at the intersection of the crossroads as Ruby stared at him.

'But Thomas Gabrie—'

'*Gebíed mé þá bóc,*' said the boy. '*Gebíed mé þá bóc.*'

He nodded at the tiny serpents. 'Take what's left of me instead,' he whispered. '*Gebíed mé þá bóc.*'

The small mouths bit into his arm again and he roared in pain as a stream of white sparks burst out of him and drilled into the ground.

He could taste his own blood. He could feel his life being sucked from his bones as parts of him began to fade. He could barely hear Ruby shouting. But he could tell what she was saying by the look on her face and the fire in her eyes, Jones too, his mouth open, his steely glare softening as he watched.

More of him disappeared as the hole in the ground grew. He could see something forming deep down in the pit. It was floating up towards him in the light. And he smiled because he knew what it was.

He watched the book rise out of the hole and lost sight of his legs, as though someone had flicked a switch and turned them off. What was left of the rest of his body blipped and began to fade too. But as he watched the serpents biting down on his arm, he felt a sense of happiness he hadn't known since being an eager and ambitious young apprentice to his Master.

He smiled at Ruby and Jones. 'Tell the Order what your friend did. Tell them that I was a good Badlander,' he said. 'I'll always remember you. I was your friend. We were Badlanders-s-s-s . . .'

And then he was smiling as the Black Amulet dropped to the ground for his arm was no longer there. And then neither was he, the boy who had been a proud Badlander, loyal to his friends and to the Order. He was nothing now, but not a No-Thing.

NINETEEN

The last thing Ruby saw of Thomas Gabriel was his smile. It disappeared as the Black Amulet lay on the ground beside a small book, open at the centre page. The hole in the ground from which it had come was gone and the crossroads had healed. She walked cautiously towards the book and as she got closer she saw strange runes drawn over the text and illustrations. She crouched down beside it.

'Careful, Ruby,' growled Jones. 'We don't know what it can do. We don't know how we're supposed to close it so it never opens again.'

Ruby reached towards the book, her fingers feeling the air around it, which was much colder than she'd anticipated. She felt a strange pull towards the pages and knew instantly that something was wrong as sounds of the wider world around her died away.

The pages rippled back and forth and all she heard was a voice which she recognized instantly as that of the Dark Magic that had taunted her. *'You're more than welcome* back to this fairy-tale world you've seen, we'd love you to stay this time.' She shook her head. Ruby heard a little peal of laughter. 'But Ruby there's no choice, not if you want to close the book.'

The force compelling her towards the open book grew stronger and as she was about to touch the pages, she understood a terrible truth: if the book was to be closed then whoever did so would pay for it with their life.

'That's right, Ruby. Anyone with magic inside them like you, dear, is just the ticket.'

She heard some faint cries behind her and tried to turn and tell Jones what was wrong but the force was too strong. It was impossible to look away from the pages. As she imagined returning to the fairy-tale world, she felt tears sting the corners of her eyes. 'Don't cry, Ruby, not now you've solved the Mystery of Great Walsingham by closing the boo—'

And then she felt a large impact slam into her body and knock the breath out of her as she was lifted into the air away from the book, and left dangling above the ground.

Sloop stood below her, magic playing out from his fingers in the form of little white strings wrapped around her arms and legs, moving her about like a life-sized puppet. Olive and the Scucca were unconscious on the ground. Jones was wrapped up tight in a bolas, Sloop's apprentice, Aldwyn, standing over him.

'Where are my Lucky Drops?' growled Sloop. 'What have you done with them?'

'What have you done to that little girl and my Scucca?'

Ruby shouted down at him, secretly relieved to have been torn away from the book and its strange force.

'Tell me where my Lucky Drops are!' screamed the man.

'They're gone,' replied Ruby. The man let out a stream of obscenities. His face turned red and spit flew from his mouth. Ruby stared at Olive and the *Scucca*, trying to see if they were still breathing.

When Sloop was done, he rubbed his face with the crook of his arm, moving Ruby about on the strings from his fingers, like she was a kite being flown.

'Although there is nothing,' he said, 'and I mean NOTHING that can be done to replace my Lucky Drops, I can still take great pleasure in making sure you play no part in solving the Mystery of Great Walsingham, thereby ensuring girls never become part of the Order. Goodness knows, it seems that we have one female too many already.' He sighed and shook his head. 'You and the boy, Jones, are remarkable. I'll admit that. When you reappeared beside your van I could barely believe it. Aldwyn and I had just finished searching the vehicle looking for my Drops. But rather than confront you, I used my head, as any Badlander would, and followed you unobserved to see exactly how things played out. And here we are.' Sloop cleared his throat and then lowered Ruby to the ground, muttering a few words of a spell as she landed heavily. The strings on his fingers detached themselves and looped round and round Ruby, trapping her like a spider might wrap up a fly.

'So tell me about this book.' Sloop nudged it with his toe.

'How does it solve the mystery here in Great Walsingham?' The strings around Ruby tightened, squeezing her ribs and crushing the breath out of her.

'You just close the book,' she gasped. 'Close it and you'll solve the mystery. Your name will go down in Badlander history.'

Sloop made a sucking sound through his lips and clicked his fingers. 'Aldwyn. Come over here.' The young boy left Jones wrapped up in the bolas and walked to his Master. 'Pick up the book. But don't shut it.' Aldwyn looked down at the book, his face pale and unsure.

'But, sir, what if it's dangerous—'

'Do it, boy!'

Aldwyn reached out with trembling hands, pausing long enough to make his Master curse at him. 'Get on with it!' The boy did as he was told and stared into the pages as he held the book. 'Now just keep holding it until I say otherwise.' Sloop watched Aldwyn intently, interested to see if there were any ill effects on the boy.

Ruby watched on too, wondering if the book was speaking to Aldwyn as it had done to her. But the longer he stood there, nothing happening, little cogs turned in her brain and she remembered that the book needed someone with magic in them to close it, so not an apprentice who hadn't Commenced.

'What do you feel, boy?' asked Sloop, eventually. 'Anything?'

'No, sir. Not a thing. Nothing out of the ordinary. Do you want me to close it, now?'

271

'Of course not! I should be the one to do that, to solve this great mystery.'

The man stroked his chin. And then he looked back at Ruby. 'As simple as that? Just close it, you say. Nothing more?'

'Yes.'

Sloop tapped his foot. 'Well, Ruby Jenkins, what a remarkable thing you almost did.' He took the book from Aldwyn. 'For it is I who will close this book.'

Sloop juddered and gasped as the book came to life, its pages rippling back and forth, and Ruby knew the Dark Magic in it was trying to take hold of him. Sloop threw the book as far as he could and stepped back, but the force from it was too strong and started dragging him quickly towards it.

'Aldwyn, do something, boy! Take that book away from me. Pick it up again.' But Aldwyn looked down and said nothing. 'Aldwyn, don't be silly, I knew the book wouldn't do anything to you. I knew all along. I knew nothing would happen.' But Aldwyn didn't move a muscle, his eyes stuck to the ground. 'Traitor,' screamed Sloop as he was dragged closer to the book, the heels of his boots dragging in the dirt. 'Traitor, you ungrateful wretch! After all I've done for you.' Sloop tried conjuring magic, and sparks sprayed towards the book from his fingers. Yet the pages swallowed them in to no effect. He turned his attention to the trees around him, trying to grasp them with his magical strings and halt his slide towards the book. But the strings weren't strong enough and they snapped under the strain.

And then, without turning, he flashed his hand back

over his shoulder and spun more magic at Ruby. The strings around her loosened and some of them sprang forth into his hands and he held on tight, dragging her over the ground behind him.

'Wherever I'm going, you're coming with me,' shouted Sloop as one foot slipped into the book. Ruby struggled to get free as Sloop began to disappear into the pages, before vanishing.

Ruby flew into the air in an arc as the strings pulled tight and sailed down after Sloop towards the open book. But as she fell, a hand came down, holding a knife and sliced the strings, cutting her loose. The book slapped shut and she landed on top of the cover:

The Classic Book Of Fairy Tales

Aldwyn stood over her and held out his hand to pull her up, the knife in his other hand.

Ruby barely checked herself over before rushing towards Olive and the *Scucca*.

'They're only asleep with a charm that my Master did,' said Aldwyn. 'You can wake them with magic.'

After Ruby had woken them, she clutched Olive close to her as the *Scucca* licked them both, its long tongue rasping their faces, its tail going round and round like a propeller.

Jones was all right too, and very much relieved, having watched everything unfold while unable to do anything, so tightly wrapped up had he been by the bolas. Picking up the book, he opened it and flicked through the pages, scanning all the usual fairy tales written for ordinary people. When he saw a picture of Charming on his steed, holding his sword, he smiled and raised the book so Ruby could see Precious too.

Sloop was in the book as well. Aldwyn noticed him in the corner of every other page so that when they flicked through the pages, he seemed to be running from something unseen, his scared face looking out at them.

Aldwyn closed the book and took a deep breath. 'I don't think my Master was a very nice man,' he told the others. 'I think he got what he deserved.' And Ruby gave him a hug when she saw that he was struggling not to cry.

They got back to the van before dawn, shivering in the cold. Despite the damage to the door, the vehicle started first time. Jones's phone was still in the holder on the dashboard and he set the Sat Nav to take them home to Ruby's cottage. When he reached the edge of the town he paused, the engine burbling.

'Is that it, do you think?' he asked Ruby, who was sitting in the passenger seat.

Ruby nodded. 'I think so.' She gave a great sigh and put her hands on her head. '*The Book of Mysteries* will tell us for sure.'

By the time they had returned to the cottage and parked the van in the rickety garage, it was light. But neither Ruby nor Jones could sleep. Nor could Olive, who was amazed that

Ruby had her own house and kept running from room to room to see what was there.

They had tea and toast and then Olive and Aldwyn fell asleep, finally, in the big armchairs in the sitting room, the *Scucca* snoring too as it lay on the floor. Ruby and Jones left them there and used Slap Dust to go and visit Raynham because they wanted to see *The Book of Mysteries* for themselves and reassure themselves it was all really over.

When Raynham opened his cottage door, he had a big smile ready for them.

'I've been expecting you,' he said, as he waved them into the sitting room. Open on the small coffee table was *The Book of Mysteries* and the page was flashing.

Case 325

The Mystery of Great Walsingham

'You did it,' said Raynham, shaking his head as though still not quite believing it. 'I felt the book start nudging me late last night and when I opened it, well ...' He paused and clasped his hands together. 'I don't know what to say. I'm pretty sure Sloop and the rest of the Order won't know either.'

Ruby and Jones looked at each other. 'I don't think that Mr Sloop will be able to say anything ever again,' she said and showed Raynham the book of fairy tales, explaining everything that had happened.

'I see,' said Raynham, when she'd finished. 'If it happened then it was meant to happen according to the *wyrd*. You haven't just solved the mystery both of you, you've changed the *Ordnung*. Turned round centuries of tradition. You've brought Badlanders into a new, modern era.'

For the first time, Ruby felt a great sense of relief that the mystery was finally solved and she suddenly felt very tired. She sat down on the sofa and stared at her trainers and thought she probably needed a new pair. The black stitching was coming loose on both shoes and a hole had almost worn through on one side above the little toe on her right foot. She found it hard to think about anything else.

'Ruby?' Jones was looking at her.

'I'm fine,' she said. 'It's just a lot to take in. I'm worn out.'

'There was one other thing,' said Raynham and he turned the page in *The Book of Mysteries* to another case that was also flashing.

Case 765

The Whereabouts of the Black Amulet

Ruby reached into her pocket and put the Black Amulet on the table in front of them and Raynham gasped as he picked it up and then nodded.

'Thank you,' he said.

Every Badlander in the land was instructed to appear on the *mótbeorh* the following evening and hundreds of men and boys turned up at the appointed hour, the air popping and crackling as they arrived using Slap Dust.

It was a still, dark night with only a smattering of stars sprinkled like glitter in the sky. But a bright and warm white glow grew above the gathering as the *wyrd* pulsed and then shone brighter as Ruby was presented.

'Members of the Order,' announced Givens. 'The *wyrd* has spoken. The Mystery of Great Walsingham has been solved and I sign it off in front of you all.' He raised *The Book of Mysteries* above his head and opened it to the flashing page which paused and then stopped and then cleared to leave a pristine white surface. There was a smattering of applause that grew louder as Givens beckoned Ruby to step up beside him. 'Sloop's challenge has been met. Although, as he is not here to acknowledge it, his apprentice must do so in his honour.'

The crowd parted and Aldwyn made his way to the top of the hill to join Ruby and Givens. He cleared his throat as he turned to look at all the Badlanders below him. Ruby gave his hand a squeeze.

'I accept that my Master's challenge to solve the Mystery of Great Walsingham has been met,' said the boy. 'And you are all witnesses to this fact. The vote to appoint girl apprentices in the Order is therefore to be passed. Neither I nor any other Badlander shall challenge this. It is now to be written into the *Ordnung*.'

The bright light of the *wyrd* erupted around them like a lightning strike, forcing everyone to shield their eyes and then they were all blinking and talking among themselves.

When Jones saw Givens beckoning him towards them, he

grasped Olive's hand. 'Ready?' he whispered to the little girl standing beside him. She nodded.

They walked up to the top and turned to face everyone. Olive gasped as she saw just how many faces were staring back at her. Ruby cleared her throat and laid her hand on Olive's shoulder.

'I take this girl, Olive, as my apprentice. The first girl apprentice there has ever been in the Order. May she be the first of many.'

Everyone blinked. No one said a word. And then a ripple of applause spread through the group on the hill. It grew louder and louder as more men and boys joined in, until it sounded like a rainstorm echoing round the surrounding countryside.

ONE YEAR LATER ...

J ones tucked in his shirt and smoothed back his hair, checking himself in the mirror one last time. He thought he looked smart enough and turned around but there was a growl of discontent from the man standing in the corner.

Maitland pointed to the bottom of the boy's overcoat and Jones saw a thread hanging off the back.

'Thanks,' he said, ripping it off and dumping it in the bin.

Maitland had taken a long time to return to him. The effect of the fairy-tale world in Great Walsingham had been pronounced, and it had been a few months before Maitland had started appearing in Jones's dreams again. Jones had waited patiently as the magical connection between them had grown stronger, eager to tell his old Master face to face what had happened. Only a few weeks ago the moment had finally arrived when Maitland had appeared to him in person. Unlike before, Jones had rushed to his Master this time, bright-eyed and smiling and spoken so fast about solving the Mystery of Great Walsingham that Maitland had told him to slow down. When the man had heard everything, he had stood there, shimmering, saying nothing for a moment, and had then hugged Jones so hard, the boy thought his heart might burst with pride. *You've made me so happy*, Maitland had whispered. *Because you've become the Badlander I always knew you could be.*

'I'm proud of you, boy,' said Maitland now as Jones checked himself once more in the mirror. 'It's a great honour to be made the keeper of *The Book of Mysteries*, and at such a young age. Only the best Badlanders are honoured in this way.' Maitland grinned and shook his head as if still unable to believe it.

'I couldn't have done it without all the lessons you taught me as your apprentice.'

'I suppose.' Maitland coughed and looked at the boy. 'I mean, you always seemed to know what you wanted and how to get it. You got all this, didn't you?' He raised his hands. 'This house with your mother and father and a life in the ordinary world, as well as being a Badlander.' Maitland shook his head again. 'I'm not sure you ever needed any Master to teach you what to do. I certainly don't think you need one now as you go on with your work.'

Jones looked at him. Opened his mouth. Maitland put up a hand to silence him.

'It's time for me to leave you in peace. All I ask is that I see you holding the book. It'll be the last thing I see.'

Jones wiped his eyes. 'Of course,' he said. 'Thank you. For everything.'

'And thank you for being so brave and allowing my legacy to live on. It's all I ever wanted, for you to be the Badlander I knew you could be. You proved me right.' Maitland walked over to Jones and hugged him harder than he ever had before. 'I'm not sure where I'm going,' he said, 'but always remember me as if I'm still here. Never forget me, Jones.'

Jones felt his eyes burning. He did his best not to cry and buried his face deeper into Maitland's shoulder.

Samuel Raynham was waiting for Jones outside his house in the sunshine, tossing bread into a pond, watching the ducks squabbling over the pieces. He led Jones inside and into his study, where *The Book of Mysteries* sat on a table. Raynham stroked the cover for a moment and to Jones it seemed as though the man was remembering all the things he had done. He picked up the book and gave it to Jones.

'Guard it well, boy. I wish you luck with its mysteries.'

Jones gasped as the book moved in his hands like something alive and then he smiled as he felt a great sense of importance with the role he had been given. He remembered what he had promised Maitland and looked up to see the man in the corner of the room. He held up the book and Maitland nodded and then waved as he started to fade from the boy's view.

'Goodbye,' whispered Jones.

'Goodbye, my boy,' said Maitland, his voice faint like a radio not quite tuned in. 'And good luck. "Be Prepared" as always, just like I am now.'

'I will, Maitland. I promise.'

The two of them smiled and then Maitland was gone.

Ruby and her apprentice crunched through the snow beside the hedge that bordered the field, their breath appearing in silver cloudbursts in the moonlight. The *Scucca* was ahead of them, nose to the ground, following a scent, arcing back and forth like a train stuck to its track. When it stopped and looked towards a small copse of trees at the end of the field, Ruby blew a short silent blast on her battered silver whistle and the hound sat, tail thumping in the snow, waiting for them to catch up. It trotted beside them as they went on, their feet punching holes in the frosty crust, skirting round the drifts that had built up in the wind earlier that day.

When Ruby stopped, Olive tapped her on the arm and shrugged, pointing at the trees ahead.

'We have to be careful,' replied Ruby. 'It could be anything in there. What's the Badlander motto?'

'"Be Prepared",' said Olive and Ruby nodded.

'So that's what we need to be. You follow my lead and keep close, your eyes peeled. Got it?'

Olive nodded and took a small silver net attached to a long handle out of her limitless overcoat pocket. Ruby pulled the gun out of the leather holster tied around her waist and moved cautiously.

'What have we got?' asked the weapon.

'Not sure, yet.'

'Well, what are we waiting for?'

'It's Olive's first hunting trip. We need to be careful. Do things by the book.'

'Jones would never believe you've just said that,' sniggered the gun. Ruby ignored it.

'I'm sending the *Scucca* in to flush out what's in those trees,' she said to Olive and gave some silent blasts on her whistle, her cheeks puffing. The *Scucca* heard them and raced round the right-hand side of the trees, then disappeared.

It didn't take long for something to happen.

They heard an excited bark, followed by some angry cursing and a human voice shouting. Branches rattled and a figure catapulted into the air above the tops of the trees and came to land gracefully in the field close to Ruby and Olive, in a spray of snow.

The man rose to his feet and looked up. He was pale with wisps of black hair combed across his head that looked as shiny as an egg. There was a smear of red blood around his lips. In his hand was a limp fox, a bright red stripe across its throat. The man cocked his head and threw the dead creature to the ground, spattering the snow with drops of blood.

'Olive?'

The little girl stood to attention at Ruby's questioning voice and looked the man up and down.

'It might be a *Gást* ... maybe?' the little girl asked with a hopeful note in her voice that made it rise up at the end. Ruby tutted and shook her head. 'Or a Shapeshifter Troll?' asked the little girl quickly. Ruby tutted again.

'Have you read any of the Pocket Book Bestiary I gave you?'

Olive hung her head. 'No.'

'Thought not.'

The man coughed and it grew into a growl. He threw back his head and gave a long howl.

'How about now?'

'A Wolfman?'

'Anglo-Saxon name?' asked Ruby quickly, her hand tensing round the gun as she aimed it at the rapidly changing man who was crouched on all fours, his clothes ripping as his body grew and sprouted a black pelt of hair.

Olive just shook her head.

'Well, use your net and see if you can remember by the end of tonight.'

Olive nodded and cast out the silver net, the end extending and growing and flopping down over the growling man, turning his noises to whimpers as the fine mesh burnt him and made him start to smoke.

Ruby fired the gun to finish him off.

When it was all over and the body had been dissolved, Ruby chose a tree at the edge of the copse on which to make her *mearcunge*. She wrote down both their names using her charmed fountain pen, along with the name of the creature they had despatched and the date, admiring the sparkling words before they disappeared. She turned and smiled at the little girl beside her.

'This is just the beginning, Olive,' she said. 'There's still an awful lot to learn.'

Olive nodded back.

And then they tramped away through the snow, the *Scucca* beside them.

GLOSSARY

of

BADLANDER

TERMS

Æfenglóm (ANGLO-SAXON)
Translates as 'evening gloom' or
'twilight'.

Apprentice A young
male Badlander trained and
assessed over a period of
time to see whether they
are fit for Commencement.
Apprentices are taken on
by senior Badlanders who
then become their Masters.
Each Master only takes one
apprentice at a time and only a
small number eventually go on
to be Commenced, usually at
around the age of 12-13 years
of age. The majority of those
who do not Commence die in
the Badlands during training.
Those who survive but are
not considered suitable for
Commencement are returned to
normal society with their minds
and memories wiped by magic
to be looked after by ordinary
people. It is generally accepted
that many of those returned to
normal life suffer from mental
disorders and depression as
they grow up. The other option
open to failed apprentices is to
become a Whelp (see separate

entry). Badlanders find their
apprentices in a number of ways,
but by far the most common
method is through the use of a
secretive network that removes
very young children from public
care who have been placed
there after being orphaned or
abandoned. However, some
apprentices are stolen straight
from their families although this
is a much rarer practice than it
used to be.

Badlander The given name
for members of the Badlander
Order, a secret society of
monster hunters. The Badlander
Order evolved in Great Britain
during the 5th century after
the arrival of Anglo-Saxons
from continental Europe who
brought with them their own
secrets and methods of fighting
monsters. Ancient Britons
adopted these techniques as
they gradually embraced the
culture and language of Anglo-
Saxons. The teachings and
organised living of early monks
also helped to create early
Badlander practice. Initially,
Badlanders were trained in the

earliest monasteries until the Order began to emerge with its own established set of rules in approximately the second half of the 7th century. The influence of monasteries may explain why the Badlander Order is exclusively male.

The Badlands

The Badlands is a term used to describe any location where creatures might be lurking. It normally refers to places right on the edge of normal people's lives. However, it is a name that encompasses a wide variety of places, from a distant valley to a park in the heart of a city, or even to a house in the suburbs. Wherever a creature is found then that location is considered to be a part of the Badlands.

The Badlander Bestiary - Pocket Book Version

A small, portable reference guide to all the various monsters found in the Badlands. The pages are blank until the user demands to know information about a specific creature at which point all the relevant information will be revealed. Because of this function it is usually used as a field guide on hunts and particularly valuable for apprentices who are learning about creatures.

'Be Prepared'

An old motto used by Badlanders to ensure that they are always ready for whatever they may encounter in the Badlands. This phrase has been adopted into the larger society of ordinary people too (for example, the Scout Movement).

The Black Book of Magical Instruction

Presented to every apprentice during the act of Commencement, *The Black Book of Magical Instruction* can only be read by those who have Commenced and been given the gift of magic. This ensures the secrets of spell-casting are reserved only for those deemed special enough to Commence. The book is vital as a teaching aid for young Badlanders, allowing them to learn how to use magic. It is interactive, leading apprentices through various lessons and answering their questions.

The Book of Mysteries

A unique book recording all the unsolved mysteries and cold cases of note in the Badlands. One Badlander – the keeper – is responsible for looking after the book at any one time and for trying to solve the difficult and puzzling mysteries it contains. A Badlander with an agile and inquiring mind is usually chosen for the task by the High Council.

Charms

Charms are often used by Badlanders to adapt or customise an object to make it more useful. Using magic is the only way to create a charm.

Commencement

The act of advancement of an apprentice Badlander by which he is given the gift of magic. Commencement is entirely at the discretion of the apprentice's Master who will formalise the Commencement by handing over a silver key. This key is worn around a Master's neck for the duration of the apprenticeship and unlocks an oak chest that has the properties to set an apprentice's Commencement in motion.

The term Commencement was agreed upon by the Order in the early 17th century prior to which various terms had been used to describe the process and its different elements.

Dark Magic *áglæccræft*

(ANGLO-SAXON) A dangerous form of magic only really understood by those who use it. All Badlanders know that once they have Commenced, the magic inside them (see separate entry for Magic) needs to be controlled otherwise it may try to corrupt the minds of anyone using it and tempt them into using Dark Magic. Therefore, many Badlanders practise forms of mediation or wear various types of undershirt to protect against this. However, magic can alter in other ways and force Badlanders into using Dark Magic: either through a bite from a creature (such as a Witch or Vampire) or if a Badlander uses a dangerous magical item of dubious provenance. Being bitten is by far the most common reason for magic changing inside a Badlander and usually results in transformation into a No-Thing, the term for a Badlander who practises Dark Magic and is required to drink blood in order to cast spells

Badlanders who want to use powerful magical items can drink bitter potions to try and guard against any ill effects.

Death Apple Tree

Identified by shiny red apples with hexagonal pips, a Death Apple Tree provides a way for a Badlander to learn about the past. Although there are many different varieties each tree grows in the same way, out of the body of a dead Badlander once a seed has been swallowed, usually in the moments prior to death. An enchanted apple will grow slowly, below ground,

within the tree's root system. If a Badlander can locate one and eat it, then it will allow them to converse with whoever swallowed the seed. In this way knowledge may be passed from a dead Badlander to a living one.

Deschamps & Sons

Deschamps & Sons is an extremely large department store in London that sells everything a Badlander might need. It prides itself on providing the highest quality products, catering for a range of tastes. The store started as a small shop in the late 16th century. After being founded by Monsieur Deschamps, who had arrived from Paris, it grew into a much larger business over time. Almost all of the shop is concealed deep underground, beneath the city of London, with the entrance at street level, to what seems, at least to the ordinary person, a small tobacconists called Deschamps & Sons. There are various Deschamps & Sons stores all over the world catering for Badlanders in different countries.

Gebíed mé þá bóc
(ANGLO-SAXON) A spell which translates literally as 'Give me the book'.

High Council of Badlanders A select group of high-ranking Badlanders. The High Council meet annually to discuss any important business relevant to the Order and are responsible for maintaining the *Ordnung* (see separate entry), ruling on any changes to it. Members of the High Council are voted in for life.

Juicing 'Juicing' is a slang term for eliminating the bodies of dead monsters. It involves the use of a magical brown dust (its mixture of elements a closely guarded secret), which is sprinkled over a corpse, reducing it to a foamy white substance. Removing evidence of monsters is an essential part of any Badlander's kill.

Badlanders who have been killed in action are also disposed of in the same way but they are honoured with the *Wyrd* rhyme which is recited as the body melts away.

Learning Book A notebook commonly kept by apprentice Badlanders. It is a simple way of keeping notes about the things they learn that are useful and important to know.

Limitless Pockets Any coat, jacket or pair of trousers a Badlander wears will usually be charmed to have limitless pockets, meaning that many objects can be carried around. To retrieve what a Badlander wants from a pocket all they need to do is insert their hand and imagine what they require. Bags can be charmed to be limitless too.

Lucky Drops Lucky Drops are extremely rare, in fact there is thought to be only one vial of them left in existence. A limited number of bottles were created by renowned "mixer" Cornelius Louchette in the early 20th century. Vials of Lucky Drops were handed out to Badlanders by lottery at the behest of the *wyrd*. The Drops were designed to bring a Badlander good fortune but only in a manner that required close consideration of the effects of greed and ambition.

Magic The most important tool in the Badlander's armoury for tackling monsters, magic is fundamental to surviving the Badlands. It is also vitally important because it allows for the creation of charms that make everyday life easier for Badlanders given the lifestyle restrictions placed on them by the *Ordnung*, allowing them to co-exist in the modern world alongside ordinary people. The gift of magic is granted at Commencement and becomes 'fused' with the apprentice receiving it.

Magic is a natural element that Badlanders have managed to control through ancient means, drawing it from the heart of the land and forcing it to work for them. Therefore,

magic is always looking for a way to release itself from being controlled by the Badlander Order. This means magic can be fickle and unpredictable, attempting to lead Badlanders astray if they are not disciplined in how they use it. As a result, Badlanders are taught to treat magic with great respect at all times.

Mearcung (-e, -a for plural) (ANGLO-SAXON) Translates as 'marking', 'branding' or 'characteristic'. The formal name given to the mark that a Badlander makes after killing and disposing of a creature to make it clear to other Badlanders what has happened in a particular location. It is also a way for Badlanders to show others how successful they have been in the Badlands, and promote their legacy.

Mótbeorh (ANGLO-SAXON) Translates as 'meeting hill'.

No-Thing A No-Thing is a term for any Badlander when the magic inside them has become corrupted. Magic may change to something dark and subversive if a person is bitten by certain types of creature (most commonly a Witch), or if the magic itself warps into something rotten because of evil intent within the Badlander themselves. Once corrupted, the magic will allow its user to perform Dark Magic, known as *áglæccræft*. This type of magic has not been examined by Badlanders very often because the study of it can be very dangerous and lead to infection. Therefore, its power and potential is little known or understood. One thing that is well known, however, is that Dark Magic requires blood to 'power it' up and allow the No-Thing to use it. Thus, No-Things are always on the lookout for people or animals to drain of their blood. It is thought that there is some connection between No-Things and Vampires but so far there has been no conclusive proof for this.

Ordnung (German) A German word, meaning 'order', 'discipline', 'rule' or 'system', *Ordnung* is used by Badlanders to describe the strict code of rules their Order must follow. It was a term adopted by Badlanders in the early 15th century when new rules for the Order were established.

Rosemary and Salt
A common mixture of two substances that Badlanders use as an all-purpose weapon against many creatures. It can cause burns on a variety of monsters. If sprinkled on the ground around the user it can also form a protective ring that repels many different creatures.

Scrying Scrying is the act of observing a person or location. It is an ancient skill that is largely vocational, meaning those Badlanders with a natural talent for scrying are drawn to trying it, usually through feeling an urge to hold a scrying object that is nearby. However, scrying still requires a great deal of practice and years of learning to perfect it. A person may only scry on a person they have met before or on a place they have visited previously.

Silvereen A silver dust, complex to create, which can be used to find hidden things, notably secret doorways and portals. A handful, thrown into the air, will coalesce beside anything out of the ordinary. The dust can be unstable and temperamental, making it difficult to use easily.

Slap Dust Slap Dust is a way of travelling from one place to another instantaneously. After a small amount of dust has been placed in the palm of one hand, all the user has to do is announce where they want to go, then slap their hands together, and they will travel to their desired location. The dust originated from a combination of charms that were mixed together by early Badlanders in the late 9th century and has been used ever since. There are many different grades and strengths of Slap Dust available to purchase.

Although the dust offers a lightning-fast and efficient mode of transport it does have its problems. Common issues are judging the right amount of dust required for a particular journey; materialising in too confined a space; lack of secrecy since the user must announce where they are going (although some rarer forms of dust only require thought) and being seen by ordinary people by accident. There is also some evidence to suggest that using the dust has an unhealthy effect on the body if used too often (A good source of information on this subject is *Why Dust Might be Bad for You* by J. Heaslip).

Tonic Different types of tonic are available for Badlanders to drink, enabling them to suppress any feelings of extreme tiredness. Given that a lot of work in the Badlands is done at night, tonics can be extremely useful although overdependence on them is not considered to be very healthy.

Tyhtnes (ANGLO-SAXON)
Translates as 'instinct' or
'conviction'.

Whelp Whelps are rare
and generally tend to be failed
apprentices who have shown
particular traits of loyalty and
who are considered too useful
by their Masters to be returned
to the care of normal people. In
very rare situations a Whelp may
be Commenced later in life if
they have shown great aptitude
and deserve their chance at
using magic.

Wyrd (pronounced like the common
English word 'weird') (ANGLO-SAXON)
Wyrd is the name in Anglo-
Saxon given to the concept of
fate or personal destiny, which
cannot be resisted. It is a noun
formed from the verb *weorþan*
(pronounced we-or-than) which
means 'to come to pass', 'to
become', or 'to happen'.

ACKNOWLEDGMENTS

Thank you to everyone who has helped support me in the writing of this book in all their different ways: Priscilla and the boys, Midge and everyone in the Creative Writing department of ICE at Cambridge University and to Nick for reading and commenting.

In particular, I'd like to thank Jane Griffiths, my editor (this was our fifth book together!), who has always believed in my stories and taught me a lot through her fantastic editing and storytelling skills. It is a great privilege to have been allowed to write a trilogy and explore my imagination and I am extremely grateful for that. Thank you!

And thank you, most of all, to you the reader for following Ruby and Jones through their adventures in the Badlands. Stay safe, live well and most of all "Be Prepared" for whatever life throws at you.